He wanted to keep her safe.

If he had the right, he would lock her up inside the house and not let her out until she came to her senses and quit this dangerous crusade of hers. Or until whoever was after her was safely behind bars. That made sense.

What didn't make sense was this absurd longing for her. And where had that insidious thought come from? That crazy idea that he might be falling in...

Absolutely not!

This was an affair. A *casual* affair. Okay, it was more than casual, but it wasn't love.

Couldn't be, he thought uneasily.

Shouldn't be.

Dear Reader,

Happy (almost) New Year! The year is indeed ending, but here at Intimate Moments it's going out with just the kind of bang you'd expect from a line where excitement is the order of the day. Maggie Shayne continues her newest miniseries, THE OKLAHOMA ALL-GIRL BRANDS, with *Brand-New Heartache*. This is prodigal daughter Edie's story. She's home from L.A. with a stalker on her trail, and only local one-time bad boy Wade Armstrong can keep her safe. Except for her heart, which is definitely at risk in his presence.

Our wonderful FIRSTBORN SONS continuity concludes with *Born Royal*. This is a sheik story from Alexandra Sellers, who's made quite a name for herself writing about desert heroes, and this book will show you why. It's a terrific marriage-of-convenience story, and it's also a springboard for our twelve-book ROMANCING THE CROWN continuity, which starts next month. Kylie Brant's *Hard To Resist* is the next in her CHARMED AND DANGEROUS miniseries, and this steamy writer never disappoints with her tales of irresistible attraction. *Honky-Tonk Cinderella* is the second in Karen Templeton's HOW TO MARRY A MONARCH miniseries, and it's enough to make any woman want to run away and be a waitress, seeing as this waitress gets to serve a real live prince. Finish the month with Mary McBride's newest, *Baby, Baby, Baby,* a "No way am I letting my ex-wife go to a sperm bank" book, and reader favorite Lorna Michaels's first Intimate Moments novel, *The Truth About Elyssa.*

See you again next year!

Leslie J. Wainger
Executive Senior Editor

Please address questions and book requests to:
Silhouette Reader Service
U.S.: 3010 Walden Ave., P.O. Box 1325, Buffalo, NY 14269
Canadian: P.O. Box 609, Fort Erie, Ont. L2A 5X3

The Truth About Elyssa

LORNA MICHAELS

INTIMATE MOMENTS™

Published by Silhouette Books

America's Publisher of Contemporary Romance

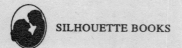

SILHOUETTE BOOKS

ISBN 0-373-27192-1

THE TRUTH ABOUT ELYSSA

Copyright © 2001 by Thelma Zirkelbach

Visit Silhouette at www.eHarlequin.com

Printed in U.S.A.

LORNA MICHAELS

When she was four years old, Lorna Michaels decided she would become a writer. But it wasn't until she read her first romance that she found her niche. Since then she's been a winner of numerous writing contests, was a double Romance Writers of America Golden Heart finalist and a nominee for the *Romantic Times Magazine* Love and Laughter Award. A self-confessed romantic, she loves to spend her evenings writing happily-ever-after stories. During the day she's a speech pathologist with a busy private practice. Though she leads a double life, both her careers focus on communication. As a speech pathologist, she works with children who have communication disorders. She writes about men and women who overcome barriers to communication as they forge lasting relationships.

Besides working and writing, Lorna enjoys reading everything from cereal boxes to Greek tragedy, interacting with the two cats who own her, watching basketball games and traveling with her husband. This winter she'll realize her dream of visiting Antarctica. Nothing thrills her more than hearing from readers. You can e-mail her at lmichaels@zyzy.com.

To Linda Hayes
with my thanks

And a note of appreciation
to my friend Barbara Rosenberg,
who brightens lives through her clowning
and who patiently answered my questions

Prologue

Elyssa Jarmon glanced over her shoulder as her friend Randy Barber's Toyota Camry maneuvered through the rain-slick streets of Indianapolis. He turned left, and the car behind them followed. The gleam of its headlights cut through the darkness.

Elyssa chuckled. "I've been watching too many cop shows."

"One of the hazards of working in television," Randy said. "If you're not on-screen, you're in front of it."

"I'm not kidding," Elyssa continued. "I could swear someone's tailing us."

Randy glanced at her sharply. "What makes you think so?"

"The same car's been behind us since we left the TV station. His right headlight's flickering. I'm a good reporter. I notice things like that."

"Look back. Is it a black Chevy?"

Alarmed, Elyssa stared at her friend. Was she imagining things, or had Randy turned pale? "What's going on?"

"Just check," he snapped.

Elyssa squinted through the back window. Rain fell harder now, impeding her view. "I...think so." She turned back, then gasped as Randy suddenly swung into Eagle Creek Park.

"Did he follow?"

"No...yes. Here he comes." She tightened her seat belt. "What's going on, Randy?"

"Damn," he muttered. "I shouldn't have offered to drive you home. I don't want you involved in this."

"Involved in what?" She looked behind them. The Chevy was close now, its lights filling the back window. "Investiga—"

Metal clanged against metal as the Chevy slammed into their rear end. Their car skidded, spun in a circle.

The Chevy hit them again. A scream tore from Elyssa's throat as they hurtled down an embankment. They seemed to tumble endlessly—rolling, pitching from side to side— then suddenly, with a grinding thud, they stopped.

Elyssa opened her eyes. She was still buckled into her seat, but her right arm hung at an angle, and her head felt as if she'd been kicked by a mule. "Randy," she whispered. A thin stream dribbled out of her mouth. She licked her lip and tasted blood.

"Here." His voice was so faint, she could barely hear it over the sound of the storm. Fighting against pain, she turned her head. Randy lay against the door, crushed by the caved-in side of the car.

Though her hands shook, Elyssa managed to unbuckle her seat belt. Forgetting her own pain, she crawled to Randy and touched his face. Her hand came away covered with blood. "You're hurt," she choked. "I'll...I'll get help."

"Too late," he muttered. "Get...the book. It's..."

"Don't worry," she told him. "I'm calling 911." She spotted the cell phone on the floor and leaned down. It was broken. She'd have to get out of the car. "I'll find some-one," she said. "Just hold on."

"No use," Randy whispered. "Tell Jenny...tell her...I...love her." He said nothing more.

"Randy," Elyssa begged, "don't die. Please." Franti-cally she scrambled across the seat, shoved at the passenger door. It didn't budge. Her right arm was useless but she turned, leaned her left shoulder against the door and pushed with all her strength. Suddenly it gave and she toppled out.

She cried out with pain, then lay for a moment in a sodden heap, trying to see where she was. Halfway down the brush-covered slope. A small tree had stopped the car from plunging all the way to the bottom. She could crawl up, find help.

She pulled herself to her knees, stared down at the ground. Mud. Glass. And a black boot.

"Thank God," she breathed and looked up.

A man stood over her. He was tall and broad-shouldered. In the rainy darkness she could just make out his features—fleshy lips, a slightly crooked nose and beetle brows. But no matter what he looked like, he was the most welcome sight she'd ever beheld. "Help," she whispered.

"No dice, lady."

Shocked, Elyssa stared at him. Behind him, up the em-bankment, she saw a black Chevy.

"You...you're the one who followed us—"

"Right. And now—" He smiled slowly, chillingly. "Lights out, love."

His booted foot shot out, connected with her cheek. She fell, tumbling over and over, down and down.

The last thing she heard was an earsplitting boom. The last thing she saw was a bright ball of fire as Randy's car exploded.

"Elyssa, open your eyes."

She wanted to, but her lids were so heavy. And they hurt. Her whole face hurt.

"Try, please." Her cousin Cassie's voice, thick with tears.

I'm trying, she thought and lifted her lids. "Cassie," she murmured. Her voice sounded shaky, weak.

"You're awake. Thank God."

Elyssa blinked, focused. She was in a bed. A hospital bed. Cassie stood beside it, crying. "Your parents just left. I'll call them." She sniffled, then tried to smile. "It's been so long. I was afraid—"

"H-how...long?" Elyssa whispered.

Cassie wiped her eyes. "You've been in a coma for fourteen days."

Two weeks. Coma. Hospital. "Did I have an accident?"

Cassie nodded. "With Randy."

"Randy." Saying his name brought unbearable pain. "He gave me a ride." That was all she could remember. She saw herself getting into Randy's car, then...nothing. "Wh-what happened?"

"It was raining. Your car must have skidded. It went off the road in Eagle Creek Park."

"I...we both got hurt?"

Cassie took Elyssa's hand. "Your collarbone was broken. You had a concussion and...and some cuts and bruises."

Three days passed before her family gently broke the news of Randy's death.

They waited another week before they told her about her face.

Chapter 1

Sixteen Months Later

Elyssa Jarmon was doing what she did best—making kids laugh. Decked out in her Lulu the Clown outfit, she entertained a group of youngsters in the cancer unit of St. Michael's Hospital.

"Watch closely now." She held out a slender china vase. "Empty. Anyway, it *looks* empty. Someone want to check?"

Hands shot up. Elyssa zeroed in on one youngster. Arms stick thin, head bald, he had the look of a concentration camp inmate. He'd clearly been absorbed in her performance but he hadn't clapped or smiled, just stared with huge brown eyes in a pale, drawn face. She thought she'd seen his fingers twitch when she asked for a volunteer. "You," she said skipping over to him. "What's your name?"

"Trace." The word barely reached her.

"Help me, would you, Trace?" She held out the vase.

The youngster peered inside. "Empty," he whispered.

"Let's fill it." She waved her hand, and instantly a flower emerged, then another. Children squealed, applauded. Trace's eyes widened, and a ghost of a smile appeared.

"Did you put those flowers there?" Elyssa asked with exaggerated suspicion.

Trace shook his head solemnly.

"Aw, I bet you did. Do it again. Come on, wave your hand."

Slowly the youngster's hand moved back and forth.

"Nope," Elyssa said, feigning disappointment, "nothing hap— No, wait. Here…it…comes."

An even bigger flower sprang into view, and to her surprise Trace grinned. Then he chuckled. The sound was creaky, as if he'd forgotten how, but he managed a laugh nevertheless. Elyssa patted his shoulder, danced back to the center of the room and brought the show to a close.

She waved to the kids as nurses began pushing wheelchairs out of the room, then as she turned to gather her equipment, she swiped a hand over one white cheek. This place was hot. She would stop at the rest room, shed her heavy costume and scrub off her makeup. And when she got home, the first thing she'd do was jump into a cool shower.

She folded a polka-dot scarf, laid it on top of a set of giant playing cards and closed her case. She was about to lift it onto her luggage cart when a deep voice behind her said, "Let me help you with that."

Startled, Elyssa turned and met the eyes of a tall, broad-shouldered man. She'd noticed him during her show, lounging against the wall and watching her with a half smile on his face. Before she had a chance to answer him, he bent over and hoisted her case onto the cart, then secured the straps.

Elyssa saw a stethoscope protruding from the pocket of his pale-blue lab coat. So he was a doctor.

His hair was light brown. No, it was more gold than brown. In fact, she thought as he straightened and turned to face her, everything about him was golden. Amber flecks in a pair of arresting brown eyes, a patch of golden chest hair visible above the opened button of the white shirt beneath his lab coat, more fine, pale hairs on the backs of his hands. Who was he? In the two weeks she'd been entertaining here, she hadn't run into him.

"Thanks for your help, Dr. ah…"

"Cameron. Brett Cameron."

She recognized the name immediately. "You're the head of pediatric oncology."

"And you're Lulu the Clown," he said, grinning at her.

She answered his smile with her own. "Sometimes known as Elyssa Jarmon."

"I'd like to talk to you if you have a minute."

"Sure."

He pushed the cart into the hall. Before they'd gone far, a nurse hurried up to claim his attention. While Elyssa waited, she studied him again.

Her impression of him as "golden" was apt; she'd heard him referred to as the golden boy of pediatric cancer. Through her access to the hospital grapevine, she knew he was the protégé of Dr. Clark Madigan, the hospital's chief of staff, under whom he'd trained at Sloan-Kettering. Dr. Brett Cameron was only thirty-four, but he'd already established a national reputation for treating young cancer victims, introducing new chemotherapy regimes and devising innovative techniques for minimizing pain. Elyssa noticed his relaxed yet authoritative manner with the nurse, the way he ruffled the hair of a youngster who walked past him, and decided she approved.

Two years ago she would have been agog at the opportunity to talk to him, perhaps have a chance to interview him on the evening news. But those days—those *heady* days—of life in the fast lane of television news were behind her.

Instead she wondered why he wanted to meet with her. She hoped he wasn't planning to discontinue her shows. Her proposal to entertain had been approved only on a trial basis.

She mentally marshaled the reasons for continuing. She was doing the children some good. They enjoyed her shows, joined in and asked for more. She'd even had a phone call from a parent who said her child hadn't stopped talking about Lulu.

And God knows, Elyssa thought, the shows were good for *her*, too. If Dr. Cameron wanted her out, he would have a fight on his hands. Circumstances had forced her to give up her career in TV news, but she hadn't lost the guts and determination that had made her a success.

The nurse turned and hurried away, and Brett ushered Elyssa down the hall past a door with Pediatric Oncology and his name on it. He opened another door, this one unmarked, and led her through a maze of narrow corridors into his office.

A typical physician's office—she'd seen enough of them recently to know—with medical journals on the bookshelf, framed certificates on the walls and a semilimp ivy plant on a small table. But she noticed a few touches she appreciated—a child's table with drawing paper and crayons, picture books and a yellow beanbag chair in the corner with a rack of books for older children beside it.

Sunlight from unshaded windows flooded the room. The windows looked out over the emergency room entrance. Elyssa glanced outside just as two orderlies rushed a gurney up the ramp and into the building. "Some view."

He followed her gaze, shrugged. "It's temporary."

That's right, she remembered. He'd have a different office, presumably with a better view, when the new children's cancer hospital opened. She remembered hearing that his mentor, Dr. Madigan, had lured him to Indianapolis to head the new facility. Being established here ahead of time would allow him input into the hospital's development. Sharp man.

Brett gestured toward an armchair. Elyssa sat and he dropped onto the couch across from her and stretched out his long legs. "Elyssa Jarmon," he said, looking at her thoughtfully. "I recognized your name on the proposal. Channel 9, right?"

"Yes." Sharp man with a good memory.

"I was a big fan of yours. I used to look forward to seeing you on the news every night. Then I went to a medical conference in Denmark. When I came back, you'd vanished." He looked at her speculatively.

She stiffened, hearing the unspoken, "What happened?" Because she'd once been a local celebrity, people thought her life was public property. Elyssa disagreed. Even if the person fishing for info had eyes that reminded her of crushed velvet and a voice like velvet, too.

"I made a career change." That was as much as she cared to say. Quickly she changed the subject. "I noticed you watching the clown show. Did you enjoy it?"

"Very much. You've been entertaining the kids for a couple of weeks now. Today was your...third visit."

"You know that?" Elyssa asked, astonished.

"You sound surprised."

"I imagine for a department head, clown shows must be way down on the list of priorities."

His lips curved in amusement. "When something matters, I do my homework. Clown shows matter." He leaned forward. "Laughter's important. It helps kids get well. I could show you some research—" Her raised brows stopped him. "Nah, you don't want to read that dry stuff. Just take my word for it, you're on the right track with these kids. Trace, for instance. Today's the first time I heard him laugh."

"I was beginning to wonder if he could."

"It'll be easier for him now. You've given him a start."

"Thanks. I hope so." Relieved, she settled back in the chair. He obviously didn't intend to cut out the shows.

He looked at her thoughtfully, then asked, "Could you do more? I'd like to have you here twice a week, unless you have another job that takes your time."

"No," she said. "Clowning Around is a full-time business. I do birthday parties, clown classes, magic classes."

His expressive brown eyes lit up. "Clown classes—that's what I want. A way for you to work closely with a few kids at a time. Would you be interested?"

She stared out the window and thought about his suggestion. She'd like to say yes. She enjoyed working with these children; they tugged at her heart. But could she afford to take another afternoon away from her business? Turn down lucrative jobs?

She looked back to find his eyes on her. He studied her intently as if he wanted to learn everything about her. Caught in his gaze, she couldn't look away. The room seemed to heat up around her.

Gracious, the man was sexy, with that lazy, relaxed veneer over a core of energy and intensity. She glanced surreptitiously at the ring finger of his left hand. It was bare.

Time was when she would have been delighted to think he might be available, might have hoped something would develop between them. But that time was past.

The accident had changed her. She wasn't disfigured—her nose was just a tad crooked and only a crisscross of tiny scars marred her cheek—but her face wasn't the flawless one that had graced thousands of television screens. And the scars inside were deeper. In the past sixteen months she'd absorbed some hard facts about male-female attraction. She was a fast learner; she didn't need another lesson.

"What do you say?" Brett asked softly.

She realized she'd been staring at him in mute fascination for long seconds instead of answering his question. She told herself to douse the sparks of attraction she once might have welcomed and to concentrate on business. "I'll do it," she said.

"Great." His smile made his eyes crinkle. "We'll find some grant money to pay for your time. When can you start?"

She knew her schedule by heart. "Next Tuesday."

"I'll have Jean, my secretary, fax you a list of kids you should work with."

They rose and faced each other, a good three feet apart. It felt much too close.

Ordering herself to be polite and impersonal, she put out her hand. His closed over it—warm, firm and much too personal. "I'd like to talk to you afterward," he murmured. "Save half an hour, okay?"

"Okay." Darn it, her voice sounded too breathy.

He walked her out, and Elyssa started down the hall. A small boy on crutches came toward her. His eyes brightened as he passed her, and she turned to watch him slowly make his way toward Dr. Cameron. "Hey, Doc, look at me," he called and hobbled to the tall doctor's side. Brett's face softened.

As he squatted beside the youngster, Elyssa felt a tug on her sleeve. She pivoted and saw a solemn, freckle-faced girl of about eight. "I liked your show. Will you come back?"

"Sure will," Elyssa said in her Lulu voice. "Next week."

She waved at the now-smiling girl and started to walk on, then paused and turned, her eyes once again drawn to Brett Cameron.

He was headed toward his office, his back to her. As if he felt her gaze, he swung around, and their eyes locked. His lips curved into a smile of such potent male charm that Elyssa caught her breath. She felt a flutter in her stomach that traveled all the way down to her toes.

Brett raised a hand in farewell, and his mouth formed the word, "Tuesday."

Elyssa nodded. "See you."

Yes, that would be okay, as long as *he* didn't see *her*.

That evening Elyssa picked up Jenny Barber and her two children at the hotel and headed to a local pizzeria. Randy's widow had moved back to her hometown in Tennessee shortly after his death. She and Elyssa kept up with each other by phone and e-mail, but Elyssa had been looking forward to Jenny's first visit here.

They'd become friends during Randy's tenure at Channel 9, though they were an unlikely duo. Elyssa stayed firmly focused on her career goals; Jenny was inclined to take in the sights along the way. Although she worked as a pre-school teacher, Jenny was a nester. She'd have been content to stay at home, raise her children and tend a garden. Elyssa was endowed with Midwestern drive and tenacity; Jenny was easygoing and as Southern as corn bread and collard greens. And yet, they'd become close.

While they ate, Elyssa studied her friend. Jenny had lost weight. Once softly rounded, she was now slender, almost bony. And the sparkle in her eyes had dimmed. That was natural, Elyssa guessed, considering the shock and loss she'd experienced.

Between bites of pizza, Elyssa told Tara and Amy, ages seven and five, about Lulu's magic tricks. Then, enticed by the video games across the room, the girls ran off to try their luck.

Elyssa smiled. "Those games'll keep them busy for a while. Now we can really talk. Is living in Knoxville working for you?"

"Yes," Jenny said, staring down at her plate. Her slice of pizza untouched, she twisted a strand of light-brown hair around her finger.

Elyssa frowned. Jenny without an appetite? And nervous? She'd never seen that before. "Really?"

Jenny looked up and smiled, but Elyssa thought the smile seemed forced. "Really. My folks and Randy's have given me so much support, and of course, Randy's buried there. It's as close as I can get to him.'' Her wide brown eyes filled with tears, and she grabbed a clean napkin and wiped them away. ''Sorry. I don't know if I'll ever be able to talk about Randy without sniffling. His death was so…so vicious.''

Vicious was a strange way to describe it. The crash was a quirk of fate, yet Jenny was talking as…as if…

''You make the wreck sound like someone caused it. Like it was deliberate.''

''I think it was.'' Jenny's eyes glittered with dark fury.

Stunned, Elyssa stared at her friend. ''It was an accident,'' she insisted, then her voice trailed off. She groped for breath. Everyone—her family, friends, the police—had said Randy's car skidded on wet pavement. She'd accepted that. Because she couldn't remember anything different. She fumbled for her glass, took a swallow of tea. ''You think someone *killed* Randy?''

''Sure as I'm sittin' here.''

Elyssa reached for her friend's hand. It was ice-cold. ''Jenny, why would anyone want to do that?''

''He was working on a story.'' Jenny leaned forward and lowered her voice. ''He wouldn't talk about it, but I know he was preoccupied, even obsessed by it. I'd wake up at night and he'd be up pacing or scribbling in a tablet.'' She raised her eyes. ''You were his best friend at the station. Do you know what the story was about?''

''No. He didn't say anything to me.'' Or did he? That last night. The memory stayed tauntingly just out of reach. ''Are you sure about this, Jenny? Maybe you're reading something into—''.

''I found some notes.'' She reached into her purse, pulled out a crumpled sheet of paper and held it out.

Elyssa's hand shook as she took the note. She recognized Randy's handwriting and, seeing it again after so many months, felt a sharp stab of pain. Before her lay a to-do list. She began to read:

Pick up cleaning, get oil changed. Nothing menacing there. But then she saw: Install home security system, make out will. "Will?" she gasped. Randy had been only twenty-eight.

Jenny nodded. "Men his age don't usually think about wills. I found this, too." She held out another paper.

An application for a gun permit, dated the day before Randy's death.

"Why haven't you said anything?" Elyssa asked. "When did you find these papers?"

"Last week. I finally made myself start goin' through Randy's things." She reached for a napkin, began tearing it into shreds. "After I found this, I remembered how edgy he seemed in the weeks before he died. Whenever we went somewhere, he'd be lookin' over his shoulder. That wasn't like him." She brushed the mutilated napkin out of the way. "I started thinking about the story he was working on and how closemouthed he was about it, when usually he told me everything. There has to be a connection." She leaned across the table and gripped Elyssa's hands hard. "Do you remember anything? I have to know."

Elyssa felt as if an electric current were racing through her body. She heard a buzzing in her ears, then a memory surfaced, but so faintly, so fleetingly, she couldn't hold on to it. It swirled away, lost in blackness. There's something, she thought, something I ought to know. But she knew nothing….

"Did you talk to Derek?" she asked. "He would have known what Randy was working on." She hated mentioning Derek's name, hated even thinking about him. Derek Graves, news director at Channel 9. Ex-lover. Prize jerk. How could she ever have thought she was in love with him?

"I called him," Jenny said, "but you know how Derek can be."

"A first-class jackass," Elyssa mumbled.

"Right," Jenny agreed. "Took you long enough to realize it. Anyway, he practically laughed in my face when

I asked if Randy was working on something dangerous. He said Randy had covered the school board meeting that week. They were debating whether or not to buy more buses. Sounds tame, doesn't it?'' She bit her lip. "Then why was Randy so nervous?"

"I wish I knew," Elyssa said. "If I could only remember…"

They both started as Amy appeared beside them. "Mama, can we have more quarters?"

"No, sugar. It's time we were gettin' back to the hotel."

"Aww."

"There'll be another day. Now go get your sister."

Pouting, Amy plodded across the room. Jenny turned back to Elyssa. "I shouldn't have brought this up, but—"

"Don't be silly," Elyssa said. "I'm just sorry I can't help." The frustration of not remembering, not knowing, gnawed at her. Surely if she could recall that last evening, she could put Jenny's mind at rest.

"If you do remember anything, you'll call me, won't you?"

"Of course."

"Thanks." Jenny said. "By the way, I brought you something." She reached into her canvas bag and pulled out a book. "I wanted you to have something of Randy's. He was reading this just before he died."

"*Everyone is Entitled to My Opinion* by David Brinkley. I've always admired him. Thank you for thinking of me."

While Jenny went to round up her dawdling children, Elyssa glanced at the cover of the famous broadcaster's book. But she was barely aware of what she held. Her mind was caught up in a question she'd never imagined she would have to ask. Was it possible that Randy's death—and her own misfortune—hadn't been accidental after all?

Chapter 2

Brett checked his watch. Five-twenty. Elyssa should be here in ten minutes, twenty at most.

He remembered when he'd seen her on TV for the first time. He'd been in Indianapolis a week, maybe two, and for once he'd gotten home early enough to watch the ten o'clock news. He'd grabbed a beer from the fridge, settled back on the couch and pressed the remote.

A face filled the screen, a voice reached out to him, and he sat up straight to watch and listen. He didn't recall the news story she'd reported, only his impression of her. Sharp, confident, the consummate TV reporter.

But there was more. Beneath the persona of dynamic newswoman, he sensed another kind of magnetism—purely sexual. He imagined those softly tinted lips forming a kissable pout; those eyes misty, dreamy; the skin beneath that trim business suit flushed with desire. He was surprised at himself. He was a man grounded in reality, not given to flights of fancy. Not accustomed to mooning over a face on the TV screen.

Yet he'd watched her often after that and indulged in a few more private fantasies. He remembered he'd been especially partial to the one that took place on his examining table.

Then she disappeared, and eventually he'd all but forgotten her. Now their paths had crossed, and the fantasies had emerged again, in full bloom. Now he wanted to find out if the emotions she stirred were real.

And if they were, what difference would it make?

A serious relationship was out of the question for him. He'd had that once with Denise—begun a love affair, then a marriage, with his heart full of hopes and dreams. How quickly they'd vanished.

Oh, he'd been warned. An older colleague had told him, "Marriage and medicine don't mix. Being a doctor is like joining a monastic order. You don't have to be celibate, but you sure as hell don't have time to make a relationship work." At the time, with a diamond sparkling on Denise's finger and a wedding soon to follow, Brett had laughed off the bitter words, attributing them to his friend's two divorces. Later he'd learned how prophetic that statement was.

The marriage was rocky from the start. They'd been too young, and Denise, he guessed, had been too needy. But when their life together had ended in tragedy, he'd blamed only himself. Would always blame himself. He and his commitment to medicine were solely responsible. He'd never risk a serious relationship again.

Instead, he poured his heart and soul into his work. And in place of intimacy, he opted for superficial affairs—a few laughs, a lot of sex, no commitment.

So why was he sitting here, filled with anticipation, waiting for Elyssa Jarmon? He didn't have time now to get involved with her, even on a casual basis. When the receptionist called to announce her, he opened the door, fully intending to heed his own advice.

But there she stood in her costume—blue checked dress

with a white pinafore, yellow pigtails tied with bright blue
bows, a turned-up smile, and freckles painted across her
nose. She looked like Dorothy in *The Wizard of Oz*. Ador-
able. And no, he hadn't imagined a thing. The attraction
was still there. Stronger, in fact.

"Hello," he said, ushering her in. "How was the afternoon?"

"Great. I have a lot to tell you."

"Why don't we talk over dinner at The Orchard?" he
suggested, forgetting what he'd told himself only minutes
earlier. "I'll wait while you get out of your costume."

She stiffened. "No!" Then as if realizing how rude she'd
sounded, she added, "I don't have my street clothes with
me."

"Bring them next week. For now, how about the cafeteria here? In costume."

"All right," she said, but she seemed none too thrilled.
In fact, she appeared downright uncomfortable.

Her reaction puzzled him. Even if she was involved with
someone, dinner in the cafeteria to discuss working with
his patients shouldn't make her uneasy. And if she wasn't
involved...

Last week he thought he'd sensed attraction on her part,
too, but maybe he'd been wrong. He would work on changing her mind. He always enjoyed a challenge.

She shoved her cart into a corner, and he followed her
out the door. She might look as if she belonged on the
Yellow Brick Road, but she smelled like... Oh, God, he
thought as his blood heated, she smelled like sex. Slow,
sweet sex on a star-laced summer night. Her scent teased
him all the way downstairs.

This early, the cafeteria was nearly empty. A couple of
interns who looked as if they were about to fall out of their
chairs from exhaustion were guzzling coffee. A dazed-
looking man, probably the father of a newborn, sat nibbling
a sandwich and grinning at no one in particular. A trio of
nurses rested their feet and snacked on doughnuts.

Brett and Elyssa moved through the cafeteria line, chose a table and unloaded their trays. Brett took a bite of spaghetti sauce that tasted as if it had come straight out of a can. "Could be better," he remarked. "But then, hospital food is—"

"Lousy," Elyssa finished, the corners of her painted mouth turning up. "I know."

Of course, everyone knew that hospitals served inedible food, but the way she spoke made Brett wonder if someone in her family had recently been ill. Instead of asking a too-personal question, he said, "Tell me about your session with the kids."

Her eyes—he'd thought they were blue, but they were violet—lit up. "I painted their faces, and they loved it. I gave them each a Polaroid snapshot. You'll have to look when you visit their rooms. But the pictures don't begin to show the kids' enthusiasm. Even Trace participated. He started talking about a circus book he'd read, then about rodeo clowns. I could hardly get him to stop."

"With his face painted, he could be someone else. Someone other than a sick little boy."

Elyssa stared at him, then dropped her gaze. "A little greasepaint makes a big difference." She toyed with a teaspoon for a moment, then began discussing the other children.

When she finished, Brett got them fresh cups of coffee. As they drank, he asked. "What made you give up broadcasting and become a clown?"

"My cousin and I worked several summers for a woman who did birthday parties. We were clowns—Lulu and Coco. It was fun, and last year I decided to start my own business."

He studied her thoughtfully. She'd only answered the second half of his question.

"Did you go in with your cousin?" he asked.

"No, but she helps me out sometimes."

Something didn't fit. Elyssa was beautiful, brainy, articulate and in his nonprofessional opinion, a woman who'd been headed straight for the top, reporting from the White House or the international scene. Why had she changed careers? And why especially had she chosen to play a clown?

Clearly, she got along well with kids. Why hadn't she gone into, say, child psychology? He'd watched her long enough last week to notice her self-assured manner with the staff, and he sure hadn't missed the confident way she walked. Yes, she belonged on some professional fast track. "Where did you go to college?" he asked.

"Northwestern."

"That's a tough school." You didn't get into Northwestern with mediocre grades or stay without high ambitions. "Then why a birthday party business?" he asked.

"Why not?" she said coolly.

"I picture you making your mark in network TV."

The long fake lashes she wore veiled her eyes, but he heard the edge in her voice when she answered. "I tried that route."

No trespassing, he thought but plunged on anyway. "And?"

"And I decided I needed a change." She raised her eyes, and now he saw the harsh glint of anger. "What are you," she asked, "a cop? I feel like I'm being interrogated."

"Hey, I'm sorry," he said. "I didn't mean to pry." Though in truth, he had. He was silent. Then with a grin he suggested, "Let's talk about me."

She stared at him with a startled expression for a minute, then laughed. "This time I get to be the cop."

"Shoot."

"Ohh, bad pun," she chided. "Where did *you* go to school?"

"University of Pennsylvania for undergrad, and Harvard Medical School."

"Ivy League," she said, tapping a finger on the table. "Why'd you choose medicine?"

"It's a challenge. And I like doing hands-on work."

"Why cancer?"

It still hurt to say the words. "My cousin Aaron died of leukemia when he was eleven."

Her eyes filled with sympathy. "That must have been terrible for you."

He nodded. "He was my best friend."

"You'd have been lonely...and scared."

He'd been devastated. To his surprise Elyssa understood. She propped her chin on her hand. "And so you became a dragon slayer."

No one had ever put it quite that way, but she was right. Cancer was a beast, and every day he tried his damnedest to defeat it. How had she recognized so easily what he'd struggled to articulate and never could? Amazed, he stared into her eyes. Eyes that seemed to see straight into his soul.

He wanted to touch her, make the connection he felt tangible. But he didn't, and the moment passed.

"Did you ever consider any other career?" she asked.

"When I was seven I wanted to be a pilot. At four, I considered becoming a trash collector but gave up on that."

"Wise decision."

Her eyes glowed with interest, he noted. She'd done this before in her work as a reporter, and she enjoyed it. Move over, Barbara Walters, he thought. But she wasn't Barbara Walters anymore, he reminded himself, and again wondered why.

"What do you want to be doing in ten years?" she asked.

"Still working in the field I'm in and making the new hospital the best damn pediatric cancer facility in the country."

"Any personal aspirations outside your career?" she asked.

Once he'd have answered yes. He'd have said he wanted marriage, a family. Not anymore. "Not at the moment."

"I suppose, with the new hospital almost underway, your life is full enough," she said.

It had been once. Remorse, as familiar as his breath, washed over him. But he'd had plenty of practice in hiding his emotions, so he nodded, then smiled at her. "When we open, you can be our resident clown."

"You've got yourself a deal, Dr. Cameron."

"Call me Brett, since we'll be working together."

"All right...Brett." She gave him the gift of a smile, and they continued talking. He hadn't spent an hour like this in a long time, relaxing and enjoying the company of a charming woman.

They'd do it again. Somewhere quiet and elegant with good food and wine and soft music playing in the background. Then they'd take the next step.

Not that he was in the market for anything serious. Just a light, carefree relationship with pleasant evenings, leading to even more pleasant nights. No strings.

When they went upstairs so Elyssa could get her things, he asked. "What's the plan for next Tuesday?"

Violet eyes sparkled. "Magic."

"Sounds intriguing. Will you tell me about it afterward?"

She hesitated long enough for him to think he'd scared her off again, but to his relief she said, "Sure."

When she left, he read charts, then his pager sounded. One of his patients had been rushed in and was in the E.R., barely clinging to life. Adrenaline flowing, he dashed out of his office, bypassed the notoriously slow elevators and took the stairs.

Three hours later, with the youngster finally stabilized and the parents' fears calmed as much as possible, he grabbed a cup of coffee in the doctors' lounge. With luck, the caffeine would keep him awake long enough to drive home, where he could snatch a few hours sleep. A message on his voice mail informed him that he was due at a meeting of department heads at 7:00 a.m. He could crash here, but he preferred a shower and his own bed.

He found he didn't need the caffeine buzz. Thoughts of Elyssa—her voice, that sassy walk, that wildly arousing perfume—kept him up even after he fell, naked and still damp from the shower, into his bed.

He was a damn fool. Slaying dragons, as Elyssa had put it, drained every ounce of his energy, claimed every moment of his time. Especially now, with the groundbreaking for the new hospital building only weeks away. He had no business starting even a superficial relationship, provided Elyssa wanted one. And judging from her response to his dinner invitation, she didn't.

Best to forget it, he thought as he drifted into sleep at last. They'd both...be...better off....

"Dinner?"

"Coffee. In the cafeteria. Dutch."

Over the past four weeks, this had become Brett and Elyssa's routine. On Thursdays, when she entertained the children, he was away from the hospital. But, on Tuesdays, after her clown class, they would meet in his office, then he'd ask her out for dinner at a restaurant and she'd refuse. Always pleasantly, but always firmly.

Every week he told himself he wouldn't ask again. But he needed to eat, didn't he? And he'd enjoy something better than unappetizing hospital chow. But that seemed to be all he'd get if he wanted to spend time with Elyssa.

Every week he became more captivated by her. Each time he saw her, his longing for her increased. He had to force himself not to lean across the table and taste her. He wanted to pull off that wig and bury his face in her hair, inhale its scent, feel its texture. He wanted to take her home, take her to bed. But what *he* wanted didn't seem to matter because she damn well wouldn't give him the chance.

Until now, he'd controlled his frustration. He'd been pa-

tient and polite. Too patient, too polite. Now was the time
to push. Lightly, for starters. "Ouch. An arrow through the
heart. You've turned me down four times in a row."

Elyssa cocked her head. "I doubt your heart is the least
bit wounded."

"Trust me, it is. You can't see the damage."

She gave him a smile, a friendly but impersonal one, and
started down the hall ahead of him.

In two quick strides he caught up with her. "Elyssa—"
Two residents left the nurses' station and fell into step behind them, trailing them into the elevator and all the way
to the cafeteria. Exasperated, Brett held his peace until he
and Elyssa were seated at a table in the corner, away from
interested ears and wagging tongues. The hell with pushing
lightly. "Are you involved with someone?" he asked.

"No." Emotion flashed in her eyes but disappeared before he could read it. "You've caught me at an inconvenient time, that's all." She glanced at her watch. "I'm doing
a birthday party at The Hungry Caterpillar at six. I have to
stay in costume."

"I always seem to catch you at an inconvenient time."

She shrugged as she stirred creamer into her coffee.
"What can I say? I have to take care of business."

"Business," he muttered. "What about pleasure?"

She didn't answer.

"I'll ask you out again," he said. "Expect it."

Her eyes gleamed with that unreadable emotion again.
"No, Brett, don't."

"Don't, what?" The frustration he'd concealed boiled
over. "Don't think about you? Don't want to be with
you?"

"Brett—" She pushed away the sweet roll she'd barely
tasted and stood up.

He caught her wrist. "Don't go. At least explain."

"There's nothing to explain." But she sat down again.
"This is a critical time for me. I'm trying to get my business off the ground."

"All work and no play—'"

"Easy for you to say. You've already made your mark. Look, Brett." She leaned forward, and the scent of her perfume teased his nostrils. "I like talking to you, but I don't want to get involved with anyone just now."

He'd thought he didn't, either, but he couldn't seem to let go. He waited until her eyes locked with his. Then he said quietly, "I'm a determined guy. I'll work on changing your mind."

"You're wasting your time."

"I don't think so." He smiled slowly, confidently, a challenge in his tone. He took a card from his pocket, scribbled on it and put it into Elyssa's hand, folding her fingers over it. "Here's my home number. When you change your mind, call me." He deliberately emphasized the "when."

This time, when she stood, he let her go.

When he returned to his office a few minutes later, he sat at his desk, ignored the stack of messages his secretary stuffed into his hand and thought about Elyssa.

She mattered. Without intending to, she drew him, made him yearn. He knew she was driven, energetic and intelligent. She liked kids, read mysteries, never missed an episode of *E.R.*, and tolerated hospital coffee. But he wanted to learn more about her, to learn…everything.

Telling him he was wasting his time wanting to be with her was like waving a red flag in front of a bull.

He would keep reminding her he was interested. Step one, he thought, and reached for the telephone.

Chapter 3

Elyssa opened her front door and pushed the cart inside. She wasn't surprised to see her cousin Cassie seated cross-legged on her living room floor. They weren't roommates, but Cassie had a key and popped in whenever she pleased.

Clad in a skimpy white camisole, purple nylon running shorts, thick athletic socks and no shoes, Cassie bent forward, brushing the underside of her strawberry-blond hair. When Elyssa walked in, Cassie straightened and flipped the damp hair over her shoulder. "Hi, I used your shower."

Elyssa pulled off her wig, tossed it on the coffee table along with her purse and dropped onto the couch. "Fine, as long as you left some cool water for me."

"Why are you still wearing your costume in this heat? Don't you usually change before you leave the hospital?" Cassie said.

"I was running late." If she reminded Cassie that she'd quit taking off her costume and makeup since she'd been meeting with Brett, her cousin would launch into a blister-ing lecture, fiery enough to make the hot August day seem like December. Instead, Elyssa kicked off her black patent leather Mary Janes and changed the subject. "How was your day?"

Cassie grimaced. "One of the kids at Billy Henderson's birthday party pinched me. Actually pinched me. Right here." She leaned sideways and rubbed her bottom. "Can you charge a five-year-old with sexual harassment?"

"Not and make it stick."

"Too bad." Cassie rose gracefully from the floor. "Go change. I'll get us some iced tea." Long-legged and limber, she crossed the room. Elyssa's gaze followed her cousin as she disappeared into the kitchen. An aspiring actress who'd recently been accepted to the city's prestigious professional repertory company, Cassie drew eyes as if the spotlight perpetually shone on her. That had always been true.

Elyssa remembered how she'd envied her cousin in high school. People *noticed* Cassie. Compared to her, Elyssa had felt invisible. Oh, she'd been smart, an A student. She'd participated in activities—had been a reporter on the school paper from her freshman year on. She'd gone on dates, but boys hadn't gone starry-eyed over her the way they had over Cassie. Of course not. Even in her early teens, Cassie had curves; Elyssa'd had angles. The only time she'd felt special was when she'd performed as Lulu.

"You're a late bloomer. You'll find your niche," her mother used to console her. And in college she had bloomed. The angles softened, her braces came off and her skin glowed. After a couple of false starts, she'd chosen a radio/TV major and by the time she'd finished her second year of college, she'd begun to shine. After graduation, she'd spent a couple of years at a small TV station, then landed a spot with KIND News. By age twenty-seven, she was their rising star.

Thinking of that, and of how abruptly the glitter had faded, Elyssa went upstairs, took off her makeup, shed her costume and slipped into a robe. No wonder she'd resurrected Lulu, she thought. She needed her alter ego to feel special again.

"How was the hospital?" Cassie called as Elyssa started down the stairs.

"Okay." Tying the sash on her robe, she returned to the living room.

Cassie appeared, carrying two glasses of iced tea. She frowned. "Just okay?"

"Mmm." Elyssa forced a brighter tone. "Trace really participated. He wanted to know about different kinds of clown costumes. I had to tell him the whole history of clowning."

"And how's Dr. Dreamboat? Still saving the world?"

"Working on it, I guess."

Cassie handed Elyssa a glass and sat on the chair across from her. "You've been having coffee in the cafeteria with him for a month now. When are you going to let him take you out?"

Elyssa picked at a loose thread on her robe. "I told him not to ask me again."

"Elyssa! You didn't."

"Yes, I did. It's wasted effort." Chin thrust out, she glared at her cousin. "I'm not going to change my mind."

"Why not give the guy a break? Give yourself one, too."

"It's useless, Cass. The first day I met him, he said he'd seen me on the news. He expects me to look like Elyssa Jarmon of two years ago." Automatically, her hand went to her cheek and traced the scar. "And even after plastic surgery, I don't."

"Close enough."

"It wasn't close enough for Derek."

Cassie's generous, usually smiling mouth, turned grim. "Derek," she muttered. "If I could, I'd strangle him with my bare hands." She leaned forward and grabbed Elyssa's hand. "Don't judge every man by Derek. He's a scumbag. He didn't appreciate what he had in you."

Elyssa opened her mouth, but before she could utter a

word, Cassie continued, eyes flashing. "You had a rough time after the accident, but you've put your life back together. You've never been a quitter. Why now?"

"You don't understand—"

"No, I don't. You're not disfigured, are you? You have a few scars, so your face isn't as perfect as it used to be. I'll grant you it's enough to keep you off the air—"

Elyssa's chin shot up again. "I handled that."

Cassie nodded. "And very well, too. But we're talking about your personal life. You can't stop living. There's a man somewhere—maybe the man you just brushed off—who won't give a damn about your face. Listen to me. You can't avoid having Brett see you, not forever. And why should you? *He isn't Derek.*"

Derek hadn't been the only one who'd reacted badly to her less-than-perfect face, but she hadn't told anyone, not even Cassie, about the others. And she didn't intend to.

Cassie slammed her hand on the coffee table. "Dammit, give the guy a chance."

A chance to hurt her? "I can't. I told you, he has expectations."

"How do you know that?" Cassie countered. "Does he walk around with a sign tattooed on his forehead that reads, I Have Expectations?"

Elyssa grinned at the image, then sobered. "I don't want to talk about it. Let's—"

They both started as the doorbell rang. "I'm not expecting anyone," Elyssa said, frowning.

"Sit. I'll get it," Cassie said. She opened the door and poked her head out, exchanged a few words with someone, then turned, holding out a flower arrangement.

Two white orchids.

"What in the world? The deliveryman must have the wrong address," Elyssa said. "Call him back."

"Card says Elyssa Jarmon."

Cassie set the vase on the coffee table, and Elyssa

reached for the card. As she read, her cheeks heated, her heart began to thud. "They're from Brett."

"Well, well," Cassie said, grinning. "Dr. Cameron's a guy with class." She leaned over Elyssa's shoulder. "What's the card say?"

"His name." She slid her fingers over the rest of the message: "I'll keep waiting for a yes."

"Now you'll have to go out with him," Cassie said.

"No, I won't." Elyssa brushed a finger over the dark-green leaves, then yanked her hand away. "Brett's an ambitious man, the kind of man who needs a gorgeous wife who gives elegant dinner parties and chairs benefits for the symphony."

"Wife!" Cassie shuddered. "We're talking about a simple dinner in a restaurant, not a lifetime commitment. Gawd, matrimony," she said in her Lauren Bacall voice and sighed dramatically. "What a crock."

Elyssa chuckled. Her cousin—independent, outspoken and in the rest of the family's opinion, outrageous—could always make her laugh.

"You know my philosophy on marriage," Cassie added.

Elyssa knew it well. Love affairs were acceptable, but Cassie believed that marriage and a career could not mix; hence, marriage had to go. Elyssa had never agreed with her cousin, but now... "My head's too muddled to think about this."

"I don't blame you." Cassie rolled her eyes. "Talking about marriage gives me heartburn. Nevertheless, you should consider dating this man. White orchids, oh my."

They sat admiring the flowers, then Cassie checked her watch, frowned and shook her arm. "Stopped. What time is it?"

"Six-thirty."

Cassie jumped up. "Omigosh, I'm due at rehearsal at seven."

"Rehearsal! You got a part."

Cassie grinned. "Nope, I'm the assistant to the assistant

stage manager.'' She turned her purse upside down on the coffee table and began pawing through the mess that spilled from it. "But I will get a part, one of these days. Aha!" She grabbed her car keys, waved them triumphantly and shoved everything else back into her bag. "See you." She headed for the door. Over her shoulder, she added, "If Dean calls, tell him I'm on my way."

Dean called. So did Dave...and Mario. Despite her views on matrimony, Cassie attracted men like honeysuckle attracted bees. How did she keep them all straight?

Shaking her head, Elyssa picked up the iced-tea glasses and carried them to the dishwasher. *She'd* always been a one-man woman. Of course, now she was a no-man woman.

She was glad she hadn't thrown Brett's card away. She'd intended to, but something had made her tuck it into the pocket of her costume, then into her robe. She took it out and called his home number. She'd be stern with him, she decided as his machine came on. "The orchids are beautiful, but I haven't changed my mind. Let's keep on being friends."

Oh, Lord! She sat down hard on the chair by the phone. She'd been in broadcasting long enough to know what she'd just done. Her words had said one thing, but her voice—her soft, husky tone—had said something totally different.

Disgusted with herself, she marched upstairs to the bathroom, yanked off her robe and tossed her underwear in the hamper. She turned on the cold water in the shower but didn't get in. Instead, she stared at her nude body in the full-length mirror on the back of the bathroom door.

Her figure was the same as before the accident, maybe a little thinner. The gash on her thigh had healed and the scar was beginning to fade. It was pink now, perhaps as light as it would ever be. Her nose looked almost straight. Even the scars on her cheek had dimmed a little. But without the clown makeup, the marks were still visible, clear reminders of that night she could never quite recapture.

What would Brett Cameron think if he saw her as she really was? A picture of him flashed in her mind—tall and tanned with a killer smile and a gentleness that almost brought tears to her eyes. A longing so sharp it nearly buckled her knees rushed though her. She knew just how his lips would taste, how his body would feel against hers.

He was a doctor, used to scars. And, compared to most, hers were minor. Maybe…maybe he wouldn't care.

But maybe he would.

She wouldn't risk a rejection from him. She'd insist she meant what she said on the phone. They'd just be friends. With a last look at her reflection, she got into the shower.

But later she took the orchids into her room and set them on the nightstand by the bed. So lovely, so romantic… The man had her on the verge of tumbling into a situation that would only cause her grief. She had to think of something else.

She reached for the book by David Brinkley that Jenny had given her. Stretching out on her bed, she opened it and flipped through the pages, reading snippets here and there. Her attention was caught by doodles and notes scribbled at the end of a chapter: ''The committee, 5, 1066, March 2.'' Beneath them was a drawing of a skull and crossbones.

Elyssa shivered. March 2 was the day before their accident.

For a moment she could only stare at the cryptic notes, then she sat up abruptly and grabbed the phone. With shaking fingers, she punched in Jenny's number in Knoxville.

''H'lo,'' Jenny said sleepily.

''Jen, did Randy usually make notes in his books?''

Jenny yawned. ''Elyssa?''

''Yes. Did he?''

''No, he was very careful with books.'' More alert now, she asked, ''Why?''

Quickly Elyssa explained what she'd found. "Does it make sense to you?"

"No, but the date—"

"I know. Jenny," she said slowly, "maybe this is important. I'll check and get back to you."

"Be careful, Elyssa. Be really careful."

"I will." She hung up and paged through the rest of the book. No more notes. What she'd found could be meaningless doodles...or it could explain what Randy had been frightened of.

As much as she hated the idea, she knew Derek Graves was the person to ask. She didn't have to look up his phone number; she knew it by heart.

Her former lover. The man who'd dumped her after the accident, when her self-esteem was at its lowest ebb. The man who, in his professional capacity as news director at the TV station, had coolly informed her that she was being offered a spot at KIND-FM, Channel 9's sister radio station. Still reporting, he'd hastened to say. He hadn't needed to add "off camera." After all, a news reporter with a ruined face would hardly contribute to a TV station's ratings. Elyssa had taken all of thirty seconds to turn down the move. She'd resigned from her job and hadn't seen Derek since.

The thought of hearing his voice again brought a sour taste to her mouth. But she had to find out what Randy's notes meant. And if Derek could help, she'd swallow her pride and call him.

Reaching for the phone, she dialed his home number.

For the first time in seventeen months, Elyssa pulled into the parking lot of the television station that had been the center of her life for three years. Here she'd been part of the frenetic scramble to get the news out. Here she'd pinned her hopes of making a name for herself in her career. And here she'd found camaraderie, friendship and love. Or what had passed for love at the time.

She glanced at the names posted at assigned parking spaces as she crossed the lot. Arthur Nixon. The chief meteorologist still drove his beloved Ford pickup. Susan Dalrimple had her own space now. She'd snagged the six o'clock anchor position that had been destined for Elyssa. And here was Derek's space. He'd moved up, too. A shiny BMW had taken the place of his Honda Accord. He must have gotten a whopping raise.

Elyssa entered the building and approached the reception desk. Lindsay Cramer, the receptionist, looked up. Surprise widened her brown eyes. "Elyssa!"

"I have an appointment with Derek."

Lindsay called him on the intercom, relayed the message. "He says to come on back. Great to see you, Elyssa."

"Thanks." As Elyssa started down the hall, she glanced back and saw Lindsay punch in another number, saw her lips moving and the excited sparkle in her eyes. Spreading the news, Elyssa thought. Probably thinks I'm here to ask Derek for my old job back. Or maybe Lindsay thought she'd come to get Derek back. Nope, Lindsay, I'm not that dumb. Elyssa missed a lot of things about this place but Derek wasn't on the list.

She reached his office, knocked and opened the door. Looking wary, he rose to greet her. She hadn't told him why she was coming. Let him sweat a little longer. She shook his hand, then took her time settling in her chair and arranging her skirt.

"Well," he said a little too heartily, "it's been a while."

"Mmm, yes," she murmured, though she was tempted to ask if he couldn't do better than that for an opener. But she didn't want to antagonize him. Derek was easily provoked.

She studied him dispassionately as he sat behind his desk. He'd gained some weight since she'd last seen him, but he carried it well. Most of it had turned to muscle, she supposed; Derek was fanatic about his daily workout. His blond hair was precisely cut and combed. His jacket—the style just right, not too conservative, not too flashy—fitted perfectly across his broad shoulders. He wore a light-blue shirt with a crisp collar and a red-and-navy tie. Funny, those fashion touches she'd once found attractive now seemed fake. Derek, she decided, was a cubic zirconium trying to pass as a diamond.

"I hear Channel 9's news at six is number one in its time period," Elyssa said.

"I'll take credit for that," he said, preening a little.

"You deserve it, I'm sure." Nothing like a compliment to soften Derek up. "Susan Dalrimple is a sharp gal."

Derek, who had started to relax, stiffened. Probably afraid she'd remind him that the six o'clock anchor spot was once supposed to go to *her* instead of Susan. She wondered if he thought she was here to threaten him. With a lawsuit perhaps? For discrimination against the facially challenged?

She decided to end his misery. "I came for some information about Randy Barber."

Relief showed in his eyes. "Ask and it's yours."

"You told Jenny that Randy covered a school board dispute over new buses before he died."

"Right." Comfortable now, Derek leaned back in his chair and smiled expansively. "It wasn't a big story. In fact, it never developed into much of anything."

"What about his next assignment?"

Derek shrugged. "I don't remember. You know, a year and a half is like a century in the life of a news director."

Did he think she didn't know that? That she'd forgotten that news focused on today? "Jenny thinks he was working on something big."

Derek chuckled. "Yes, she told me that herself. I didn't want to disabuse Jenny of her illusions, but Randy was a novice. He wasn't experienced enough for the, quote, big story."

Didn't want to "disabuse" her? Pretentious jerk. Derek knew damn well that Randy had been a good newsman,

even for a rookie, but he obviously felt he could get away
with saying that now. Who, after all, would Elyssa tell?
Certainly not Jenny. "Whatever Randy was working on
made him nervous. Jenny says he thought he was being
followed."

"Really, Elyssa, Jenny is being paranoid. Or Randy was.
School buses are not the stuff of diabolic plots. Besides,"
he added slyly, "if anyone would know, you would. You
were with Randy when he died."

Elyssa shut her eyes. "I still can't remember anything
after we got in the car. Maybe I never will."

Derek leaned across his desk and patted her hand. "I'm
sorry. I know how tough this is for you." His voice softened. "Jenny was thoughtless to put you through this."

Elyssa fixed the carefully manicured hand covering hers
with a hard stare until Derek removed it. The fact that she'd
once welcomed his hands on her body made her want to
shudder. "Jenny didn't put me through anything," she said.
"I came on my own."

"Don't tell me *you're* becoming paranoid, too."

With an effort Elyssa controlled the urge to walk around
the desk and slap the condescending smile off Derek's face.
"I found some notes dated the day before Randy's death.
I thought you might know what they mean." She took out
the paper on which she'd copied Randy's scribbles and
handed it to Derek.

He glanced at it, then gave it back. "Looks like a kid's
secret code," he said in an amused tone. "Where did you
find it—buried in Randy's backyard?"

Something told Elyssa he wasn't as amused as he tried
to appear. "Does it mean anything to you?"

Derek shook his head.

"Could it be related to a news story?"

"It could be related to something, but I don't know what.
What is all this, sweetheart? Have you taken up a new
career? Elyssa Jarmon, girl detective?"

This time her temper did flare. "Don't patronize me,

Derek. And don't—don't *ever*—call me sweetheart." She rose from her chair. "Thanks for your time."

Elyssa took a deep breath as she walked into the hall. She shouldn't have lost her temper, but damn! Derek was such a slime. She glanced over her shoulder. Through the half-open door she could see him staring after her, a troubled expression on his face.

Elyssa spent two fruitless hours in the library, hunting for the meaning of Randy's note. She left with barely time to hurry home and get into costume for her Tuesday-afternoon clown class.

She clamped down on her anger and shut out thoughts of Derek as she worked with the children. She'd given each of her students a magic trick to learn and perform today for the others.

Trace was last. He looked good today, Elyssa thought, with a hint of color in his usually sallow cheeks. He hung back after the other children left the conference room. "Dr. Cameron says I might get to go home pretty soon."

"Really! That's great news." She hunkered down beside his wheelchair. "I'll miss you, though."

"I thought maybe I could get my grandma to bring me by on Tuesdays if…if I could still be in the class."

Elyssa swallowed. "Of course you can. In fact," she added, smiling at the youngster, "I'd be disappointed if you didn't come back. You're good at magic."

"You think so?" His eyes brightened. "Maybe I could do some shows if I go back to school. One year I played soccer, but…but it's too late to try out for fall leagues."

She tried to imagine Trace on a soccer field, with his stick-like legs that barely supported him for walking, and winced. "Magic would be a great hobby for you," she said. "Next week I'll bring some information about the Junior Magicians."

"Cool." His smile seemed to take up his whole face. He gave her a thumbs-up and guided his chair out the door.

Would he get well? Get another chance to play soccer, go to school with his friends? Would he grow up, have a girlfriend, an after-school job? Elyssa prayed he would. She knew she shouldn't get emotionally involved with these kids, but Trace had touched her heart.

She made herself a note to look up the information on Junior Magicians, then packed her equipment and headed for Brett's office. Her heart, dammit, fluttered in her chest.

Jean Torry, the receptionist, looked up when she came in. "Dr. Cameron's not available."

"Oh." She'd told him not to ask her out again, hadn't she? Apparently, he wasn't interested in settling for half a loaf. Trying to conceal her disappointment, she backed toward the door.

"He had an emergency up on three," Jean continued. "He said to tell you he doesn't know when he'll be back."

She shouldn't have felt relief at the explanation, but she did. "Tell him I'm sorry I missed him."

Since Brett wasn't there, she'd go back to the library, she decided. Maybe she'd overlooked something. But she had to get out of her costume. Should she change here? Risk running into Brett? Jean said he'd be upstairs a long time. She headed for the ladies' room.

Inside the rest room, she discarded her wig and false eyelashes, creamed her face and removed the makeup, then changed into navy slacks and a rose-colored blouse.

She brushed her hair and pulled it into a pony tail, applied lip gloss and stepped back, still thinking about her visit with Derek. She'd always had a good instinct for interviews. Derek hadn't told her everything. This wasn't the first time he'd acted that way. It was just like him to hold back, the jerk.

She supposed he could be stonewalling because someone at the station had recently gotten a tip about Randy's death and was checking it out. That was unlikely, but if it had happened, Derek wouldn't want to hand over a sensational story to her and ruin Channel 9's chance for a scoop.

Tough! To the station, Randy's death would be one story out of hundreds; to her it was the most important story of her life.

Bundling her costume into her case, she slammed it shut and stepped back into the hall. She passed the small lounge area and the staff elevator. Its doors slid open and two doctors in green scrubs stepped out.

One of them was Brett.

Her heart dropped to her toes. She couldn't let him see her.

She quickened her steps. He wouldn't notice her, she told herself. He hadn't seen her since the accident without her wig and makeup. Why should he recognize her? Besides, he was deep in conversation with the other doctor. *Just keep walking.*

"Elyssa."

If she didn't stop, he'd think he made a mistake. A few more steps and she'd be around the corner.

"Elyssa, wait."

His voice was closer now. A hand touched her shoulder. She stopped, felt every muscle from her neck down freeze. Rooted to the spot, she heard Cassie's words playing in her mind: *You can't avoid having him see you, not forever.*

No, she couldn't. Dreading what she'd see in his eyes, she turned and faced him.

Chapter 4

Elyssa's grip tightened on the handle of her cart. When he hurt her—as she knew he would—she wouldn't let him see it.

Warily she searched his face for revulsion...but saw only pleasure. His expression was as warm and admiring as ever.

He pressed the elevator button and when it opened, beckoned her forward. Dazed, she stepped inside. The door slid shut, and he pressed the Stop button. "Why were you running away?"

"I wasn't. I—"

"Elyssa." His voice was quiet, firm.

All right, no use to pretend any longer, no use to deny. She looked past him, focusing on the panel of buttons by the door. "I didn't want you to see me."

"Because of this?" he asked softly, tilting her face up to meet his gaze. A gaze that was so tender, Elyssa felt a lump rise in her throat. She nodded, not trusting herself to speak.

Brett shook his head, then slowly, gently, he brushed his

finger over her scarred cheek, touching her as if her skin were the finest silk.

Wide-eyed, Elyssa stared at him. His touch was whisper soft, but it meant so much. No one had touched her *there* since the accident.

He stepped closer. "How could you think the scars would matter?"

"I..."

"They don't." His gaze was steady. "Don't run away from me again," he murmured. "Please."

"Okay," she breathed.

"Good." He smiled now, a glint of mischief in his eyes. "Would you join a starving man for dinner?"

"I would." A laugh bubbled up. And she felt the first crack in her frozen heart.

He released the elevator. "I'll wind up things here and come by for you in an hour. Give me your address."

She scribbled it on the slip of paper he pulled from his pocket and stepped out of the elevator on the ground floor. As she walked down the hall, she found herself smiling at everyone she passed. On the way home she didn't notice the heat, only the brightness of the sun. The raucous honking of horns on the busy streets sounded cheerful. Even her next-door neighbor's basset hound, who usually eyed her with suspicion, seemed almost friendly today.

She parked in her garage, hurried inside and called Cassie. Her cousin's machine picked up. "Cassie here. Leave your number and message and I'll ring you back." The accent, which changed weekly, was presently British upper crust—Eliza Doolittle after Professor Higgins transformed her from a guttersnipe to an English lady.

"I'm having dinner with Dr. Cameron," Elyssa said. "I ran into him without the makeup, and it turned out okay." She was certain she'd have a reply on her machine when she got home, knew just what Cassie would say: "I told you so."

The laughter she'd restrained earlier came out free and full as she went to get ready.

Brett frowned as he drove through Elyssa's neighborhood. He wondered who had rejected her and how the guy could have been such a fool. Why couldn't he have seen past a couple of scars to the beauty inside? A wave of anger surged through him. Whoever he was, the bastard had hurt her. Badly.

Lucky he and Elyssa had run into each other in the hall this afternoon or he'd never have convinced her to go out with him. She'd have stayed in costume, hiding behind her clown face indefinitely. Thank God for chance meetings.

He pulled up before a two-story Victorian set back on a quiet street. Oaks shaded the front yard. Pansies planted on either side of the porch steps nodded a welcome. On the porch were two wicker rocking chairs with a small wicker table between them. Did she sit there on summer nights, watching the stars?

She opened the door to his knock. "Hi," she said.

"Hi," he answered, then simply stood and looked his fill. She wore a pale blue silk blouse and matching pants. Shiny silver loops dangled from her earlobes, and she wore a trio of thin silver bracelets on one arm. Her soft-brown hair hung loose, flowing in glorious waves to her shoulders. On television she'd worn it pulled back in a sleek twist, but this... God, he wanted to run his hands through it, then run them on a long, thorough journey over the rest of her.

She flushed under his intent gaze. "You didn't say where we were going. Is this okay?" She glanced down at her outfit. For the first time since he'd known her, she sounded uncertain.

"Perfect," he said hoarsely, his eyes drawn to the dainty pearl buttons on her blouse. He'd like to unfasten them one by one...

The hell with dinner; he wanted to take her to bed.

Firmly he stifled that thought. They'd taken a major step

today, and she wasn't ready for the next one. He'd wait. He was a patient man. Oh, he could be rash at times, but when something really mattered, he knew how to bide his time, how to take care. He did that every day, when he battled disease, beating it back inch by inch. He'd do that now, too. "I've made reservations at The Orchard," he said, and took her arm.

The restaurant was quiet and elegant, with subdued lighting, attentive service and a menu food critics consistently applauded. A perfect setting for the evening he'd been waiting for since the first time he'd seen Elyssa.

As the maître d' led them to their table, someone called his name. Brett turned and saw a group of senior staff members from St. Michael's. He stopped to greet them.

"Well, I see Clark lets you out sometimes," Dr. Herbert Raines said.

"Not only that, but he recommends restaurants." Brett grinned as he met the eyes of Clark Madigan, the hospital chief of staff, who'd convinced him to leave Duke University Hospital and come here.

Madigan returned the smile. "Dr. Cameron deserves an evening out at a fine restaurant now and then. He's doing a first-rate job."

Brett acknowledged the smiles and nods from around the table, then said, "Gentlemen, I'd like you to meet Elyssa Jarmon. She's been entertaining the kids in the cancer unit."

To his surprise Madigan's eyes cooled. He shook Elyssa's hand but said only a curt hello. Not his usual style. Clark Madigan was charm personified. But not tonight.

None of the other doctors were particularly cordial, either. But Brett put that out of his mind. He wasn't here to speculate on his colleagues' moods. The evening he'd been longing for had finally come to pass, and he wanted to focus on Elyssa.

"Sorry for the interruption," he said when they were seated.

"I don't mind." Her eyes teased. "I'm enjoying being with a famous doctor."

"You're pretty well-known yourself."

She flashed a wry smile. "Former celebrity." She paused, then said, "Brett, I want to tell you about my accident."

The waiter hovered, order pad in hand. When they'd made their choices, Brett said, "I know about the accident," then, noting her surprise, added, "but not the details. I ran into the coordinator of volunteer services the other day, and she told me you'd offered your services because you were grateful for the care you'd gotten at St. Michael's after your wreck. That's all I know."

Elyssa picked up her water goblet, set it down. "It happened last year in March. Randy Barber, a friend from the station, gave me a ride home from work. Someone ran into us and Randy was...killed." Her lip trembled, and Brett quickly reached over and covered her hand with his.

"I was in a coma for two weeks," she went on. "When I woke up, I didn't remember anything about the wreck. I still don't."

"Not remembering's a way to protect yourself from something too painful to face. You may be better off if you don't."

"No." The intensity with which she spoke surprised him. "Last month Jenny Barber, Randy's wife, told me she believes what happened wasn't an accident. She wanted to know what I could remember. She wanted my help." Her face was stark with anguish. "I couldn't give it to her."

Wanting to soothe, he stroked her hand. "It's not your fault."

"Maybe I'm not trying hard enough to remember," she said, and he saw that the thought brought her pain. "Since Jenny talked to me, I keep wondering if I could have done something that night, something that would have kept

Randy alive.'' Her free hand fisted on the table. ''And if what happened wasn't an accident, if someone deliberately ran into us, then I need to know who and why. I have to find out.''

Her words made him uneasy. He didn't like the idea of Elyssa investigating a possible murder. But surely she didn't intend to conduct a serious inquiry, not on her own. Or did she? ''That's a job for the police,'' he said.

''The police report said the wreck was accidental.''

''Well, then.''

''I think they're wrong.'' Her eyes flashed, and he suddenly saw the determined reporter.

''You won't learn much a year and a half after the wreck,'' he pointed out.

''Maybe not, but I have to try. Yesterday I found some notes Randy made the day before he died. Under them he drew a skull and crossbones. I'm researching the notes, but so far I haven't come up with anything. I've started asking questions, too.''

Brett felt a prick of alarm. ''Be careful.''

''I will. I've done investigative work before.'' She touched her cheek. ''I was in the wrong place at the wrong time, and that wreck ended my career. That's reason enough for me to try to find out who caused it.''

''I understand how you feel,'' he said, ''but watch your step. And get some help if you need it.''

While the waiter served them, Brett studied the crisscross of tiny lines on Elyssa's cheek. An idea occurred to him, but he needed to present it tactfully. ''Some cancer patients have scars,'' he said carefully. ''You could help them come to terms with that.''

She frowned. ''How?''

''By visiting them, talking to them, letting them see that you've gone on with your life in spite of the injury.''

''I wouldn't know what to say.''

''The Department of Social Work has a training program for breast cancer survivors who talk to patients. I could give

them a call, tell them what I have in mind...if you feel up
to it.''

''How can I help people 'come to terms' as you call it
when I'm not sure I have?''

''Coming to terms—healing—is a process,'' he said.
''You're building a new career, doing something with your
life. You're farther along the road toward healing than
most.''

''I'll think about it.'' Her expression was solemn but he
saw the spark of interest in her eyes. She'd say yes, he
thought, and by helping others heal, would help herself.

He steered the conversation to lighter topics—the summer's blockbuster movie, politicians she'd interviewed, a
forthcoming book by a former senator that was expected to
set Washington on its ears.

When their plates were removed, he reached for her
hand, toyed with her fingers. A faint flush lit her cheeks.
He touched her wrist and noted with satisfaction how her
pulse jumped beneath his fingers. No matter what he and
Elyssa said aloud, below the surface another conversation
took place: *I want you. Soon. Want me back.*

They continued talking, lingering over coffee and dessert. Brett barely noticed the time passing until he glanced
around and saw that the restaurant was nearly empty. Their
waiter stood in the corner, eyeing them balefully. Brett
beckoned to him. ''I think he wants us out of here.''

Elyssa took one last bite of cheesecake and set down her
fork. ''That was delicious.''

''We'll come again.'' *Often.* Patience was a virtue, but
so was persistence.

A sliver of moon glinted in the star-dusted sky as they
climbed Elyssa's porch steps. The daytime heat had abated,
but the air was still thick and muggy. In the oak trees crick-
ets buzzed, the only sound that broke the stillness.

Elyssa got out her key. ''I enjoyed the evening.''

"So did I. Here, let me get the door." He took the key from her, unlocked the door and followed her inside.

"Do you want some coffee?"

He shook his head. "I'm doing early rounds. What I want—" he stepped closer, put his arms around her "—is this."

She only had time to register that this was the move of a confident man, before his lips covered hers.

She'd imagined kissing him more times than she could count, but now it was real and she was lost. Lost in the pressure of his lips, the taste of his tongue, the warmth and rhythm of his breath. She felt his heart beat in tune with hers.

She kissed him back, her tongue tangling with his. She could hold him like this, kiss him like this forever.

"I want you," he murmured against her mouth.

Oh, I want you, too. So much. But she'd learned to be cautious. She'd learned how easy it was to go with your emotions and end up paying the price.

She drew back and put a hand to his chest. "Brett, we're moving too fast."

"Not nearly," he whispered, sprinkling kisses along her jaw.

"For me we are. I need some time."

He sighed. "I'll give it to you then...grudgingly." His lips curved in a half smile. "But don't make me wait too long."

She didn't answer. She wasn't sure how much time would be long enough.

"One more kiss," he said and pulled her close again.

When they drew apart, his eyes were as dazed as hers.

Brett kept strictly to the speed limit as he drove home. He didn't trust himself to drive too fast; his blood still pounded from Elyssa's kisses. They'd packed a punch he'd never expected.

"Whoa," he told himself. This didn't feel like the light-hearted affair he had in mind. This felt...serious.

But he knew his limitations. He couldn't let this relationship become anything but casual. "Back off, Cameron," he ordered himself. "She's right. You're moving way too fast."

Still under the spell of Brett's kisses, Elyssa wandered through the house. She measured coffee into the coffeemaker for tomorrow, turned off the downstairs lights and slipped off her sandals. Dangling them by the straps, she climbed the stairs.

In her room she glanced at the bed. If she hadn't stopped Brett—stopped *herself*—they'd be there now. She'd done the right thing, she told herself firmly, as she ran her hand over the pillow. She needed to probe her heart and mind before she took the next step.

She went into the bathroom and slowly undressed. How would it have been to undress for Brett? To watch him undress? To feel flesh against flesh?

Her lips still tingled from his kisses. Her skin was still warm. She looked in the mirror. Dreamy, half-closed eyes gazed back. She touched her lips. How long since someone had kissed her like that? *Never before,* she thought. *Never.*

She slipped into a nightgown and was strolling back into the bedroom when the telephone rang. She jumped, then laughed. Probably Cassie, dying to hear all the details of her evening. Or maybe Brett was calling to say good-night.

She picked up the receiver. "Hello."

"Elyssa Jarmon?" The male voice sounded faraway, disembodied.

"Yes."

"This is a warning."

Her hand tightened on the receiver. She checked her caller ID. "Anonymous." Nervously she glanced out the window. The blinds were open, and she stood in a revealing gown, exposed to any eyes that cared to look. Hand trembling, she reached over and shut the blinds.

"Stick to clowning."

"Wh-what do you mean?"

He laughed. "You know damn well what I'm talking about. You keep following in Randy Barber's footsteps, you're in trouble." The line went dead.

Her legs shook as she sank down on the bed. She sat for a few moments, taking deep breaths, then when she was sure she could stand, she raced downstairs. She peered outside but saw no one. No strange cars, either. Then she checked all the doors and windows and made sure her alarm system was turned on.

Upstairs again, she tried to calm herself by considering what she should do. Be logical. Make a list.

She grabbed a pencil and wrote "call the police," then crossed it out. She doubted she'd get much response by reporting one phone call. She'd done a story once on a woman who'd received dozens of calls from a stalker before the police paid attention to her plight. And in this case, what could they do when Elyssa couldn't tell them who the caller was?

The pencil dropped from her nervous hands. Logic and planning hadn't calmed her yet. *Think.*

She could call the telephone company and put a block on anonymous calls. Or tape the next call—if another one came—and try to figure out who was on the line. Yes, that made sense.

Frowning, she stared at the phone. That voice. She'd heard it before, she was certain. But where?

Chapter 5

Elyssa woke with a throbbing headache. She'd sat up for hours, gripping the fireplace poker, the nearest thing to a weapon she could find. When she finally lay down, every noise from outside, every creak and groan in the house had her leaping out of bed and grabbing her makeshift weapon. At last, near dawn, she fell into a troubled sleep.

Now she sat up, rubbed her eyes and massaged her temples. Along with the headache, she felt groggy and vaguely nauseated. She'd never had a hangover but she suspected they felt like this. "Coffee," she muttered and trudged downstairs.

By the time she'd drunk half a cup, her mind began to clear. Last night she'd been so shaken, she hadn't asked herself the obvious question, how did her caller know she was investigating Randy's death? She'd told only two people—Brett and Derek. Now that she'd tipped him off, was Derek trying to frighten her away from a story *he* wanted?

The voice last night wasn't Derek's. She would recognize it in an instant even if he tried to disguise it. Would he have gone so far as to get someone else to call and scare her off so she'd leave this story to him and Channel 9?

With Derek, anything was possible. Well, he wouldn't get away with it. She grabbed the phone and punched in his number.

"Derek Graves," he answered in the too-smooth voice she'd come to detest.

"This is Elyssa." She got straight to the point. "Someone called me last night to warn me—no, to *threaten* me— that I'd better stop looking into Randy's death."

"Good grief, Elyssa, what have you been up to?"

"Up to?" Though anger threatened to bubble over, she kept her voice level. "All I've done is talk to you. What have *you* been up to?"

"What do you mean?"

"Who did you tell about our conversation yesterday?"

"Nobody." His tone implied that their discussion was so insignificant, he'd forgotten it the moment she left. "What did this caller have to say?"

Elyssa always paid attention to nuances of voice, and now she heard just the smallest tinge of uneasiness in Derek's. Was he afraid the caller had mentioned his name? "Standard threat," she said. "Essentially, he told me to watch my back."

"Good advice. I hope you pay attention."

Her temper boiled over. "Why the hell did you say that? What do you know? You did sic someone on me, didn't you?"

"Good God, do you hear what you're saying? You really are becoming paranoid."

"I'm not paranoid. Jenny thinks Randy was murdered—"

"Murdered!"

"Yes," Elyssa said, "and I'm beginning to agree with her."

"If this bizarre idea is true, then investigating could land you in a mess of trouble. I'm concerned for your safety, sweet—uh, Elyssa." He paused, and his voice deepened. "What happened to him could happen to you."

"Don't lose any sleep over me," Elyssa said coolly. "I'll stay alert, but I won't stop digging until I know what happened." Then she said what she wished she'd told her caller last night, "Don't try to scare me off." She hung up before he had a chance to say another word.

Elyssa sat across the desk from Amanda Pryor, coordinator of volunteer services at St. Michael's. They'd been high school classmates but had lost track of each other. Elyssa had been surprised when she'd made an appointment to present her proposal for clown shows and found an old friend.

Bright posters adorned the walls of Amanda's small office, lush plants crowded the windowsills, and the bulletin board held letters from former patients praising the volunteer staff.

"Your program's going great," Amanda said. "Want to expand? The kids in the orthopedic unit could use some entertainment."

"I'm not ready for that yet," Elyssa said. Hoping Amanda wouldn't notice, she checked her watch. This was not her regular day at St. Michael's, but she'd mentioned to Brett that she'd be here, and they'd arranged to meet in the cafeteria. *Ten minutes.*

"Let me know when you're ready. Meanwhile, we'll authorize the programs in the cancer unit for another four months." Then she smiled slyly. "I hear you're seeing Dr. Cameron."

Elyssa's mouth dropped open. "I just went out with him Tuesday night."

"But you've been staring into each other's eyes in the cafeteria for weeks."

Elyssa's eyes traveled upward. Heaven help her. "Um, I guess word gets around fast here," she muttered.

"Yep, faster than the Internet." Amanda grinned mischievously. "The things I could tell you..."

"You already have." From Amanda Elyssa had learned that the head of neurology, who'd been married to his wife for twenty years, was involved in a hot affair with a male resident; that two aides in obstetrics had engaged in a nasty altercation over a trivial misunderstanding; and that the hospital would soon announce its participation in trials of what was considered the most promising AIDS drug in the last decade.

Even in high school Amanda had had such a proclivity for gossip that she'd earned the nickname Miss Tattles. She'd loved the name; she'd even titled her column in the school paper Miss Tattles' Tales. Now she leaned forward, her eyes sparkling with interest. "So is it serious?"

"Are you kidding? After one dinner?"

Amanda sighed dramatically. "Love at first sight."

"That, my dear, is a myth."

Later when she saw Brett coming toward her, she told herself that just because seeing a man made you breathless, it didn't mean love. At first or even second sight.

"A consultation came up," he said, "so I only have a few minutes. I should have called you and canceled...but I wanted to see you." His lips curved in the sexy smile that made women go weak in the knees. "So, how about a quick cup of coffee? We can sit on the patio."

Elyssa cocked her head and smiled at him. "Is this a date?"

He chuckled as he paid for their coffee. "A cheap one."

The patio behind the cafeteria was quiet, with only a few tables filled. The worst of the midday August heat had dissipated, leaving the promise of evening in its wake. They drank their coffee, and Elyssa told Brett that Amanda had extended her contract. "I know I have you to thank for it," she added.

"Don't thank me. You earned that extension."

When they finished their coffee, he walked her to her

car. In the garage he nodded to a tired-looking man in scrubs, then glanced over his shoulder and raised a hand in greeting as a silver Lincoln Town Car drove slowly past.

He held Elyssa's door open, leaned close and to her surprise, kissed her hard. "Drive carefully," he said, and shut the door.

Her heart pirouetted wildly from his kiss. And she thought, maybe love at first sight wasn't a myth after all.

Brett glanced at his watch—10:00 a.m. Clark Madigan rarely kept a colleague waiting when he scheduled a meeting, but this morning Brett had been cooling his heels in the chief of staff's outer office for nearly twenty minutes. He wondered what Clark wanted to see him about. When Clark called at nine saying, "We need to talk," he'd sounded agitated. Something about the plans for the new hospital or the departmental budget, Brett supposed. He flipped through the latest issue of the *New England Journal of Medicine,* then glanced up when the door opened.

"Come in, Brett," Madigan said. "Sit down."

Wondering at the seriousness of the older man's expression, Brett sat across the desk from Madigan. Had they lost the grant they'd been counting on from the National Institute of Health?

Madigan frowned, then said, "The woman you were with the other night, Elyssa Jarmon. How long have you been seeing her?"

Brett blinked. *This* was what his mentor wanted to talk to him about? Why?

An idea dawned, and Brett's lips twitched. Maybe Madigan had been planning on matchmaking. His daughter was married, but Brett had heard something about a niece who'd recently moved to Indianapolis. Uh-uh, Clark. Thanks, but no thanks. Determined to thwart Madigan's plans before they got off the ground, Brett smiled easily. "That was our first evening out together. The first of many, I hope."

Madigan tapped his pen sharply on the desk. "Break it off before there's a second."

Brett's mouth dropped open. "Excuse me?"

"Stop this…affair before it goes any further." Madigan's voice was stern. "She's a poor choice."

"And why would that be?" Brett asked. His voice revealed no emotion, but below the desk, his fist clenched. Who did Clark think he was talking to, one of his interns?

"Some time ago Ms. Jarmon aired a story about St. Michael's," Madigan answered. "She ruffled some feathers."

"I don't think that's relevant," Brett began.

"It's relevant," Madigan said sharply. "Those feathers are still ruffled." He leaned forward. "You have a bright future here, Brett. Don't tarnish it by getting involved with someone who could jeopardize your standing in the medical community."

Brett fought down his anger. "Look, Clark," he said, willing his voice to stay calm, "I always appreciate professional advice, but what I do with my free time and who I spend it with is personal. It has nothing to do with my career."

"On the contrary, it has everything to do with your career." Madigan put his pen in his pocket. "Think it over. I'm confident you'll come to the right decision."

The two men rose. Brett forced himself to shake the proffered hand, say a cordial goodbye and leave.

Come to the "right" decision? Like hell, he thought as he strode down the hall. Clark Madigan had misjudged him. Challenging Brett's actions made him that much more determined to continue on course. Madigan could say whatever he liked. Brett would damn well see who he wanted to.

He was still steaming when he shoved open his office door.

For the rest of the morning he saw patients. He couldn't afford to indulge in anger at Madigan now; these sick youngsters needed his full attention. And by the time he

finished his morning appointments, his fury had ebbed. He
wouldn't waste time pondering the older man's motives nor
would he be foolish enough to start a feud with such a
powerful individual. He'd simply ignore this morning's
conversation and do as he pleased.

What pleased him was being with Elyssa.

He leaned back in his chair, shut his eyes and pictured
her. But imagining wasn't enough. He picked up the phone
and dialed her number. As soon as he heard her voice, he
forgot all about Madigan. "Hi," he said. "What are you
doing?"

"Getting ready for a birthday party."

"I'll miss seeing you this afternoon."

"No, you won't. The party's at St. Michael's in an hour.
You caught me just as I was putting on my clown
makeup."

"You don't sound like a clown," he murmured. *Or feel
like one in my arms.* "More like a siren. You have the most
alluring voice."

Her laugh was low and husky. "You're trying to seduce
me."

"Yeah." He grinned. "Is it working?"

A hesitation, then she said primly, "No."

"I'll try harder then." But the seduction *was* working,
he knew. He hadn't missed that brief, uncertain pause before she answered. "I'll see you later."

She knew the instant Brett came into the room.

Elyssa had her back to the door as she entertained the
children, but she heard it open, and although several people
had gone in and out since she'd begun her show, this time
was different. Something in the air changed.

She couldn't help it—she turned, and her eyes locked
with his. He smiled and then, the rat—he winked at her.

Her fingers fumbled with the balloon she was tying, and
whatever she was about to say fled from her mind. Oh,
Lord, in seconds she was going to melt into mush right in

front of a roomful of people. With an effort she tore her gaze from his and managed to finish her performance.

Afterward he strolled up to her. "I enjoyed the show, Ms. Jarmon." His eyes twinkled as he shook her hand.

"Thank you, Dr. Cameron," she said politely, then added under her breath, "You distracted me."

"Did I?" he asked with an innocent smile.

"You know you did. And you enjoyed it."

"Yeah." He patted the birthday girl on the shoulder and wished her a happy day. Then, without waiting for the group around Elyssa to disperse, he took her cart with one hand, closed the other over her arm and led her away.

"Where are we going?" she asked, hurrying to keep up with his longer strides.

"My office, the broom closet—anywhere we can be alone." He tugged her into his office, locked the door and put his arms around her.

His kiss was hot and hungry. She shut her eyes and closed out everything but him. His scent, his taste.

She felt his hand on her breast, and a wild rush of pleasure engulfed her. Her legs went weak, and she clutched his shoulders to keep from sinking to the floor. He made a sound of approval and pulled her nearer.

And then he lifted her. She clung to him dizzily as he set her on the edge of his desk. "Let me closer," he said urgently, and she spread her legs, wrapped them around him. He pressed against her, his heat searing her right through her clothes.

The scream of a siren startled them both. They jolted apart, and both of them glanced out the window as an ambulance squealed to a stop. Elyssa's breath still came in staccato pants as they turned back to each other.

Shocked at her response to him, Elyssa lowered her gaze. "I know this is going to sound fake, but the other night I said we were moving too fast. Maybe you won't believe this, but I still think so."

"Maybe you won't believe this, but I think you're

right.'' She heard the smile in his voice and looked up. ''Shall we take a step back?'' he asked.

''That would be good.'' Not ''good,'' she thought, but sensible. She smoothed her clothes. He offered his hand and helped her down from the desk.

When her feet were on the floor, he didn't let go. He smiled at her, his eyes crinkling. ''Let's not step back too far. Spend the evening with me.''

When she hesitated, he said, ''I won't ravish you, Scout's honor. We'll make it a 'friendly' evening—rent a movie, order a pizza and neck on the couch, okay?''

She smiled and reached for her cart. ''Okay. Pepperoni and mushrooms on the pizza. And don't rent one of those macho action movies.''

''Please don't ask for a chick flick.''

''Something in between. Oh, and we'll see about necking on the couch.''

She reached for the door, then glanced back as he pulled a handkerchief from his pocket and wiped his cheek. She chuckled. ''You don't have to worry. It's special clown makeup. It doesn't come off.'' She opened the door. ''See you later.''

At seven, when he was ready to leave the unit, Brett's pager went off. One of his patients, a youngster who'd gone home several days ago, had suffered a severe reaction to her chemo and was on her way to the E.R. ''Be right there.''

Quickly he phoned Elyssa. ''I'm sorry,'' he told her. ''I have an emergency. I could be here all night.''

''We'll get together another evening,'' she said. ''No problem.''

But it was a problem, and one that wouldn't go away. Regardless of what he'd said to Madigan about his personal life, he didn't *have* a personal life. There simply was no time. How could he have forgotten what he'd learned long ago? Medicine and relationships didn't mix.

But, he reminded himself, what he had with Elyssa

wasn't a relationship. What they had was pure old-fashioned lust, the kind that exploded like a firecracker, burned beautifully and brightly for a time, then fizzled. That he could manage.

She was disappointed, Elyssa admitted, but sitting around and brooding was useless. She'd spend the evening with Cassie. After the scary phone call earlier this week, she wasn't keen on being alone.

"Come on over," Cassie said when Elyssa called. "We can pig out on tuna bulgur salad and tofu pumpkin pie."

"Yum-yum."

"Sorry. It's no fat or no dinner."

Elyssa picked up a Big Mac and fries on the way. Bulgur—whatever that was—might be healthy but it wasn't her idea of a Happy Meal.

Cassie leased a town house in a suburban area across town. 'Burb living wasn't Cassie's style, but the town house had been a steal, so she put up with a neighborhood full of SUVs and swing sets, Girl Scout cookie sales and Little League games.

Clad in a black body suit and ballet slippers, Cassie opened the door. Her hair was damp, and a fine sheen of sweat covered her face, no doubt from her daily exercise regimen. "Come on in," she said. "Dinner's on the table, and I want to hear all about your night out with the gorgeous doctor. Every juicy detail."

"There's not much to tell," Elyssa said, following her into the kitchen.

"How long did you spend with him?"

"Three hours, I guess."

"Then you must have *something* to tell," Cassie insisted as she led the way to the table. "Come on, out with it. Everything from how the food tasted to how *he* tasted."

Elyssa chuckled and ignored Cassie's disapproving stare as she slid her burger onto the plate. To please her cousin,

she served herself some salad and swallowed a forkful.
"We had a wonderful time."

"Hmm," Cassie said. "So why aren't you with him tonight?"

"He had an emergency." She leaned her elbows on the
table. "I miss him."

"Well, hallelujah! It's about time you let yourself enjoy
being with a man. I can't understand why it's taken so
long." She held up a hand before Elyssa could answer.
"Don't blame it on Derek. You know he's not worth it."

"He's not the only one who hurt me," Elyssa said softly.
Now that she was having a good experience with a man, it
was easier to confide a painful one.

"Who else?" Cassie sounded like a mother lion ready
to protect her cub.

"Max Dewitt."

"Sounds familiar," Cassie said. "I think I've seen his
name in the paper."

"Probably. He's the CEO of Dewitt Consulting."

"Oh, yeah. I didn't know you were seeing him."

"I wasn't," Elyssa said. "He had a press party when he
launched his company. We talked, he got me a drink, and
we talked some more. That's all."

Cassie's eyes sparkled. "That was all for *you,* but *he* fell
madly in love."

"It almost seemed that way," Elyssa said. "He started
calling, coming by the station, sending flowers."

"Rich and romantic. So far so good. What about his
looks?"

"He's tall, tanned and handsome, with inky black hair
and a black mustache. He reminded me of Antonio Ban-
deras as Zorro. But I was involved with Derek and I wasn't
interested."

"Foolish girl. Zorro, or rather Antonio, is a hunk." Cassie pushed the bowl toward Elyssa. "More salad?"

"Um, no thanks. I'm full."

"Of saturated fat. You've scarfed down a whole order

of fries. Do you know what that does to your cellulite, not to mention your cholesterol?'' She took the last serving of salad for herself. ''So what happened? Did you brush him off?''

''I tried to. Then I had the accident. When I was in the hospital, he sent flowers every week. Afterward, when Derek broke things off and I really needed a boost, I went by to see Max to…to thank him for being so kind. I thought he was still interested—after all, I'd heard from him only a few weeks before. But once he got a look at me, it took him all of two minutes to show me the door.'' She stared down at her plate. Even after all this time she still burned with humiliation, remembering how Max's gaze had swept over her, how his eyes had grown cool and how quickly and ruthlessly he'd ushered her out of his office.

''Maybe he was busy.''

''Maybe, but he started seeing someone else. I was at the movies a few weeks later and I saw him with Lynette Harris, this gorgeous red-haired business reporter for the Indianapolis *Clarion*. *Her* face was perfect.'' She touched her cheek, feeling the ridge of scar tissue where once-smooth skin had been.

As she stood across the lobby from Max, she'd longed for the day when she could prove something to him, could find some way to show him—and herself—that she was still desirable. She imagined him seeing her surrounded by admirers and oblivious to his presence. A childish dream, the kind she'd had when she was a teenager with a mouthful of braces. Scars weren't like braces that eventually came off, leaving a perfect smile. Scars were forever.

Cassie glowered at her. ''Stop acting like a victim.''

''I'm not—''

''You damn well are.'' Cassie stomped off to the kitchen and banged her plate on the counter. Elyssa heard her open the refrigerator, then slam it shut. In a moment she returned, bringing the pie and two dessert plates. She sliced the pie, slapped a piece on one plate and shoved it toward Elyssa, then scowled at her. "You have no right, no reason to treat yourself this way." She picked up her glass of mineral water and gulped. "What makes you think your face turned him off?"

"Isn't it obvious? As soon as he saw me, he froze me out."

Cassie gave a disgusted snort. "When did you go to see him?"

"Mid-June, I guess."

"Hah! Wasn't that just after you left Channel 9?" When Elyssa nodded, she said, "Well then, how about your loss of power? My guess is *that's* why he lost interest."

"I...don't know."

"Hasn't Dewitt Consulting gotten a huge amount of publicity in the *Clarion* this year? In fact, I think I recently read a gushing column by none other than Lynette Harris. Convenient isn't it, that he hooked up with a *business* reporter?"

"I hadn't thought of that," Elyssa murmured, giving her cousin a sheepish smile.

"Lucky you have me to do your thinking for you," Cassie said with a smirk. "Forget Max," she advised. "You've found a man who's made it clear he cares about you—not your face, not your position." She began clearing the table. "So why not have an affair?"

"Elyssa picked up her plate and followed Cassie into the kitchen. "I'm afraid we'd be moving too fast."

"Pooh! Anyone would think you were an elderly turtle, the way you're crawling along. Remember what Shakespeare said—'She who keepeth tight hold of her heart risks strangling it to death.'"

Elyssa raised a brow. "Shakespeare? In what play?"

"Ummm...can't remember."

Elyssa chuckled. "Regardless of what ol' Will said, Brett seems to understand. Tonight he suggested necking on the couch."

Cassie rolled her eyes. "Sounds like the fifties. A

twenty-first-century woman would take his hand, lead him upstairs and slip into something more comfortable. Like skin. And then have safe but awesome sex.''

Elyssa laughed and shook her head. Then she pictured herself and Brett, cuddling on the couch, sharing wine and kisses, sharing warmth and breath...

"Wake up," Cassie said, interrupting Elyssa's fantasy. "Come on, I'll give you a pedicure.''

"Deal," Elyssa said, "but I want a normal color. No navy, no black, no chartreuse.''

"Spoilsport." Cassie led the way to the bathroom.

An hour later with her toenails painted mulberry pink and Cassie's emerald green, Elyssa hugged her cousin and left.

The night had grown misty. Elyssa wondered if it might rain. They could use it; the summer had been dry. She wiggled her toes as she drove. No one was better than Cassie at getting you out of a funk. She flipped on the radio and sang along with Shania Twain as she drove along the freeway feeder.

A car pulled out of a side street a block behind her. Since her accident Elyssa been careful about observing the speed limit, but the fellow behind her, driving a dark-colored vehicle, apparently had no such compunctions. He was in her lane and coming up fast.

Within seconds he was right behind her. "Dammit, stop tailgating me," Elyssa shouted, and honked her horn. Her heart slammed against her ribs.

She swerved to the right lane of the feeder so he could pass her, but he didn't. Instead, he pulled alongside her and matched his speed to hers. She couldn't see him through the mist. Probably a crazy teenager high on something or some fiend who got his kicks by terrorizing women driving alone.

A memory flashed through her mind but so quickly she couldn't hold on to it. All she could do was concentrate on driving...and pray.

Her phone was in her purse, across the passenger seat. She tried to reach for it, but the dark car edged closer. She slowed; he slowed.

Suddenly he swerved into her lane, crowding her over. His car was bare inches from hers. To her right was an undeveloped area—no houses, no streets to turn into. Just an empty field with a ditch running alongside it.

Elyssa knew that half a mile farther a concrete wall shielded a residential area from freeway noise. Her breath hitched. If he kept edging her over, she'd slam into it.

He inched closer. She couldn't see him or hear him but she knew he was enjoying her fear.

She had no choice. She swung right and her car careened into the ditch.

With a blast of his horn, he roared away and disappeared into the night.

Chapter 6

Elyssa leaned her head on the steering wheel. Her hands trembled, her heart thudded in her ears. "Idiot driver," she muttered, her voice shaking as she tried to decide what to do first.

She should call the police and warn them about the guy before he killed someone. But she hadn't gotten a license plate number, hadn't even noticed the make of the car.

What if he came back? She'd better get out of here. Her motor was still running, but when she pressed the accelerator, the car didn't move. Over the groaning of the engine, she heard a grinding sound. Shakily, she got out and surveyed the car in the dim streetlight. No apparent body damage. She got back inside, locked the door and tried again. No luck.

More than anything she wanted to go home, take a warm bath and try to calm down. But for now she was stuck. At least she wasn't hurt. She could be grateful for that.

She reached across the console for her purse. The contents had spilled but she found her cell phone. She picked it up, then her hand stilled. She'd done this before. In a darkened car...somewhere.

She tried to shake off the feeling of déjà vu. "You've used the phone in your car at night a thousand times," she told herself aloud, then forced herself to call for towing service.

After waiting for almost an hour, she finally saw the tow truck's flashing light. Another hour passed before she got home. The bath seemed too much of an effort now. She peeled off her clothes, tossed them on a chair and belly flopped onto the bed. Within seconds she was dead asleep.

The dream was murky, confused. She was walking alone down a deserted street. The night wind whipped around her with a sorrowful moan. She heard footsteps behind her and turned but saw no one, only heard the steps coming closer. She began to run but the thudding steps continued, gaining on her. A hand closed over her shoulder—

She shot up in bed, heart pounding. Nightmare, she thought. Not real. No one lurked in the shadowy corners of her bedroom. No sound broke the nighttime stillness. She should lie down and go back to sleep, but she couldn't seem to move.

And then the thought—worse than the nightmare—emerged. Was tonight's incident connected to the phone call she'd received the other night? Was the near miss on the road another warning?

Tomorrow she'd call Cassie and ask her to substitute at the hospital. And as soon as she'd made arrangements for transportation, she'd go downtown and talk to the police.

Sergeant Abel Huffstetter was a thick-jowled, balding man with an annoying habit of tapping his foot while Elyssa talked and an even more irritating one of interrupting her to take phone calls. Now he glanced up from the thin file in front of him. "Ms., um, Jarmon, Randall Barber's death was investigated—" he glanced back at the folder "—seventeen months ago and found to be accidental. Report says his car skidded and went down an embankment.''

''I know.'' Elyssa spoke patiently, though inside her stomach churned. ''I was a passenger in the car. But I believe his death wasn't an accident. I think someone wanted him dead.''

The sergeant eyed her skeptically. ''Doesn't say nothing here about foul play.''

''I understand,'' she said, deciding that ''Abel'' didn't live up to his name. ''But isn't it possible that Ran...Mr. Barber's vehicle was so badly damaged that no one could tell if there'd been a collision?''

He shrugged again. ''Could've blown up for another reason. Maybe a gas line broke.''

''Or maybe his car had been tampered with and—''

''Beg your pardon, ma'am, but if you thought that, why didn't you say so at the time?''

''Because,'' Elyssa said, ''I was unconscious for two weeks afterward, and even after I woke up, I was hospitalized for nearly two months.''

He stared at her silently. Elyssa could almost read his mind. Over a year had gone by since she'd been released from the hospital, and she hadn't said a word about the accident in all that time. ''I couldn't remember anything about the accident after I woke up,'' she told him. ''I still can't.''

''So you're here now to...?''

''To ask you to reopen the investigation.''

He coughed, or tried to, in order to disguise a laugh. ''Seventeen months later? That car's long gone and any other evidence, too.''

Elyssa leaned forward. ''Look, someone tried to run me off the road last night, and I think the two incidents are connected.''

The sergeant sighed. ''Lady, people get run off the road all the time. Driving's a dangerous pastime. The streets are full of kids out for a joy ride, incompetent drivers and drunks who shouldn't be behind a wheel.''

He'd all but called her paranoid. Indignant, Elyssa said, "I got a threatening phone call the other night. The caller told me not to follow in Randy's footsteps or I'd be in trouble. That doesn't 'happen to people every day.''' She leaned back in her chair. There. Let him try to refute that.

"You contact the police and report the call?" he asked.

"No, I'm reporting it now." She knew that cops often discounted what civilians told them; she'd heard plenty of stories to that effect. But after the phone call *and* last night's scare she knew she had to get a formal complaint recorded in the file. It might help the case later on.

"Well, Ms. Jarmon," he said, "if you can't recall Mr. Barber's accident, what makes you so sure that phone call had anything to do with it?" He sat back and folded his arms across his chest as if to say, "Gotcha."

"Because the call came one day after I started looking into Randy's death. Because the caller mentioned Randy's name. And because a couple of nights later, someone tried to *run me off the road.* Aren't those reasons enough?"

"Like I said, there's not much chance we could uncover anything after so long. I don't suppose you got the number of where that phone call was made?"

"It was listed on my caller ID as Anonymous."

Damn, the jerk was smirking at her. He pushed the folder away. "Well I'd suggest you call the phone company. They can fix your phone so it won't accept anonymous calls."

"Any other suggestions?"

"I'd think twice about going out alone at night. And I'd get a good security system."

"You're not going to help me, are you?" Elyssa asked.

He shrugged, clearly his response for any question he didn't choose to answer. "There's nothing more we can do." He shut the file, stood and added, "You can call if you get any more information."

This time Elyssa didn't bother to hide her feelings. "You

mean if someone bashes me over the head, you might take me seriously?'' She didn't wait for another shrug; she stalked out. Frustrated, fuming, she strode through the parking lot. She passed her rental car twice before she recognized it.

Suddenly her anger drained, leaving her weak. Clutching the keys, she leaned against the car. The unfamiliar vehicle seemed a symbol of her life these days—alien, bewildering. And so lonely. Maybe she should get a dog, she thought. Not just for protection but for companionship.

Once, in a situation like this, she'd have called Derek and leaned on him, but Derek was long gone and best forgotten. Once she'd had a support system—Randy, other friends at work. But Randy was dead and, like rats abandoning a sinking ship, her former colleagues had deserted her the minute she left the station. Now she had only Cassie—though of course Cassie could count as a whole support system on her own. But Elyssa didn't want to involve her cousin in a potentially dangerous situation.

There was Brett, but their relationship was too new, too tenuous. True, the attraction between them was powerful, but that was physical. The emotional side of their relationship was untested.

She swallowed the tears that threatened, straightened and unlocked the door. ''You're on your own, babe,'' she muttered, and squared her shoulders. So be it. She'd call on every skill she possessed, use every contact she had to find out what really happened that night in Eagle Creek Park. She'd search until she convinced herself that Randy's death was a quirk of fate or until she uncovered the identity of a murderer. Meanwhile she'd apply for a gun permit.

He had to see her.

Brett slipped out of his office, avoiding the questioning glance of his secretary. He didn't want to stop and discuss tomorrow's appointment schedule. He wanted to watch

Elyssa interact with the kids, listen to her laugh and kiss her again as soon as he got her alone.

Whistling, he strolled down the hall to the small auditorium where she entertained. He opened the door and stopped short.

The woman at the front of the room, dressed in a traditional clown suit and wearing a cone-shaped hat over a multicolored wig, wasn't Elyssa. Disappointment, surprisingly intense, coursed through him. He started to leave, then changed his mind. He'd wait and find out why Elyssa wasn't here.

He checked his watch frequently, impatiently, mentally reviewing what he still had to do today. One of his residents had questioned the dosage of a youngster's medication, and Brett thought the young man had a good point. He'd look into it. And he had a procedure scheduled at four. Still, he didn't want to leave without finding out where Elyssa was.

Despite his preoccupation, he noticed that Coco, as she referred to herself, was enthusiastic and funny. Everyone seemed to enjoy her performance. The children giggled, asked questions, and waved hands excitedly when she asked for volunteers to participate in a trick.

She had to be the cousin Elyssa had mentioned. But she wasn't the woman he'd come to see. Where the hell was Elyssa?

Finally she finished. She made an exaggerated bow, and the children applauded. Brett started toward her, but one of the nurses stopped him with a question. By the time he finished talking to her, Coco was on her way out. He hurried forward and waylaid her before she reached the door. "I'm Brett Cameron, and—"

Her mouth curved into a wide smile. "I'm Elyssa's cousin, Cassie Jarmon."

"Where's Elyssa?"

Her smile disappeared. "She had a wreck last night."

"A wreck!" He felt the blood drain from his cheeks. "Is she all right? Is she in the hospital?"

"No, she's okay. She's home—"

He didn't wait for her to elaborate. "Excuse me," he said, swung around and sped out of the room.

On the way to his car he called his office and said he had to leave the hospital and wasn't sure when he'd be back They could page him if they needed him. Meanwhile, his chief resident could cover for him.

He wanted to call Elyssa but he didn't have her number handy. He wished he knew a shortcut to her neighborhood. He drove as fast as he could through the burgeoning afternoon traffic. If a cop stopped him for speeding, he'd just point to his lab coat and stethoscope and say he was answering an emergency call.

He pulled up in front of her house, left the car unlocked and rushed up the walk. He punched the doorbell and paced back and forth, waiting for her to answer. Finally he heard footsteps, and she opened the door.

"Brett, wh—"

"Are you hurt?" His eyes raced over every inch of her, checking for injuries.

"N-no. Just my car was damaged."

"Thank God." With a groan of relief he pulled her into his arms. "Thank God," he murmured again, and then he kissed her.

Elyssa felt the fierce emotion he poured into the kiss. Passion. Need. She forgot they'd agreed to slow down, forgot to hold back and wait for trust to build slowly. He was here when she needed someone. When she needed *him.*

Her mouth opened beneath his, and she told him with lips and tongue what she couldn't yet put into words, that her hunger was as ravenous as his.

She pulled back for an instant and gasped, "Come inside."

They stumbled into the living room, to the couch. He pulled her onto his lap. "What happened yesterday?"

"I...ran the car into a ditch. I think the axle's broken."

He buried his face in her hair and tightened his arms around her. "God, I pictured the worst."

Touched by his concern, she stroked his back. Beneath her he grew hard. The feel of his arousal thrilled her, and she bent to kiss his hair.

He turned his face up to hers, and their lips met again, pressing hard, tongues invading, then receding.

"I need to touch you," he said hoarsely and pushed her T-shirt up. She wasn't wearing a bra, rarely did when she was home alone. His hand covered her, and she gave a little cry of pleasure, then pulled away and struggled with the T-shirt until she got it over her head. She tossed it on the floor, then took both his hands and brought them up to her and luxuriated in the feel of him molding her breasts. He bent his head and kissed her, circling her nipples with his tongue. His teeth scraped against her tender skin, and sparks of pleasure shot through her.

She wanted to be closer, to feel his skin against hers. "Take off your shirt," she gasped, already working with the buttons. He helped her, their fingers bumping in their haste to remove the barrier between them. When the last button was undone, she didn't wait for him to take off the shirt but spread it wide and pressed herself against him. She moaned with pleasure, delighting in the feel of his skin, the tickle of his chest hair and the solid wall of his chest.

He shucked his shirt and fell back against the sofa cushion with her atop him. He slipped one hand beneath her skirt, squeezed her bottom, and she cried out again.

"More," he whispered, working at her zipper. "Everything."

She reached down to help, but the high-pitched sound of a phone stopped her hand in midair.

Brett froze, too. "My cell phone." It shrilled again, and Elyssa rolled away and sat up as he fumbled for it. He finally found it on the floor where it had rolled out of his shirt pocket, but by then the ringing had stopped. He checked the number. "Hospital. I need to call back." He punched in a number, waited. "Dr. Cameron," he said hoarsely. "Yes, tell her to start an IV. I'll be there in ten minutes."

He looked up and sighed. "Sorry. I'm afraid the hospital's destined to come between us." He buttoned his shirt.

He was upset, Elyssa thought, and angry. Angrier than the situation warranted. Wanting to soothe, she stood and touched his hand. "It's all right, Brett."

"Is it?" he asked, his tone bitter.

There was more here, much more, than frustration at interrupted sex, Elyssa thought. She cupped his cheek, turned his face so their eyes met. "Yes," she said firmly, "it really is all right. I've met your patients, remember?"

He circled her wrist with his fingers, brought her hand to his mouth and kissed her palm. "Spend the weekend with me. I won't be on call then, and I know a place where we can be alone."

She hesitated for a moment, and wondered why. If the phone hadn't rung, they'd be making love right now. But there was a difference, wasn't there, between the wild, *impulsive* lovemaking they'd started today and something planned?

He took her face between his hands, caressed her jaw with his thumb. "Don't make me wait any longer."

Why hold back when she knew she didn't want to? She covered his hand with hers. "I won't."

She pulled her T-shirt on and they walked to the door, hand in hand. She opened the door, stood on tiptoe and kissed him lightly.

He turned so their lips met for a kiss filled with promise. "I'll pick you up at three tomorrow."

"Okay." She stood in the doorway watching until he drove away.

Brett turned the corner and headed for the freeway. He was still dazed, but not just by how wildly their passion had erupted, how close they'd come to having sex and how

angry he'd been when the page had come. What truly
amazed him was that when the phone had rung, he'd been
so lost in her he hadn't realized who would be calling. For
the first time in his career, he'd forgotten the hospital, totally erased it from his mind.

He wasn't surprised that he and Elyssa had nearly gone
to bed; he'd expected that to happen soon. But the other—
forgetting his work—that was a first. What the dickens was
happening to him?

Chapter 7

The doorbell rang at 3:05. Elyssa paused with her hand on the knob, feeling suddenly shy. But when she opened the door and saw Brett there, his eyes gleaming with anticipation, the shyness melted away. And when he took the bag from her and kissed her lightly on the cheek, she felt as if they'd been together like this for ages.

"I have to make a quick stop before we leave town," he told her as he opened the passenger side door of his classy silver Jaguar. "I need to sign some papers that should've arrived in today's mail."

On the way Elyssa asked him about Trace, the solemn-faced youngster who had become a favorite of hers. They'd talked about his participation in her class, but they'd never really discussed his illness. "What are his chances of recovering?" she asked.

"The prognosis is good for acute lymphoblastic leukemia, the type Trace has. It's a rough road, but more than 70 percent of these kids are eventually cancer-free." He glanced at her dissatisfied expression and said, ''I know that sounds clinical.''

''It does. Trace isn't one percent or one-hundredth of a percent of some anonymous group to me.''

''Not to me, either,'' he said. ''He's a nine-year-old kid who used to play soccer, who idolizes superheroes, and whose favorite video game is Pokémon. His mom works too hard, most days she's half-dead on her feet. His grandmother takes up the slack but it's tough on her, too. She has rheumatoid arthritis and sometimes she can barely hobble to his room, but she's at the hospital every day.''

Surprised, she said, ''I didn't realize you knew so much about your patients.''

It was his turn to be annoyed. ''Why shouldn't I?'' he asked stiffly, his hands tightening on the steering wheel.

''Of course you should. But some doctors don't.''

''*I* do. I don't have kids of my own so I spend a lot of time with my patients.''

Substitutes for children he didn't have? She suddenly wondered if he'd ever been married. He hadn't said. She could ask Amanda, but she didn't feel comfortable prying into Brett's life behind his back. Besides, Amanda would talk—she was already talking—and Elyssa didn't care to feed the gossip mill.

The way Brett had spoken just now, the dark expression on his handsome face, made her wonder if he was lonely. Funny, she'd never imagined that he, too, might be lonely.

He said nothing more, and she turned the conversation back to Trace. ''He's a great little boy,'' she said. ''He's lucky to have you as his doctor. If anyone can make him well, you can.''

''Families may want to believe that, but often recovery is out of a doctor's hands. We do what we can, and then we pray.''

She nodded. She'd received the best medical care after the accident, but the scales could have tipped either way. She was about to say so when he stopped the car. Elyssa hadn't paid attention to their route, and anyway she'd assumed they were going to the hospital.

But now she saw that they'd pulled up before a charming old Victorian house in one of the most prestigious sections of Indianapolis. "What a beautiful home," she said. "Whose is it?"

"Mine. Want to come in and see?"

"I'd love to." As they mounted the porch steps, she looked around with interest. "You didn't have this built. It's authentic, isn't it?"

"Yes," he said, and opened the door. Elyssa admired the etched-glass panels and matching fanlight, as Brett added, "It'll take a lot more work to restore the house completely, but I've made a start downstairs."

As he led her through the spacious, lovingly refurbished rooms, Elyssa exclaimed with delight. Not only was the house beautifully redone with meticulous attention to detail, but the furnishings were lovely. They were contemporary and comfortable. By the fireplace was an inviting armchair in buttery yellow leather, and in the center of the room a grouping with a sleekly modern couch and love seat in midnight blue. A blue and yellow vase on the mantel picked up the color scheme.

The smooth lines of the furniture fit her taste exactly. She'd always thought Victorian furniture stuffy, though she loved the architecture. Her own cottage was Victorian. But not like this regal home that could almost be called a mansion. Hers was small, slightly shabby, like a once-lovely woman past her prime.

She'd begun her own remodeling with her kitchen—updating appliances, installing new countertops, adding a center island, which she loved. Someday she planned to remodel the rest.

"Your house isn't at all like I expected," she murmured.

"Oh?" He raised a brow.

"I imagined you living in the suburbs in an ultracontemporary."

Brett shook his head. "This suits me."

Me, too, she thought. She knew she was foolish to feel such a connection to a man because of their similar tastes in homes, but she did.

Brett picked up a letter lying on the floor by the mail slot and opened it. "I overextended myself to buy this house and fix it up," he said, "but when I saw it, I had to have it." He took a pen from his shirt pocket, scanned the document and signed his name. "Be back in a minute. I need an envelope and a stamp."

Elyssa wandered around, admiring the ornamental marble fireplace, the decorative brass doorknobs with matching push plates. She already knew enough about Brett to understand that his response to the house was typical of him—if you see something you want, go after it. He went after *her* when he saw her, didn't he?

When he returned, she said, "So your surroundings are great but you're existing on bread and water, huh?"

"Not quite. Some unexpected funding came through." He opened the door, locked it behind them and reached for her hand, lacing his fingers through hers. Again she noticed how well their hands fit.

He dropped off the envelope at a nearby post office, then headed out of town. "The place we're going to is off the beaten track," he told her. "Quiet, remote, kind of rustic."

"Romantic?" she asked.

"Mmm, I haven't done the romantic part. I've gone there alone a couple of times to relax, but, yeah, it qualifies."

She was glad he hadn't been there with someone else. She wanted this weekend to be special, just for them. And she certainly didn't want him comparing her with some other woman. "Tell me about it."

He took her hand again. "They have a restaurant with pine-paneled walls and low lighting. In the evenings a harpist wearing a long black dress plays classical pieces and show tunes. The food's great. We'll have dinner there tonight, with wine..."

"…and we'll share dessert," she suggested. "Something decadent."

"Chocolate?"

"Or cheesecake. With cherry sauce." Her tongue slipped out to lick the imaginary sauce, and his fingers tightened over hers.

He turned his head and smiled at her. "I want to watch you savor that first taste…"

"Then I'll feed you a bite."

He chuckled softly, then raised her hand to his lips. "I'd rather nibble on you." He nipped her finger, then soothed the tip with his tongue. The feel of his tongue—moist and gentle—sent a pulse of sexual desire zinging through her body.

"After dinner," he continued in a voice as deep and soft as a caress, "we'll go for a walk…"

"…in the moonlight." She leaned her head back on the seat, shut her eyes and pictured the moon glinting on his shadowed face. She imagined the smell of summer flowers, the sounds of the night—the breeze whispering through the trees, water gurgling softly in a creek.

"Then we'll go back to our room," he said. "We'll leave the light off, open the curtains." His voice roughened, sending shivers of anticipation down her spine. "I want to undress you in the moonlight. I want to take my time, shut my eyes and see you with my fingertips."

"See? With your fingertips?"

"Doctors learn to rely on touch as much as sight, sometimes more. Try it. Close your eyes."

"Um, okay." She cradled his hand in her palm and moved the fingers of the other hand in a slow and careful tactile exploration of each of his fingers. "Let's see. All five fingers, that's good. They're long and slender. There's a tiny bump here," she added with a smile, enjoying the discovery. "I guess it's where your pen rests when you write."

She turned her attention to his palm and traced it slowly

with her fingertips. "I can't feel the lines…but, oh, you have a callus right here under your ring finger." She turned his hand over. "You have a scar below your thumb, a deep one, about a quarter of an inch." She opened her eyes and glanced at him. "How'd you get it?"

"Fishing."

"I didn't know you were a fisherman." There were a lot of things about him she didn't know. There was so much to learn—his childhood memories, first car, favorite songs…

"My dad used to take me fishing in the summers," he said.

"So what happened? Did a shark bite you?"

"Nope, knife slipped when I was cleaning a fish."

"Poor baby." She kissed the tiny indentation, then, as he'd done, laved it with her tongue. She heard his breath catch from the sweet torture she was inflicting, and knew she'd aroused him as much as he'd excited her.

She lifted his hand and held it to her cheek. "Examination's over. What's the verdict, doctor? "

"You can say the Hippocratic oath anytime."

She kept his hand in hers, trailing her fingers over it again. "I want to undress you, too," she said softly, "and touch you…everywhere."

She'd never realized before that half the excitement of lovemaking was the anticipation. Her body was already preparing itself for him—heating, softening, moistening.

"And then—" She broke off. "How much farther to the hotel?"

"*Too* far," he said, then added, "Only a few miles."

Finally, as the sun was setting, they turned off the highway and onto a gravel road. Trees grew on either side, forming an umbrella of greenery over the drive. Through the woods Elyssa saw a creek almost like the one she'd imagined. She opened the window, drew in the scent of pine and luxuriated in the air that was degrees cooler than in the city.

"This is heaven," she sighed. Here she wouldn't have to worry about ominous phone calls or nighttime car chases. Here she was safe, but most of all, here she was with Brett. And soon he would be her lover.

They drove into a clearing, and there was the hotel, actually a lodge with rustic wood shingles. As they got out of the car, she caught a glimpse of a swimming pool to the left of the building, but then the woods closed in again. "No golf course?" she asked. "No tennis center?"

"Uh-uh, just the pool and the forest." He put his arm around her as they started toward the lodge. "And you and me."

"Perfect," she murmured.

The staff was efficient, handling check-in in minutes. An earnest young bellhop, probably a college student with a summer job, carried their suitcases upstairs. He set them precisely on the luggage rack, then bustled about, opening the curtains and pointing out the TV remote.

Elyssa paid little attention as the young man opened the sliding glass door to show the balcony overlooking the pool. She watched Brett. On his face was a lazy half smile. His eyes traveled slowly over her, pausing at her lips, lowering to her breasts. His gaze was so intent, she felt as if he were touching her. Her nipples tightened, pressing against her T-shirt.

He raised his eyes to hers, and their corners crinkled just a little. She couldn't tear her gaze away from his.

"I want you," he mouthed. Her cheeks heated.

"Your tub's a whirlpool," the oblivious bellhop said proudly, throwing open the bathroom door. "You turn on the motor right here."

"Ummm," Brett said.

"Uh-huh," Elyssa echoed. Neither of them glanced at the bathroom. Their eyes remained on each other.

"If you'd like extra towels, just call housekeeping. Or I can get you some now," the bellboy offered eagerly.

"No, thanks," Elyssa said. Her voice came out soft and dreamy. *Now go away.*

"Would you like some ice?"

"Ice? Um, no." *No.* She didn't want this heat to go away. Her gaze was still locked with Brett's, her eyelids heavy, her lips parted.

"Shall I—"

Brett yanked his wallet out of his back pocket, pulled out some bills without glancing at the them and stuffed them into the young man's hand. "We're fine," he said sharply and strode to the door. Their unwanted guest departed. "Overstayed his welcome," Brett muttered, grabbed the Do Not Disturb sign and jammed it over the doorknob. Then he turned back to Elyssa.

She stood in the center of the room, her body taut with sexual tension, ripe with desire.

Brett leaned against the door, chest heaving, eyes fixed on hers. His gaze was incendiary. How long until she simply ignited into flame?

She took a step forward, so did he. In a few long strides he crossed the room and pulled her hard against him. "No more waiting," he groaned. "I want you *now.*"

She was already pulling off her T-shirt. "Yes," she said breathlessly. "Now."

Chapter 8

Mouth still clinging to hers, Brett tore at his shirt buttons while Elyssa worked on the snap at his waist.

Hurry! The word raced through his mind. No matter how quickly they were moving, it wasn't fast enough. He pulled off the shirt and tossed it to the floor. His jeans and the rest of their clothes followed, landing haphazardly as he walked her backward to the neatly made bed.

They didn't bother with the spread; they tumbled down on the bed and rolled across it in a tangle of arms and legs. He kissed her urgently, devouring her mouth, her shoulders, her breasts. He was starved, and she was a feast.

He couldn't remember making love like this. As in all aspects of his life, he was a man who valued control, a lover who prided himself on finesse. He'd never experienced this desperate hunger, this consuming need to possess and be possessed.

"Touch me," he rasped. She circled his nipples with her tongue. "Yes, there. And there." No matter where or what he asked for, she gave.

Elyssa clutched at him, almost violently. His skin was roaring hot; hers, too, as if they'd dived together into an inferno—but a good one, a glorious one.

While his hands kneaded her buttocks, slid up and down along her spine, hers raced over his belly, then lower until she closed over him—rigid, pulsing.

"I want you inside me," she pleaded. She couldn't wait any longer. She'd been waiting forever.

He cursed, muttered, "Sorry. Condom." He leaned over the edge of the bed and pulled a foil-wrapped packet from the pocket of his jeans. He tore it open and fitted it over his shaft. That was his last rational act before he kissed her again.

His kiss was fierce and reckless. It robbed Elyssa of breath, of sight. He said something, but she couldn't hear the words. She was beyond that, too.

Then he positioned himself above her. In the last instant she opened her eyes and saw him. And in that infinitesimal pause between past and future, she opened herself to him. Body, mind and soul.

With one strong movement he entered her, filled all the lonely, empty spaces. For a moment she held him deep inside, utterly still. Whatever happened later, for now he was hers. Over the pounding of her heart, the thrumming of her blood, two words flashed into her mind, as if they were written in flame. *At last.*

Did she say them aloud? Did he?

She couldn't tell, for he began to move and she with him. In a rhythm as old as time, as new as this moment. She clasped him tightly while pleasure built and swelled and swirled through her and around her. Until her muscles clenched, everything that was female tightening around the male length of him, holding him as if she'd never let him go...and then she exploded and so did he.

Later they sat propped against the pillows, he in his jeans, she in his shirt, and nibbled on cheese and crackers and shared the wine they'd ordered from room service.

She'd never felt this way before—sated from their tempestuous joining and utterly relaxed as if she floated, weightless, somewhere in the cosmos. Yes, they'd had incredible sex, but that wasn't all. She felt as if they'd connected on some elemental, almost spiritual level that she hadn't known existed until now. What would he think if she told him?

He'd be scared to death. She was a little shaken herself at the intensity of her emotions.

So she hid her feelings, kept the conversation light, and concentrated on actions, not emotions. That seemed the safe thing to do. "Our plans got sidetracked," she teased, offering Brett a cracker piled with cheese.

"Mmm-hmm, did you mind?" he asked. She hadn't buttoned the shirt, and he trailed a finger from her throat to her breast.

Immediately her nipple peaked. She suspected from now on it would do that if he only looked at her breasts. She was already programmed to respond to his slightest cue. "Not much."

"Not *much?*"

She laughed. "Not a bit."

His smile displayed masculine satisfaction. "Sure you didn't miss the romantic dinner?"

With wide-eyed innocence she turned her face up to his. "Can we have it now?" She was amused at how quickly the smug look faded. Chuckling, she kissed his cheek lightly. "Of course I didn't miss it, or the moonlight, either."

She sipped the wine, handed him the glass. He placed his lips on the same spot hers had touched. That seemed remarkably intimate, and she felt a shiver of delight.

"We'll have dinner in the restaurant tomorrow. And the moonlight now." He set the glass on the bedside table and turned off the lamp. "Meanwhile, as long as we're in bed..." He turned on his side and pulled her back into his arms. "I need you again. Medical emergency."

"In that case, Doctor..." She wrapped herself around him and let the magic begin.

Birdsong awakened her. Perched on the balcony a mockingbird trilled a morning greeting. Sunlight wafted through the window and across the bed where Brett still slept, his head pillowed on one arm, his other arm spread across the mattress. He took up nearly three-quarters of the space. If they were going to sleep together regularly, she'd have to train him better.

Turning on her side carefully so as not to wake him, she studied him. In the morning light his tousled hair seemed even more golden than in the artificial lighting of the hospital. The hair on his chest and belly was a paler gold. He must've been a towheaded baby, she thought, imagining him with a cap of soft, blond fuzz.

His body was perfect, so different from hers. He was without a blemish. Except for an intriguing birthmark on his left buttock.

With a painful catch of her breath, Elyssa gazed at her own naked form. The scars seemed larger, more vivid—and uglier—than the last time she'd examined them. Quickly she pulled the sheet up to her shoulders. Last night in their first frenzied coupling they'd taken no time to scrutinize each other's bodies, and after that they'd made love in the dark.

She told herself she was foolish to feel ashamed of her body, but she wanted desperately to slip out of bed and close the drapes. The movement would probably rouse Brett; doctors were known to be light sleepers.

He hadn't minded her face. So what if her body was imperfect? Still, she huddled beneath the covers, dreading the moment when his eyes would open.

Eventually she dozed. A soft kiss woke her, and she

turned to stare into Brett's slumberous eyes. He glanced at the cover. "Cold?" he asked.

"Yes," she lied. Her hand fisted on the sheet.

"Come here. I'll warm you."

She didn't resist when he loosened her fingers. Doing so would have made her look foolish. Instead, she felt nervous, afraid she was about to be judged and found wanting.

"Making love's the best way to raise body temperature." He drew the sheet down, leaned over her and kissed first one breast, then the other. He trailed his tongue over her belly and kissed his way down to her knees, murmuring his approval along the way. "So lovely," he said, raising his eyes to hers.

"I-I'm not."

"You are, in every possible way," he insisted. And her heart soared.

The morning seemed magical. They started with a pre-breakfast hike. Except for the birds and a few squirrels scurrying up and down the tree trunks, they met no one. Beneath the canopy of trees the air, still cool, was laced with the scent of earth and leaves...and Brett. He hadn't bothered to shave, so there was no aftershave, nothing but the smell of soap and man.

He put his arm around her in a natural but somehow possessive move. He'd staked his claim and like any male he intended to declare it.

"I grew up in Philadelphia, but we spent summers in North Carolina on the coast," Brett said as they ambled through the woods. "I used to get up before everyone else and walk along the beach. There'd be nothing but the sand dunes and the sound of the surf. I'd imagine I was exploring the moon or Mars." He bent to pick up a pine cone. "Then I learned that neither of them has an ocean."

"And once you did, was the pretending over?"

"Nope." He tossed the cone away. "I just figured I'd

discover the first Martian sea and prove the scientists wrong.''

''But you didn't become an astronomer or an astronaut. Were you ever sorry?''

''No, after my cousin, Aaron, died, I never wanted to be anything but a physician. I read a lot of science fiction though.''

Elyssa wrinkled her nose. ''It's too far-fetched for me.''

''The best stories are based on scientific principles. Robert Heinlein's. Arthur Clarke's—I've probably read *2001: A Space Odyssey* twenty times.''

She shrugged. ''What else did you do at the beach?''

''Tried to keep out of my sisters' way, or think up plans to terrorize them.''

''Them?'' she asked. ''How many do you have?''

''Four. It wasn't bad, except when the two younger ones hassled me, like wanting me to be Ken when they played Barbie.''

''A real live Ken. If I'd had a brother, I'd have done the same thing.''

''And gotten the same response.''

''Maybe, but I can be pretty persistent.'' She sighed dreamily. ''I was in love with Ken for six whole months.''

His brows lifted. ''And then?''

''Then I discovered Luke Skywalker. He was so much more exciting. Ken seemed...plastic by comparison.''

''I found my hero in comic books,'' Brett said. ''Batman—living in that great house, sliding down the Batpole, saving the city. What a guy. And what a cool car. I *craved* that car.''

The path wound around a clump of trees, and they came upon the creek Elyssa had seen the day before. They sat on the bank, and Elyssa took off her tennis shoes and socks and dangled her feet in the water while they watched the dragonflies hovering over the creek.

Elyssa wiggled her toes, disturbing a school of minnows.

"You know," she said, "I envy you growing up in a big family. I was an only child."

"There's something to be said for that," Brett said, leaning back on his elbows, "at least I thought so when I was growing up. The little ones were always listening in on my phone conversations, sometimes joining them. They almost killed my romance with Chelsea Drew, the eighth-grade siren."

"Lucky for you. The Sirens lured men to their death."

"But what a way to go."

She punched him on the shoulder and he fell back on the bank, pulling her with him for a kiss, then another. Then she looked over her shoulder. "We're putting on a show. You can see the creek from the road."

Brett glanced toward the drive, apparently unconcerned. "So you can." His grin was full of mischief. "Shall we continue the performance?"

"No way. Anyhow, I'm starving. Let's go back."

She put on her shoes, and they retraced their steps, swinging hands companionably. Halfway to the hotel Brett reached in his pocket, then stopped. "The room key must've fallen out of my pocket at the creek. I'll be right back."

Elyssa rested one hand against a tree trunk and shut her eyes. She loved it here...the peace, the isolation. She felt as if she and Brett were the only two people on the planet. Why had she waited so long to let him get close to her? Why—

The sound of rapid footsteps directly behind her disturbed her reverie. Suddenly she was jostled hard, the impact knocking her against the tree. She lost her balance and slid to the ground. Whoever hit her didn't stop. When she sat up and looked, he'd already disappeared into the woods.

Who in the world—

Oh, God, could *he* have followed her here? Her tormentor—the man who'd threatened her, who'd run her off the road? Terrified, eyes darting from side to side, she jumped up and shouted for Brett.

While she waited for him, she took a breath. Of course it wasn't that man. A person like that wouldn't resort to something as tame as a shove. Besides, what would he have to gain by trailing her here? No, he was the kind of guy who'd wait until she was alone, unprotected. This was surely nothing more than an accidental push by someone too rude to stop and see if she'd been hurt. She was just edgy, overreacting because of the stress of the past few days. By the time Brett burst out of the woods, she was embarrassed that she'd screamed.

He rushed to her side and grabbed her arm. "What's wrong? What happened?"

"Nothing much. I'm sorry I scared you. Someone ran into me and I fell." She gestured vaguely. "I think he went that way."

Brett scrutinized her. "You scraped your thigh." He ran a gentle finger alongside the abraded area. "I'll take care of it later. Stay here." He sped off in the direction she'd pointed.

Disgusted at her behavior, Elyssa kicked at a clod of dirt. "You're acting like a ninny," she scolded herself. "Stop it." If she started jumping like a scared rabbit every time some clumsy oaf bumped into her, she wouldn't be able to stop. The incident reminded her that she hadn't gotten around to applying for a gun permit. She'd do that next week.

She heard someone coming and stifled the urge to shrink back against the tree. Instead, she straightened her shoulders and waited. Brett appeared, looking stern, with a teenage boy in tow. He couldn't have been more than fourteen, but he was big, solidly built and, at this moment, miserable.

"This is James," Brett said. "He has something to say to you." He nudged the boy forward.

"I'm sorry," the youngster mumbled, hanging his head. "I, uh, didn't know I bumped you so hard. I was listening to music.'' He gestured to the earphones hanging around his neck. ''I, um, guess I wasn't watching where I was going.''

This was her attacker? She'd reacted to a kid. ''It's okay.''

James smiled weakly and glanced at Brett, who nodded.

The boy scurried off, and Elyssa would have started back to the hotel, but Brett held her still. He knelt down. ''Let's have a look at that scrape,'' he said, in doctor mode now.

She needed to make light of this, if only to restore her dignity. ''Will I live, Doctor?'' she teased.

''With proper medical attention. We'll clean it off and put some antibiotic ointment on it.'' He stood and held out his hand.

As she stretched hers out to meet his, she realized, to her chagrin, that it was trembling. She snatched it back, but not fast enough. Brett noticed, too.

''What's wrong, baby?'' he asked. ''You're shaking. Were you hurt somewhere else?''

''No, of course not. I was just—'' the words stuck in her throat, and unable to stop herself, she shuddered ''—overreacting.''

He drew her into his arms and stroked her hair. ''That kid's as big as an ox and strong, too. Of course you were scared.'' He held her close for a few moments. ''Okay now?''

Mortified, Elyssa swiped at a tear that was making its way down her cheek. ''Yeah, I'm just a little edgy. A...a couple of nights ago, after you brought me home from the restaurant, I got a threatening phone call.''

Alarm showed on his face. He tightened his arms around her. ''What did they say? Did you call the police?''

She repeated the caller's words, recounted her experience with the police, then added, ''The accident the other night—I think someone deliberately ran me off the road.''

Brett's face darkened. ''And you thought *this* was another attempt to terrorize you, didn't you?'' She nodded, and he gripped her hands fiercely. "For God's sake, Elyssa, forget about looking into your friend's death. You can't change what happened. Let it alone. Please."

Vehemently Elyssa shook her head. "I can't. Don't you see? I need to know what happened now, more than ever." His expression didn't change. Earnestly she continued. "If I could remember, maybe I could let it go, but that night's a blank. I need to know the truth. But someone doesn't want me to."

"That's clear enough."

"And doesn't that tell you they're scared of what I'll turn up?" she asked. "That's why they're trying to frighten me."

"They're succeeding, aren't they? They're damn well frightening me."

She tugged her hands away and paced a few yards down the path. "I'm scared, but I won't let them make me a victim, too."

Brett strode after her, took her shoulders and turned her to face him. "Let the—" An elderly couple strolling by stared at them, and he lowered his voice. "Let the police handle it."

"I told you, they won't."

"I'll talk to them."

The anger she was feeling abruptly vanished, and she cupped his cheek. "Brett, that's very sweet of you—"

"I'm not feeling 'sweet,' and I can hear a *but* coming."

She stood on tiptoe and kissed his cheek. "*But* I need to handle this on my own." Suddenly she saw how she could convince him. "When you asked me to think about working with cancer survivors, you talked about healing. This is part of my healing process."

"All right. I don't like it, but I understand," he said just as she'd hoped. They started up the path toward the hotel, then he stopped. "Promise me this. Don't take it too far. If anything else happens, you'll call me."

His concern warmed her, but at the same time she knew she needed to take care of herself. "Brett—"

He held her in place. "Promise."

Making a phone call wouldn't compromise her independence, she decided. She promised.

By mutual consent they didn't discuss the threatening phone call, Elyssa's suspicions about Randy's death or anything connected to it for the rest of the weekend. Instead they relaxed. They let themselves get talked into a bridge game with a couple from Chicago, then went upstairs and made love in the hot tub. They lingered over the gourmet dinner they'd missed the night before but passed on the moonlight walk. Elyssa had had enough of the woods.

The next day they indulged in the lavish brunch served in the dining room, then drove back to Indianapolis. But they'd be back, Brett promised himself. Being with Elyssa could become a habit. Not a commitment, of course, but definitely a habit.

As they neared home, his thoughts inevitably turned toward his patients. That proved something, didn't it? The priorities in his life hadn't changed. Couldn't. He flipped open his cell phone and called the hospital.

When he hung up, Elyssa said, "I did a story on St. Michael's once."

He remembered his conversation with Clark Madigan. He said she had ruffled some feathers. "That must've been before I moved here. Tell me about it," he said.

"We got several calls from patients who'd gone to the emergency room there, saying that they were subjected to tests they thought were unnecessary. I gave a list of their symptoms and the tests that were run to two independent physicians, of course without saying where these patients were seen. Both of them agreed the tests *were* unwarranted *and* costly. I aired the story, and I'm afraid a few heads rolled."

No wonder the senior staff members disliked her. She'd

damaged the hospital's reputation, and by definition, theirs. But she'd been right to publicize unethical practices. MDs who scheduled unwarranted tests and ran up the costs for patients were reprehensible and deserved to be terminated. He glanced at her admiringly. "You were a good reporter."

"I still could be," she said bitterly.

He figured he understood what she meant. She'd "left" the station shortly after recovering from her accident, and he doubted *she'd* made the decision. "Did they fire you?" he asked.

"Of course not. If they had, I'd have slapped them with a lawsuit. No, they offered me a 'promotion,' to news director on KIND-FM. I could read the subtext of that message and I didn't like it, so I quit." She twisted her hands in her lap. "They didn't even wait for me to heal enough to see if makeup would cover the marks on my cheek."

He reached for her hand and squeezed. "Bastards."

"Yeah, and the worst part was, the man I was…involved with delivered the message. I don't know if he was responsible for the decision, but he clearly didn't dispute it. So my career and our relationship ended on the same day."

A mixture of disgust and, yes, dammit, jealousy coursed through him. Jealousy that she'd had another lover. Disgust because those at the station had made her suffer, picked the guy to deliver the blow, and the rat hadn't even backed her up. "Couldn't you have gotten a job at another station?"

She stared out the window, then said, "I didn't try. And after a while I quit thinking about it."

He could think of a number of reasons for that. She feared the pain of another rejection, or she just wanted to put the past behind her. He didn't probe but tightened his hold on her hand.

When they reached her house, he took the key from her. "I want to check your alarm system."

"Go ahead," Elyssa said. "It's state-of-the-art."

It seemed to be. Reassured, he pulled her close for a long, lingering kiss.

When they drew apart, Elyssa sighed. "I'm glad I didn't wait any longer to make love with you."

"Me, too. What made you decide?"

"I trust you," she answered gravely.

Trust. She'd given him a precious gift, one he sensed wasn't easy for her to bestow. The bastard who'd sacked her at the TV station had killed her trust.

Now she'd given it freely to *him*. Did he deserve it?

His wife would have answered with an unequivocal, No.

Soon, he thought with soul-wrenching sorrow. Soon he'd have to tell her about Denise.

Chapter 9

Later that evening, Brett studied Trace Malden's chart. "You didn't tell me he had a fever when I called."

Sue Chen, the charge nurse, met his eyes squarely. "He didn't until a few minutes ago. We just checked his temperature."

Brett tucked the chart under his arm. "Let's take a look."

They found the youngster lying on his back, staring at the ceiling. The TV was off, which was unusual; the nine-year-old normally had ESPN blaring the baseball game or the sports news. "How're you doing, pal?" Brett asked, noting Trace's glassy-eyed stare and labored breathing.

The boy coughed. "Don't feel so good."

"Been coughing much?"

"Yeah."

"Since when?"

"This morning, I guess."

Brett laid his hand on the child's forehead. He was burning up. "Let's check you over," Brett suggested, and quickly took vital signs. The boy's fever was nearly 104. "Get a chest X ray," Brett told Sue, "and blood work, stat." She hurried out. He turned back to Trace and brushed a hand over his matted hair. "I'm going to call your mom."

Instantly alert, Trace stared at Brett. "Am I gonna die?"

Brett put his hand over Trace's bony one. "I want your mom here because you're running a fever and you're not feeling well. I think you may have pneumonia. We're going to take some blood and check your chest and then we'll give you medicine to treat it. But it'll take time for the medicine to work."

He believed in being honest with his patients, telling them as much as they could grasp and cope with. Most of these kids knew a great deal about their illnesses. Pretending or painting rosy pictures didn't work. It frightened them and made them distrust the medical staff. "You'll feel better having someone with you tonight," he added.

The boy stared into Brett's eyes, gauging the truthfulness of his words, then he nodded. "Okay. Tell her to bring my baseball cards. I left them at home last time I went."

"Sure thing." Brett glanced at his watch. "I have some other kids to see, but I'll be back before I leave. Meantime we're going to give you some oxygen to help you breathe easier."

He went back to the nurses' station to check with Sue on how long it would take to get the blood work and X rays. "When you get the results, page me immediately," he told her.

As soon as he could, he returned to Trace's room. The boy was alone and frightened. It would take his mother some time to make arrangements for someone to stay with her other two children and to drive to the hospital from Edinburgh where they lived.

Brett was sitting with Trace when the blood and X-ray results came in. As he feared, the boy had pneumonia. It wasn't uncommon in immunosuppressed children, but that didn't make it easy to treat. When Mrs. Malden arrived, looking as pale as her son, Brett explained what was going on and the course of treatment.

It was nearly midnight when he got home. He ran his hand over his face. His cheeks were rough with stubble and his eyes ached. He kicked off his shoes and lay down, still dressed.

God, he was exhausted. But his mind refused to shut down. What chemo dose was best for Ramon Guiterrez? Was Darcy Kaplan ready for discharge? And what about the sudden coolness between himself and Clark Madigan? He'd have to set up a lunch meeting somewhere quiet, away from the hospital, and try to heal the breach between them.

Elyssa would want to hear about Trace, but she was probably asleep, and after what had happened to her last week, he didn't want to frighten her with a midnight call.

If he were living with her, how would she feel about his coming home in the wee hours, exhausted but wired, his mind burdened with thoughts of his patients? He remembered Denise's reaction only too well. One night, as their marriage floundered, she'd castigated him as usual for being late. "You think I have another woman," he said tiredly. "It's not true."

"Oh, I know you don't have a woman," she snapped. "You don't have time. You're too much in love with medicine." She was right.

And now medicine was his mate, his...life.

Best to keep that in the forefront of his mind. Best to remember that he could never consider a long-term relationship with Elyssa. But he didn't want to give her up, not when they'd just found each other. He would keep things casual between them, and he'd be careful—very careful—not to get in too deep.

The next morning when he got an update on Trace's condition, he called Elyssa. She was upset when he explained that the boy's condition was grave. "Can I visit him?" she asked.

"We've transferred him to Intensive Care to keep him isolated. His immune system is virtually nonfunctional."

"Oh, no," she said. "Does this mean he's going to... die?"

"We don't know," Brett said gently.

"I wish I could do something," Elyssa said. "Maybe I'll come by and sit with his mother and grandmother for a while."

"That would be good," Brett said. "And you can do more than that. The isolation room has a window. You can wave to him."

"I'll wear my costume," she said, sounding more cheerful.

"After you've visited Trace, come by and see me, too. I have a full day and a late night, but I can take a break."

"I'll be there," she said, "and I'll bring you a surprise."

Late that afternoon Elyssa walked to the tiny window and peered into Trace's room. Her heart constricted when she saw him lying pale and inert in the bed. Tubes ran into his skeleton-like arms; monitors beeped; an oxygen mask covered most of his face. A nurse, masked and gowned in hideous hospital green, stood by the bed, taking his pulse with a gloved hand. Nothing softened the room's cold, otherworldly atmosphere—no teddy bear, no baseball posters, nothing to cheer a frightened child. He might as well be in an alien world. And he looked like a creature from such a world—thin, lifeless.

When the nurse came out, she saw Elyssa and turned back. "Trace, you have a visitor," she called.

The boy's head swiveled toward the tiny window. Elyssa waved exuberantly and smiled her Lulu smile. Slowly his lips curved, and a tiny hint of life emerged in his eyes. She held up a poster board on which she'd printed with colored markers: "Get well soon, Trace. Love, Lulu." He nodded and smiled faintly. Elyssa waggled her head and gave him a thumbs-up sign.

"I'll be back," she mouthed, then moved away from the window and leaned her head against the wall. This was what Brett encountered every day. How did he survive?

She swallowed her tears, then went to change before visiting with Trace's grandmother. As she removed her costume and makeup in the rest room, she promised herself she'd be strong for Trace and his family, and for Brett, too.

Brett opened his office door. Elyssa was in street clothes and carried a large brown paper bag. She kissed his cheek, then patted the bag. "I brought you a snack and your heart's desire."

He pulled her close for a kiss, deep and satisfying. God, she felt right in his arms. He wanted to bury himself in her. *Needed* to. When he was with her, he felt that he'd found a sanctuary where the defeats he suffered every day couldn't touch him. "You're my heart's desire," he said softly.

She drew back and smiled at him. "This is one you've had much longer." She reached into the bag and brought out a gaily wrapped package. "Open it."

Brett tore off the paper and opened the box. "The Batmobile!" he said and burst out laughing. He lifted her off the floor and spun her around, then set her down and kissed her exuberantly. "Just what I needed."

She reached in the bag again. "I have more goodies." She set a basket on his desk. "Garlic bread. Mineral water. Caesar salad with low-fat dressing. I'd have brought a hero sandwich to go with the car, but it isn't nutritious."

"This is great. Will you join me?" he asked.

"Of course. I brought two forks."

He pulled a chair to the side of his desk for her, and they dived in. "I didn't realize I was hungry," he said. He'd been too immersed in the routine of patients, treatment, emergencies.

"How often do you forget to eat?" Elyssa asked.

He thought for a minute, then shrugged. "Fifty-fifty, I guess."

She gave him a stern look. "You'd lecture your patients if they didn't eat three meals a day."

"But they're sick." He broke a piece of bread, offered half to Elyssa. "And hospital chow often makes me sick."

"I'd tell you to order out, but you wouldn't listen." When he smiled and shrugged, she touched his hand and said softly, "I worry about you."

Brett stared at her in surprise. She was focused on *his* needs, not hers. She was the antithesis of Denise in every way.

Carefully he removed her hand. "I should tell you about my marriage."

He saw her flinch and swallow hard, but her voice was steady when she said, "All right."

"Denise and I met at a party my third year of med school. We married the week after I graduated. We had a weekend honeymoon, and then I started my residency. Right away I was loaded down with twenty-four- or thirty-six-hour shifts and the stress that went along with them— being terrified at holding human lives in my hands, wanting to prove myself, feeling exhausted half the time." He sighed. "Denise couldn't deal with it. And I couldn't give her what she needed."

Young, needy and lonely in an unfamiliar city, Denise had taken it out on him. How well he remembered the tears, the complaints, the accusations. From the vantage point of years, he realized Denise was immature. But half the blame was his. Worn out by the constant demands of his medical training, he hadn't given her the time and attention she craved.

The knowledge of that aroused the guilt he always bore like an albatross around his neck. If he'd been more aware, more sympathetic, everything might have been different.

He brought himself back to the present. Elyssa sat still, waiting. With that uncanny ability he'd noticed the first

time they talked, she seemed to absorb not only his words
but his emotions, too.

"A few months into my second year of residency, Denise got pregnant." *Pregnant.* Such a powerful word. It
could bring profound joy or unbearable pain.

"She was ecstatic," he continued, "and so was I. All
the tension between us disappeared, and we began planning
for the baby, spinning hopes and dreams...."

He felt then that their marriage, despite its rocky start,
had been given new life. He was wrong. He sat now, staring
out the window as the gray shroud of twilight obliterated
the day.

Elyssa laid her hand on his. "What happened?"

"It was January. I was scheduled at the hospital for
twenty-four hours. I told Denise I'd be home as soon as I
finished. I meant to. I was on my way out of the E.R. when
they brought in three kids who'd been in a fire..."

"You stayed," Elyssa murmured.

"Yes." He could hear the scream of the sirens, the sobs
of the mother following the gurneys. He could see the
nurses dashing from one cubicle to another, see himself
racing back into the E.R., feel the adrenaline rush as he
pulled a curtain aside and joined the battle to save a child.

"Afterward, I went to the residents' lounge to get my
jacket, and I sat down..."

He'd been half-blind with fatigue. He'd decided to sit on
the couch for just a moment, then go home. His eyes had
drifted shut.

"I fell asleep," he said. "Three hours later I woke up.
I knew Denise would be furious. I called, but she didn't
answer."

He'd glanced out the window at low-hanging clouds.
Wind-tossed papers blew across the sleet-covered parking
lot. He remembered the knot in his gut as he'd told himself
surely Denise wouldn't go out in this weather. Maybe he'd
dialed the wrong number. He tried again. Still no answer.

He'd thought of stopping on the way home and buying

flowers as a peace offering, but he forgot that now. Alarmed, he dashed, coatless, out of the hospital.

"The garage was too far. I got a cab home. When we pulled up, I saw an ambulance." The words came out one by one, mechanically, but the emotions ran beneath them like a firestorm. He'd relived this scene countless times, recast it, reversed it, to no avail. It always had the same ending.

"Two paramedics were kneeling on the ground at the bottom of the porch steps. I ran across the yard and saw Denise...."

He could see her still, her face white as marble, the snow stained scarlet with her blood. He could feel the icy wind sting his cheeks, hear Denise's words—weak, toneless. Painfully, he met Elyssa's eyes. "She said, 'The baby's dead.'"

"Oh, Brett." Elyssa's hand tightened on his.

"She'd been feeling ill and was on her way to the obstetrician's office when she slipped on the stairs. I asked why she didn't call me, and she said, 'How could I trust you to come? You're never here for me. You were hours late already.'"

His voice thick with tears long unshed, he continued, "They took her to the hospital and straight into surgery. She'd lost a lot of blood."

Torn with grief and guilt, he sat in the waiting room, head in his hands. Denise's parents were on their way from Vermont, but he hadn't thought to call anyone else. He was alone.

He heard footsteps but didn't look up. Then he felt a hand on his shoulder and heard the voice of Denise's obstetrician. "I'm afraid we have bad news,"

He'd looked up, puzzled at the doctor's words. What bad news? He already knew they'd lost the baby.

"Your wife's blood volume was very low when she got here. We started transfusions, but she went into cardiac arrest. We couldn't save her. I'm sorry, son."

That was the last clear thing he remembered. What happened later—Denise's parents arriving, her mother's sobs, the funeral—all of that seemed to occur in a fog. He was numb and stayed that way for weeks. For months.

He didn't tell Elyssa all of that. He simply said, "She died in surgery."

Elyssa rose, put her arms around him and drew him against her breast. "I'm so sorry."

Brett sat for long moments, feeling the tenderness of her embrace, the steady beat of her heart against his cheek. He wanted to stay like this, to let himself sink into her softness.

"I don't know how I got through the rest of that year," he said, "but I did. I asked myself some hard questions that spring."

Now, with Elyssa holding him, her hand stroking his hair, he wanted to let himself pretend for a little while that he'd come up with different answers. But he couldn't. What happened that chilly winter day was his fault and his alone.

Elyssa said nothing. He was grateful that she didn't press the issue of his blame. People—family members, close friends—had argued that the loss of the baby and Denise's death weren't his fault. Their attempts to cheer him, to alleviate his guilt, always made him feel worse.

He felt a sudden need to distance himself from the pain he'd recounted. He stiffened and drew away.

Elyssa, as always, seemed to understand. "Thank you for telling me about your marriage," she said quietly, then began methodically stuffing plates and forks into the paper bag. "I see now why you understand your patients and their families so well. You've gone through a terrible tragedy yourself and because of that, you can help them deal with theirs." She dropped the bag into the trash can. "You've helped me. I've decided to follow your suggestion about working with cancer patients. I made an appointment with social services."

"That's good." She, too, would know how to relate to people who'd been through hell; she'd been there herself.

She steered the conversation to other subjects—her visit to Trace, some new lessons she was planning for her clown class, a funny experience she'd had at a birthday party. She brought him back to the present, made him laugh. She was an exceptional lady, and he would be honest with her. He owed her that.

"Elyssa," he said when she was ready to leave, "after Denise died, I realized I couldn't be a good husband and a good doctor. I made a commitment to medicine. I can't make another." The words sounded cold in his own ears, but he had to say them. He wanted her to understand where he stood.

Her lips curved into a saucy smile, the kind of smile that went straight to a man's loins. "Why, Dr. Cameron," she said, "what makes you think I want one?" Then she walked out of his office and shut the door behind her.

"Liar," Elyssa muttered as she headed for the hospital garage. Of course she wanted a commitment. What woman didn't?

Well, Brett wasn't ready to give one. She understood why and she ached for him, though she didn't believe for a moment that what happened to his wife and unborn child was his fault. No, it was one of those random acts of fate, like her accident. The point was that *he* believed it.

At least he was honest about his unwillingness to commit. Unlike many men, who promised more than they intended to deliver.

So she'd protect the heart that was already his, enjoy his company, treasure the intimacy they shared…and see that he was taken care of. Good heavens, the man needed a keeper—skipping meals the way he did. She'd make a point to drop off some nutritious snacks when she went by the hospital. She'd be there a lot—looking in on Trace, visiting cancer patients, besides giving her regularly scheduled clown shows and classes. And if Brett couldn't get away, well, there was always the broom closet.

He was busy around the clock that week, and she saw him only in passing. She, too, was occupied with birthday parties and hospital commitments. In her spare time she continued to track Randy's comings and goings the last weeks of his life. She questioned other friends of his, seeking information about his mood and his activities during those final days. Because Randy had been covering the purchase of new school buses, she requested the minutes of that week's school board meeting. She learned nothing. She surfed the Internet, trying to make sense of Randy's scribbles, to no avail. Her inability to discover any relevant information frustrated her, but she didn't stop digging.

At least she had no late-night phone calls or near accidents in the car. But just in case, she applied for an Indiana Personal Protection Firearms Permit. She filled out the form, had it notarized and brought it back to the Citizens' service office. "Go to room 108 to be fingerprinted," the clerk said.

The process took only a few minutes, but under the stern and, she thought, suspicious gaze of the woman who took her prints, Elyssa felt like a criminal. She half expected to be tossed into a cell.

"You'll get the permit in two to ten weeks," the woman said.

"But I need it now. Isn't this all computerized? It should be faster."

"Two to ten weeks," the woman repeated in a robotlike voice as she stared at a spot on the wall over Elyssa's shoulder.

A lot of help that would be if her midnight caller decided to confront her on a dark street. But you couldn't argue with bureaucracy. "I'll look forward to it," Elyssa muttered.

If she were still on television, she'd do a story on the overlong waiting period, get viewers so riled up they'd write and complain. Since that wasn't possible, she decided that if the permit arrived one day after the ten weeks were up, she'd lodge a complaint with the State of Indiana.

More than a week passed before Brett could take a Saturday afternoon off. He called Elyssa, and they arranged to get together with her cousin and a friend at Larchmont Park in Cassie's neighborhood.

When they arrived, Cassie greeted Brett with a knowing smile. Then she glanced at Elyssa and the two exchanged some sort of secret female message. Cassie was communicating her opinion of him, he guessed. He must've passed muster because Elyssa grinned.

Cassie introduced her friend, a shy young actor named Nathan Stein, then announced, "We're going to fly kites."

The last time he'd done that he'd been about twelve, Brett remembered as Cassie pointed to the two kites lying on a nearby picnic table. All of her gestures seemed larger than life, appropriate for an actress.

Brett liked her. How could he not? She was part of Elyssa's life, and besides, with her sparkling green eyes and wide smile, she seemed capable of charming anyone. She'd certainly charmed Nathan, who, Elyssa explained in a low voice, was Cassie's boyfriend-of-the-month.

"Pick a kite," Cassie said.

"The one with the happy face," Elyssa decided.

"Okay, men against women," Cassie said. "Let's see who can keep theirs up the longest."

The men won easily. "Only because we let you," Elyssa said. "Our mothers told us we wouldn't get boyfriends if we beat guys."

"Okay," Brett said. "Let's try again, but this time give it all you've got."

This time the men were soundly beaten. "See?" Cassie gloated. "We're women of steel."

Brett pulled Elyssa back against him and kissed her temple. "But where would you be without boyfriends?"

"I'll answer that," Cassie said. "Independent."

Nathan sighed.

They watched a kids' baseball game, then drove to Cassie's for hamburgers which they cooked and ate on the patio. "Thank heaven she's over her vegetarian phase," Elyssa said.

They were just finishing when Brett's phone shrilled. He stepped inside to take the call. It was the hospital, of course.

How would Elyssa react? Many women loved the idea of dating a doctor but were annoyed at the realities of a physician's life. Most didn't bother to hide their displeasure at the inevitable interruptions. Once that happened, they were history.

When he returned, Elyssa asked, "It's not Trace, is it?"

"No, but I have to go in. I'm sorry to break this up."

Elyssa seemed unperturbed as they said their goodbyes and left. In the car Brett took her hand. "I won't be long at the hospital. Come with me." He leaned closer and kissed her. "Afterward we'll think of...something to do."

"Okay."

At the hospital he unlocked his office. "I have to see a little girl who came in yesterday and isn't doing well. After that, I'll check on Trace."

"Good. I want to know how he's doing."

Elyssa picked up a copy of *Time* and settled down on the couch in Brett's private office. Strange how quiet the hospital seemed on a weekend evening, she thought. There were surely as many sick patients as during the week, but everything seemed to function in slow motion as if even illness took a break.

Nearly an hour later Brett came back, smiling. "Trace' fever broke," he said. "He's going to be okay."

Elyssa jumped up. "Oh, thank God." Brett opened his arms and she ran into them. He lifted her off the floor and they hugged each other, laughing with relief.

Elyssa kissed his cheeks, his chin...and then his mouth. And the laughter stopped. Oh, she'd missed his taste. If she were blind, she'd recognize him just by that. A flavor that was sexy and male. And Brett.

She invited his tongue into her mouth, engaged in an erotic dance of thrust and retreat. He pushed her shirt up, took her breasts in his hands and leaned down to kiss them through her bra. His teeth grazed her throat; his breath was hot against her skin. "God, I want you. It's been too long."

She tugged him toward the door. "Let's go home."

"No," he said hoarsely, "Here." He pulled her to the couch.

Like the first time, no titillation was necessary, no finesse. Lust consumed them, fierce and primitive. Within seconds they were naked. He was over her, then deep inside. They moved together, their bodies slick with sweat, their breathing harsh. Faster, faster. And with one wild cry she climaxed, and Brett followed.

Exhausted, they lay tangled in each other's arms. "Wow," Elyssa managed finally. "That was…awesome. But what if someone had come by for you?"

"If someone needed me, they'd page me. But to be safe, I locked the door." He nuzzled her neck, then raised his head and smiled at her. "I've imagined having you in my office."

Lazily she stroked his back. "Really?"

"On the examining table." He chuckled at her gasp of surprise. "We'll try that another time. For now…" He sat up and handed her the T-shirt she'd worn.

Not bothering with the bra, she pulled it on, then reached for her jeans. "My house or yours?"

He considered only a moment. "Yours is closer."

"Okay," she murmured, not sure she had the energy to walk to the garage. "When we get there, you can carry me up the stairs."

"All right, Scarlett." He fastened his jeans and put out his hand.

She smiled as they strolled out together. Ah, romance.

Chapter 10

"Before we adjourn," Dr. Madigan said, "I want to announce that Dr. Stevenson is a nominee for vice presiden[t] of the American Medical Association."

Brett automatically added his congratulations to the res[t] rippling around the conference table. His mind was else where. On Elyssa as it so often was these days. Last nigh[t] they'd gone to a foreign movie and sat in the back row. H[e] couldn't remember anything about the movie except that i[t] was Italian, though he hadn't bothered to read the subtitles Instead he'd been horny as a schoolboy, nuzzling, kissing touching her. They'd barely made it home before they wer[e] naked....

"...and Dr. Cameron will present at the cancer sympo sium in November." More congratulatory murmurs. Ma digan turned to Brett. "You'll be discussing the wor[k] you've done with Warren Frank at Columbia, right?" Bret[t] nodded and Madigan added, "He's a good man. You'l[l] need some good people for the new hospital."

"I'm already working on convincing him to come."

"Good. Keep at it."

"Sure thing." The conference was in Toronto. Maybe he'd take an extra day, ask Elyssa to come with him....

Not a good idea. He was getting in too deep, too fast. Three days away would give him—give them both—some breathing space. He began gathering papers as the meeting came to a close.

Madigan's secretary, Lee Anne Scarborough, said something to him in a low voice, and he added, "Oh, yes. Patricia and I have booked a block of tickets for the revival of *A Chorus Line* on opening night, September 17. We'd like all of you to be our guests. Your wives or significant others, too, of course." More murmurs, this time of thanks. "Let Lee Anne know."

As the group began filing out, Madigan said, "Brett, hold on a minute." He waited for Lee Anne to shut the door, then said, "I was impressed with your new resident at grand rounds today."

"Thanks, I'll let her know," Brett said.

Madigan jotted notes on a yellow pad as they spoke; he was known for multitasking. He glanced up. "How's she fitting in?"

"Very well. By the way, I should tell you I'm going to ask Elyssa Jarmon to the theater."

"As you like." Madigan's expression didn't change. In fact, he seemed unconcerned. Brett was surprised. The older man wouldn't have forgotten their previous conversation—Clark never forgot anything—but apparently his displeasure at Brett's choice of companions had evaporated.

Good. He had no intention of giving in to Madigan's demand that he drop Elyssa, but he also didn't want friction between himself and his mentor. He didn't know why or when Clark had had a change of heart, but he was pleased.

He was even more delighted later when he called Elyssa and she said she would go. Once she spent time with Madigan, Brett was certain she'd charm the older man as thoroughly as she'd enchanted him.

* * *

What she and Brett felt for each other wasn't love, Elyssa reminded herself daily. Even though they *made* love at every possible opportunity, in every possible way. Late one night they finally christened the examining table in his office.

"It's not a serious relationship, just a casual affair," Elyssa assured Cassie as they pedaled side by side on stationary bikes during their early-morning workout at Yolanda's Gym.

Her cousin swiped a hand over her sweaty brow. "We'll see." Her eyes narrowed as she glanced at Elyssa. "You're spending every minute at the hospital."

"I'm working with cancer patients. Oh, Cass, it's so rewarding. Wait till I show you the letter I got yesterday."

When they'd showered and changed, she rummaged in her purse, pulled out a thank-you note and held it out.

Cassie smoothed the paper and read aloud:

"Dear Ms. Jarmon,
   Your visits to me while I was recovering from a double mastectomy meant so much. Though I was told I had a good prognosis, I was severely depressed. My lover couldn't deal with the idea of the change in my body and backed away. I felt less a woman, not just imperfect but unlovable. But you made me see that a perfect body isn't the essence of who I am or who I can be. I have a long way to go, but you've given me the example and the courage to make the journey.
                                    My heartfelt thanks,
                                    Rhonda Grayson."

Cassie looked up, her eyes damp. "That's nice. Making such a difference in someone's life is remarkable. And I bet it's helping you, too."

"It is," Elyssa said. "I'm learning to live with my own

scars. I'll never be completely happy about them, but I realize I don't have to be completely sad, either.'' She put the note away. ''Let's have breakfast at the Health Nut.''

The small café, half a block away, took advantage of its proximity to Yolanda's, advertising pre- and postworkout specials. This morning it was noisy and crowded but they were lucky enough to get the last vacant table.

Cassie ordered, then tapped her finger on the table impatiently while the waiter took Elyssa's order for an egg-white omelet. ''Now back to Dr. Dreamboat,'' she said. ''How 'casual' can this relationship be? You're not the kind of person to sleep with a man unless you care for him. You *are* sleeping together, aren't you?''

Embarrassed, Elyssa glanced around to see if anyone at nearby tables was listening, then decided no one could hear over the clatter of dishes and the noise of conversation. ''Yes, but he doesn't want a serious relationship.''

Cassie sniffed. ''So macho. The lone cowboy, never tied down to anyone but his horse. Or in this case his stethoscope.''

''It's not funny,'' Elyssa said. ''He was married once, and it ended tragically.''

''What happened?''

''His wife miscarried when he came home late from the hospital and then she died. He feels responsible.''

''That's terrible,'' Cassie said. ''Is he?''

''I don't think so. What happened was just an accident. But he won't risk another commitment.''

''He'll come 'round.''

''I wish I could believe that,'' Elyssa said with a sigh, ''but…''

The waiter appeared with their tea and asked if they'd like something else—cream, lemon, mineral water, *anything*. He gazed at Cassie like a lovesick puppy.

When he left, Elyssa said, ''I wish I could be like you. Every man who looks at you falls in love. Even our waiter.''

Cassie stared after the waiter in surprise, then shrugged. "But I don't fall in love back. Actually, I'm thinking of swearing off romance. It interferes with my career goals."

Elyssa stared at her cousin in awe. "And just like that, you'll give up men."

"Yep." Cassie sipped her tea. "What else is new?"

Elyssa chuckled at the abrupt, Cassie-like change of subject. "I'm still looking into Randy's death."

Cassie's sunny expression immediately turned grim. "You know what I think about that. Especially since you told me about the phone call and the car chase."

"I'm being careful. Last week I applied for a gun permit, and yesterday I bought a .38 special."

Cassie's eyes widened. "A gun?"

"Titanium—lighter than aluminum, stronger than steel."

"Do you know how to use it?"

"Sure. I took riflery in camp one summer, remember? A revolver should be easier to fire."

Cassie looked skeptical. "But would you actually shoot someone?"

Elyssa hesitated. "Yes, in self-defense. Of course, I can't carry it with me yet. I have to wait for the permit."

"Somehow that doesn't make me feel any better. I wish you'd forget this."

"Brett says the same thing, but I can't."

Cassie gave a disgusted snort. "Well, dammit, if you end up in another ditch and I have to fish you out, don't say I didn't warn you."

"If I could just remember something about that night— whether Randy *said* anything—I wouldn't be up against this darned brick wall."

"Okay," Cassie said, "I'm going to make a suggestion. I know someone who knows a woman named Mariah Hart. She's a hypnotist/psychic who specializes in helping people recall past lives and past experiences. You could call her and set up an appointment. Maybe she can help you remember."

"A psychic? Cassie, those people are fakes."

"Not all of them. Police departments use them."

"But—"

"You're not having any success going through normal channels," Cassie pointed out. "What have you got to lose?"

Elyssa stared down at the table and fiddled with her spoon. "Nothing, I guess."

"Well then," Cassie said, looking smug.

"Okay, get me her number."

When they talked on the phone that night, Elyssa was surprised at Brett's reaction to the news that she planned to see a hypnotist. She'd expected him to be appalled, but he was neutral. Of course, she didn't mention that the woman also purported to be a psychic.

"I know doctors who use hypnotists for stress reduction and pain management," he said, "but I don't put much stock in them."

"Cassie's friend says Mariah's very good."

"*Cassie's* friend?"

Oh-oh. "Just because Cassie suggested her, are you going to put her down?"

Brett chuckled. "You have to admit your cousin's off-beat."

"True," Elyssa admitted, "but she'd never recommend someone who would hurt me."

"I'm sure she wouldn't, but when it comes to hypnosis, I'm a skeptic. Besides, I'd hate for you to get your hopes up and be disappointed."

"If it doesn't work, I won't be any worse off than I am now. Besides, what's my alternative? I've tried everything."

"At least let me check her out and see if she's licensed."

Elyssa agreed, and he asked, "When are you going?"

"Next Wednesday."

"I'll go with you."

Nothing could have surprised her more. "Why?" she asked suspiciously. "To pick up the pieces?"

"Maybe." Then his tone changed. "Or I could be looking for an excuse to spend an evening with you." Elyssa could almost see his lips curve.

"Then, thanks. I'd love to have your company."

When she told Cassie that Brett was going, her cousin said smugly, "You see? Only a man who's hopelessly in love would tag along to something like that."

Hopelessly in love or not, Elyssa was glad to have company. As the evening of the appointment approached, she alternated between feeling hopeful and foolish. She was more of a skeptic than Brett, she decided. If she weren't so desperate, she'd call the whole thing off. Instead, she hurried home from a birthday party and changed into an ankle-length denim dress. Mariah had told her to wear comfortable, loose-fitting clothes.

"How much did you tell her about yourself?" Brett asked as he turned into Mariah's neighborhood.

"Only that I had an accident and can't remember it."

"Good," he said.

She couldn't resist the urge to tease. She lowered her voice to a whisper. "And don't worry. She knows nothing about you." He shot her a baleful glance, and she added, "I told her I was bringing a friend, that's all."

When Brett parked on a tree-lined street in an old inner-city neighborhood, Elyssa let out a sigh of relief. "I'm glad her house looks so...so normal." It was a small cottage with a swing hanging on the porch and a riot of late-summer flowers blooming in the yard.

"I'd feel better if she practiced in an office," Brett said.

"Snob."

"Probably," he agreed good-naturedly.

"I wonder if she'll be as...ordinary as her home," Elyssa murmured. She doubted it. As a reporter, she'd interviewed people who were out of the mainstream. She wondered if Mariah would try to call up Randy's ghost. The idea made Elyssa shiver.

Brett took her hand as they started up the walk. "You're ice-cold," he remarked. "Are you okay?"

"Sure, I…"

"Having second thoughts? If you are, we can turn around and forget this."

For just an instant she was tempted to agree, but the door of the cottage was already opening. A tall, striking woman with waist-length black hair came out on the porch and waved.

Trapped, Elyssa waved back.

"Hello." Mariah called. Her voice was low and whisky smooth, with a slight accent that Elyssa couldn't place. When they reached her, Elyssa saw that her eyes were black as onyx, her skin golden. Her dress, made of some black, gauzy material, flowed to her ankles. She wore gold bangles on her arms, gold teardrops in her ears, and, heavens, a tiny gold hoop in a pierced eyebrow. Exotic, Elyssa thought, like a gypsy.

Suddenly she remembered going with a group of friends to a fortune-teller's booth at a carnival when she was about fourteen. The woman insisted the girls come in singly and led each in turn past a beaded curtain into a grubby, dimly lit room that reeked of fish and garlic. Elyssa remembered the bony hand grasping hers, the hoarse voice saying she'd meet the man of her dreams and have three beautiful children. When they'd compared notes afterward, the girls discovered that the "fortune-teller" had told each of them the same thing. Would Mariah be equally hokey?

Elyssa put out her hand; the psychic took it in a firm grasp and held it for a long moment. She shut her eyes and seemed to center all her consciousness on Elyssa's hand. Elyssa felt as if a surge of electricity passed through Mariah's fingers and into hers, then told herself she was over-reacting. And forgetting her manners. She introduced Brett and watched Mariah grasp his hand with the same intense focus. Then she invited them inside.

Mariah's living room was nothing like the carnival fortune-teller's lair; it was tidy and clean and smelled faintly of lavender. The psychic nodded toward a sofa, and Elyssa and Brett sat, displacing a fat Persian cat, who glared at them before flicking her tail and marching haughtily out of the room.

Elyssa's nerves began to flutter. She felt as if she were about to dive into unknown waters. Could she bear to relive Randy's death? Would she learn what really happened? She suddenly wondered if she wanted to.

"Would you like a cup of herbal tea before we begin?" Mariah asked. "It will relax you."

"Yes, thank you." Was her nervousness that evident? But then, most people who visited Mariah were probably anxious.

Mariah served the tea in small cups that looked as if she'd filched them from a Chinese restaurant. She didn't make small talk. Instead, she studied Elyssa as she drank. "You were a newscaster."

Didn't take much psychic ability to know that. Anyone who'd watched Channel 9 and had a good memory for names and faces would recognize her. Elyssa nodded.

"And then you had the accident you mentioned. I'm sorry your station didn't keep you on. You were good."

"Thank you."

"But what you're doing now is satisfying, hmm?"

Elyssa stared at Mariah in surprise. Since she wasn't on TV, it was an easy guess that she'd started another career. Or *was* it a guess?

"And you want to know what happened the night you can't recall, hmm?" Elyssa nodded, and Mariah said, "Finish your tea and we'll begin. Come."

Elyssa turned to Brett. "Do you want to wait here?"

No way in hell, Brett thought. "I'm coming with you." He glanced at Mariah, daring her to tell him no. She stared back. The two of them engaged in a silent battle of wills until Mariah gave him a half smile, turned and gestured for them to follow.

Brett glanced around as she led them down a short hallway. This place—the whole scenario—unsettled him. The flowery scent. Mariah's exotic get-up. The odd feeling he'd experienced when she gripped his hand. Even the cat disturbed him.

He'd come because the idea of Elyssa alone in such a place aroused every protective instinct he possessed. If anything went wrong, he intended to get her out of here immediately.

They entered a room that was unfurnished except for a couch and several straight chairs. Heavy satin drapes in deep burgundy covered the windows and darkened the room. The odor he'd noticed when they entered the house was stronger here. Trappings that would reel in desperate people, Brett thought cynically.

Yet on the wall was a framed certificate, attesting that Mariah was a licensed hypnotherapist. That *should* have alleviated his misgivings, but it didn't.

He didn't like the way she insinuated that she knew more than Elyssa had told her. Had she quizzed Cassie's friend about Elyssa? Surely she hadn't figured anything out on her own.

Barely sparing him a glance, Mariah instructed Brett to take a seat. Then she turned to Elyssa. "Lie down now and make yourself comfortable."

Elyssa sat on the couch and slipped off her shoes, then she hesitated. "I'm...a little nervous."

Brett was out of his chair in an instant. "You don't have to do this." He started toward Elyssa. "We can—"

Mariah blocked his path. "Stop. She'll be all right."

He pushed past her, but she grabbed his arm. "I've done this thousands of times, and I'm in charge here, *Doctor*."

Shocked, he met her eyes. Her gaze was clear and calm and totally confident. Brett stepped back.

Mariah pointed to a chair. "Sit, be quiet. Not a word."

She walked to the couch and stood beside it. "You're going to be fine," she said firmly, gently. "Lie back." Eyes fastened on Mariah, Elyssa lay down. "Close your eyes now," Mariah said. "Relax. Take a deep breath..."

Still stunned, Brett sat and frowned at Mariah. How did she know he was a doctor? What was going on here? Used to being in charge, he suddenly was not in control. Out of his depth. He didn't like it.

He leaned forward, his eyes riveted on Elyssa. She lay rigidly on the couch, her hands clenched. Beside her, the hypnotist stood relaxed, eyes half-closed, her voice droning.

"Breathe in...out." Mariah's voice was soft, hypnotic. "Picture a screen in front of you. See the number seven on it. Now six...five..."

As Mariah slowly counted backward, Elyssa felt as if she were drifting. Floating in a dark, slow-moving river... farther from shore...farther...

"Four...three...two..."

Her breathing deepened, slowed. Her surroundings receded into the distance. She heard the rhythmic sound of water, felt the night—velvet and heavy—close around her. And she heard Mariah's voice. "One."

"Elyssa, can you hear me?" Mariah spoke quietly.

"Yes." Her voice was high, breathy.

"You're going back in time. Back to the night of your accident. You'll know every sound, every feeling."

Brett felt a shudder of unease. For the first time he wondered if Elyssa might actually remember the accident. If she really was able to relive that night, how traumatic would the experience be? He glanced at Mariah. She was still, serene.

"Tell us what happened. What do you see?"

"I'm at the station, ready to leave. My...car. Won't start. I go back inside...ask Randy for a ride. He says yes...."

"Go on."

"It's raining. Have to run to…the car. We're laughing…getting soaked."

Nothing new. Brett had heard Elyssa say this before. Mariah was mesmerizing, but face it, she was a quack. Had to be. All right, somehow or other, she'd found out about *him.* But she couldn't help Elyssa relive anything she didn't already remember.

"We drive along…. It's dark…rainy. Oh, I see lights…lights shining…somewhere."

"Tell us about the lights"

"Lightning maybe…or the dashboard? Can't tell."

"Think, try to remember." Brett saw that Mariah was no longer relaxed. Her muscles were taut, her concentration intense.

"Don't know. The rain…it's coming down harder, pounding on the roof, on the windows…can't see…I'm afraid."

Afraid. Brett's adrenaline began to pump. He edged forward. Over her shoulder Mariah gestured him to sit back.

"What frightens you?" she asked. "The rain?"

"The…the light. Randy's afraid, too."

She'd never mentioned fear before, Brett thought. He glanced at Mariah. The psychic's eyes were on Elyssa.

"He…he turns. Fast," Elyssa said. "Tires squeal. I…we're in the park…"

"Yes. In the park. Go on."

"Oh! The noise, the crash." Her voice rose, became shrill, terrified. She writhed on the couch. "Oh, no! We're falling…falling…can't hold on." She sobbed now, clutching her head. "It…it hurts…. Oh, God, Randy."

Brett shot out of his chair. "Enough."

Mariah grabbed his arm, her grip amazingly strong. "Quiet!" Her voice was low, fierce. Brett shook her off, but she seized his hand.

"Stop this," he snarled at her, jerking her arm. "For God's sake, she's in pain." He could feel every sharp, excruciating jab along with her. "Stop it *now*," he ordered.

They stared at each other, Brett rigid with fury, Mariah unyielding as stone.

"Listen to me," Mariah demanded in a harsh whisper. "This is what she wanted, why she came. I'll help her the best I can, but *let her be.*"

They both turned toward Elyssa. She lay curled up on the couch, moaning. "Elyssa," Mariah said firmly, "let go of the pain. Take a breath, let it go."

"Let...go," she echoed, and incredibly she did. She sighed deeply and lay still, her hands falling open at her sides.

"Do you hear anything?" Mariah asked.

"A...a voice."

"Is it Randy's?"

"Don't know. It's...garbled. It's...way up there." She gestured vaguely.

"What do you see?" Mariah prodded. "Try to remember."

"Nothing...nothing. Just the dark." Her voice faded.

Mariah glanced at Brett. "That's all," she said in a low voice. "She's remembered as much as she can, for now. Elyssa," she said softly. "We're going to wake you now. Watch the screen again. One...two..."

At seven, Elyssa's eyes opened. Brett rushed to the couch, knelt by her side and felt for her pulse. It was rapid but steady, probably steadier than his. He brushed her damp hair from her face. "Are you all right?"

"Yes, just tired." She sat up. "I...I didn't remember everything, did I?"

"You remembered enough," Brett said. He never wanted to see something like this again.

"But not everything I needed to know," Elyssa said.

"Your mind won't let you remember yet," Mariah said, "but you will. Very soon. Out of the shadows the light will dawn."

The way she said it, as if making a solemn promise, gave Brett chills. She took Elyssa's arm, and he loathed seeing even that small contact. It was all he could do not to jerk Mariah's hand away.

"Come," she said. "You must go home now and rest."

They walked back to the front door, and Mariah opened it. Suddenly she turned to Brett. "Cancer!" she said.

Bewildered, he stared at her.

"Cancer," she repeated. "It festers and grows. You must overcome it before it wins."

How did she know he dealt with cancer? Cassie's friend had filled her in—that was the only explanation. He didn't want to talk to the woman any longer. He wanted to get Elyssa and himself out of here as fast as possible. "I'm working on it," he said shortly.

"See that you do," Mariah said. "Quickly, before it's too late."

"Sure." He didn't bother to point out that battling cancer would take his lifetime and likely longer.

He put his arm around Elyssa as they walked to the car. This was a night he'd like to forget. "How are you feeling?" he asked as they drove away.

"Disappointed. But I didn't let myself expect too much."

They reached for each other at the same time. He didn't want to say, I told you so, so he simply enveloped her hand in his and held it tightly.

"Did you and Mariah talk about your work while I was asleep?" Elyssa asked. When he shook his head, she asked, "Then how did she know what you do?"

"I imagine Cassie's friend told her."

Elyssa shook her head. "The friend's been in Europe all summer. She gave Mariah's phone number to Cassie months ago when Cassie got interested in psychic phenomena."

"Then Cassie told her."

"Cassie's never spoken to her. She just gave me Mariah's card. I called her myself." She frowned. "What do you suppose she meant when she said you had to overcome cancer quickly?''

"I don't know."

A shiver ran up his spine. He'd always been a pragmatist. Now he had to wonder what powers Mariah Hart possessed. Had he been wrong to take her astounding message literally? What, he asked himself, had she been trying to tell him?

Chapter 11

Trace was out of Intensive Care and back in his regular room. He was weak, thinner than ever, but he was a fighter and he had come through. "Do you think I'll get well someday?" he asked wistfully when Elyssa visited him.

"You will. You beat the pneumonia, and you're tough enough to lick the rest," she told him, and prayed she was right.

His eyes brightened with hope and he doubled his fists. "Yeah," he said, "I'm Superkid."

Elyssa swallowed the tears that welled in her throat and squeezed his shoulder gently. His bones seemed so fragile, she feared they'd break. They talked about the upcoming World Series and about a new Harry Potter book Trace was reading. She didn't want to tire him, though, so she brought the conversation to a close. "So long, Superkid," she said. "I'll be back tomorrow."

"I'll be here," Trace said.

I hope, Elyssa thought. She blew him a kiss and closed

his door softly. For the hundredth time she wondered how Brett coped with this every day.

There he was in the hallway. Three intense-looking residents trailed him, but he stopped and squatted beside a thin, bald-headed girl, focusing completely on what the child was saying. As always when he interacted with kids, he wore a smile.

Elyssa stopped and watched. She loved seeing Brett with his patients. He was thoroughly dedicated to the youngsters in his care. He'd make a wonderful father, she thought, picturing him with a chubby toddler in his lap and a golden-haired girl at his feet.

Oh, God, what was she doing? She wasn't seeing him as *a* father but as *the* father...of *her* children.

What a fool she was. Hadn't he made it perfectly clear that such a scene wasn't in his future? In *their* future.

What would he say, what would he do, if he guessed what she was thinking? When he looked up and met her eyes, he winked. And her cheeks turned crimson. She reminded herself that, unlike Mariah, he couldn't read minds. Thank heaven for that.

"You're flustered. I'm flattered," he murmured as he came up to her. He tucked a strand of hair behind her ear, then brushed his fingers lightly over her cheek.

She turned a brighter shade of red. "Stop," she whispered. "People will notice."

"I think they already have." He shifted the chart he carried to his other hand. "Unfortunately, I can't spend time with you this afternoon. I have a procedure scheduled in twenty minutes and a meeting after that." He leaned closer and lowered his voice. "So the broom closet's out. I'll call you tonight."

"Fine." Relieved he didn't have time to talk now, she watched him hurry away. She *was* flustered...and disgusted with herself. Why couldn't she keep their relationship light and sexy instead of longing for permanence? These crazy feelings she had about him had to stop. But how could they, unless she quit seeing him?

Could she do that?

She headed for the elevator. She had to get away and think. When she passed the cafeteria on the main floor, she slowed. Caffeine, that's what she needed. Something to clear her mind. She went in, bought a cup of coffee and slumped in a chair, sipping thoughtfully.

What was it with women? Couldn't they learn to enjoy men without envisioning a lifelong commitment? Couldn't they treat men the way men treated them? Or was it genetically impossible?

Like all women, she'd mistaken sex for love, and foolishly she'd fallen in love. With a man who was strong and gentle, tender and passionate. And unavailable for marriage.

She dropped her head into her hands. Why couldn't she be like Cassie, decide to swear off men, and just do it? Because she didn't have her cousin's iron will, at least not where Brett was concerned. She couldn't just walk out of his life and not look back.

Relentlessly she turned her thoughts from Brett and watched the people at nearby tables as she slowly finished her coffee. Then, no closer to a solution to her situation with Brett, she tossed her cup in the trash and left the cafeteria.

She glanced at her watch as she stepped out of the elevator on the basement level. Nearly seven. Maybe she'd stop somewhere for dinner instead of going straight home, she decided as she started into the tunnel that connected the hospital building with the garage.

As she walked through the tunnel, she went over her schedule for tomorrow. Replenish her stock of balloons, reconfirm the party next Thursday for Cynthia Alman—

The lights went out.

What in the world? A transformer must've blown, she decided, and quickened her pace through the shadowy passage. Her footsteps tapped on the concrete floor as she passed a short, narrow hall that led to a mechanical room, and rounded a corner.

Silly to be edgy. She'd walked this way a hundred times. But she clutched her purse and moved faster.

Not fast enough.

Heavy footsteps sounded in back of her, moving quickly. She hadn't heard them before. Somebody must have come out of the mechanical room. She started to run.

Hands grabbed her from behind, and she was pulled up short and yanked back against a hard chest. She tossed her purse on the floor. "Take it," she croaked just before a thick, callused hand snaked around her neck and covered her mouth. The odors of sweat and tobacco filled her nostrils.

She heard a chuckle, then a voice rasped in her ear. "You think I want your money?"

He backed up, dragging her with him. She tried to scream, but he had her muzzled. She thought of sinking her teeth into his hand but couldn't open her mouth. She struggled, trying to jab him with an elbow or kick him with her heel, but he had her off balance, half carrying her. She knew where they were going.

Into the side hall where, in the darkness, no passerby would notice them. He pulled her backward into the passageway. One shoe came off. Would someone see it and come looking for her?

"I warned you before," he growled in her ear.

On the phone. She recognized his voice. *Keep talking,* she begged him silently. If he did, maybe she'd remember where else she'd heard him.

"Stop screwing around with stuff that's none of your business." He tightened the arm he'd flung across her chest, almost cutting off her breath. "Drop it," he snarled, "or I'll carve up your other cheek."

His right hand came up to her face, and Elyssa felt the cold steel of a knife blade against her skin.

Nausea gripped her, and for a moment she thought she would pass out. *No!* She couldn't—*wouldn't*—let this happen. *Think,* she ordered herself. If she fainted, she'd be at his mercy....

Faint. She let herself go limp, sagging against him. Off balance, he staggered back, and she felt a sharp pain in her arm.

Then he dropped her, and she screamed. He cursed and backed away.

She landed smack on her bottom, tried to get up and fell back. Winded, she sat and prayed someone had heard her cry.

Yes! She heard footsteps racing toward them. Her assailant ran off.

Hands reached for her. One of the pediatric residents. She grabbed hold of his hands and let him pull her up, then leaned against the wall, gulping air.

"What hap—? You're bleeding."

Astonished, Elyssa stared down at her arm. That was the pain she'd felt. Blood dripped from the cut, staining her dress, pooling on the floor. In the dim light from the red exit sign, the bloodstains were an ugly black. "He had a knife," she murmured. "He must've slashed my arm when he dropped it."

She twisted around to look down the passage. The knife was gone. So was the man.

"There's a stairway to the outside past the mechanical room," the resident said. "He must've gone that way, but let's not worry about him. You need to get to Emergency." He bent to pick up Elyssa's purse and shoe. She gaped at them, surprised they were still there, then she slipped the shoe back on.

The young man took Elyssa's other arm, then stared at her. "You're the clown, aren't you?" When she nodded, he said, "I'll page Dr. Cameron."

"No, don't," Elyssa muttered, but he ignored her.

She didn't have the strength right now to argue. Besides,

her mind was so muddled she didn't know how she felt: she didn't want Brett to come; she did want him to come. She didn't want to become dependent on him; she needed him.

"Come on," the resident urged. "Lean on me."

"I'm okay," she insisted, and made it back to the hospital elevator without help. Inside, she leaned against the wall while the elevator creaked its way to the first floor, then her rescuer found a wheelchair and rushed her to the E.R.

He left, then returned with a nurse who handed her a gauze pad. "Hold this over the gash. We'll get to you in a minute."

"Dr. Cameron will be right down," the resident said.

She shut her eyes and waited for Brett to come.

She identified his hurried footsteps when he rushed into the E.R. waiting room. She opened her eyes.

"What happened?" He dropped to his knees beside her, his face white. She didn't answer, and he examined her arm, glanced at the hovering resident and nodded. "Thanks for calling me, Neil." Then he turned back to Elyssa. "How did you get cut? Did you have a wreck?

She was tempted to say yes, but she supposed the resident, who was on Brett's service, would relate what had really happened. No lying, but she didn't have to tell Brett everything. After all, the resident didn't know what her attacker had *said*. "Someone came up behind me and grabbed me when I was walking through the tunnel."

Brett's face turned to stone. "Dammit, where was Security?"

A nurse appeared. "Excuse me, Dr. Cameron. We're ready for her now."

Brett shook his head. "Page Dr. Halliday. Tell him I'm bringing a patient upstairs." He began pushing the wheelchair toward the elevator.

Elyssa turned her head to scowl at him. "I'm not a patient."

"The hell you're not," he muttered.

She'd never seen Brett angry before. She decided not to argue. "Who is Dr. Halliday?"

"Plastic surgeon." He jabbed the elevator button. Two doors slid open at the same time. Brett chose the empty car and shoved her wheelchair inside.

"Okay," he said, glowering down at her. "Tell me what you've left out. Did someone try to snatch your purse?" His eyes swept over her, zeroed in on the purse clutched in her hand. He shook his head. "Did he try to...to molest you?"

"No."

He stood silently, staring at her as the elevator ground its way upward. Elyssa could tell the moment the thought flashed into his mind.

His voice came out sharp, cold. "This wasn't a random mugging, was it?"

She pretended not to understand. "What do you mean?"

"You know damn well. This was about Randy, wasn't it?"

She sighed and nodded.

Brett spoke between clenched teeth. "Dammit, this Randy business has gotten out of hand. First the phone call, then the ditch, now this. What's next? Will I get a call from the morgue?"

Elyssa was tempted to tell him *he* wouldn't get the call. He wasn't the "responsible party." He wasn't her husband, had made it clear he didn't intend to be.

But he'd rushed downstairs the minute he heard she'd been hurt. Was he the twenty-first-century version of the knight in shining armor, riding to the rescue of *anyone* in distress? Or did he care more than he admitted? She reached for his hand. "Nothing happened to me."

"Nothing? You're bleeding, dammit," he said, his voice cracking. Before he could say any more, the elevator door opened, and he pushed the wheelchair out.

Dr. Halliday met them at the door of his office. "You

caught me just as I was leaving," he said to Brett, then smiled at Elyssa. "John Halliday. I'm going to stitch your arm. Right this way."

Brett wheeled Elyssa into John's examining room and helped her onto the table. As he watched his colleague clean the wound, he tried to pull himself together. When he'd gotten the message that she'd been hurt, his heart had nearly stopped. His emotions had spun out of control. He wasn't sure what he'd felt. Shock first. Then fear that she'd been seriously injured, that he'd be too late to tell her... what?

When he'd seen the gauze wrap on her arm, seen blood trickling through it—her blood—and found out what had really happened, rage had taken over. Rage at her attacker, at the hospital's lax security, at Elyssa. Why in hell did she have to be so stubborn about this so-called investigation of hers? Her friend was dead, her face was scarred. Nothing could change those facts. Damn her, couldn't she see that?

He leaned against the wall, watching as John expertly stitched the wound. The acrid odor of antiseptic filled his nostrils, and he felt sick. Abruptly he sat but resisted dropping his head between his knees. He would not make a fool of himself in front of a colleague, he told himself, as the room spun slowly around him.

He glanced at the pad John tossed in the waste container, then looked quickly away. This was ridiculous. Watching a simple procedure shouldn't bother him. He'd watched hundreds of surgeries, performed endless numbers of procedures on countless patients himself, but he'd never been lightheaded, not even the first time he'd walked into an operating suite.

But watching when someone you loved was injured was completely different.

He froze. Was he thinking *loved?* he wondered, stunned. No, of course not. He meant *cared about,* didn't he?

Before he had time to ponder his surprising reaction,

John's voice intruded. "All done. Elyssa, I'd like to talk to you in my office. Brett, would you excuse us?"

Still dazed, he nodded. He sat woodenly in the chair as the door closed behind them. He should go out to the waiting room, he told himself, but he couldn't seem to move. He felt like a puppet waiting for the puppeteer to pull the strings.

His pager sounded, and he almost jumped out of the chair. He ordered himself to calm down and went into the waiting room to call in.

"Dr. Cameron, Jean from your office wants to know if you're finished for the day," the operator said.

"Yeah, you can pick up my calls." He hung up, stared at the phone in his hand. He needed to...

"Call Security," he muttered, "and the police."

Elyssa sat across from John Halliday, nodding as he explained how to care for her arm. He gave her a pain pill to take immediately, wrote a prescription, then sat back and steepled his hands. "Tell me about your cheek," he said.

Briefly she explained that she'd been in an accident. No use mentioning that today's episode was connected.

Halliday hesitated a moment, then said, "I could make your cheek look much better."

She'd had plastic surgery after the accident. It had been a disappointment. "Somebody's already tried."

"Then he's not as good as I am," Halliday said.

Six months ago, even one month ago, if someone had suggested this, she'd have been thrilled, eager for the surgery, for another chance. Now she felt...indifferent.

She frowned, wondering if the unnerving events of the day had clouded her mind. No, she realized, her disinterest was real. She cared less about the scar than about finding out who'd caused it. "I think I can live with my cheek as it is, but if I change my mind, you'll be the first to know." They shook hands.

As she left the office, she heard Brett's voice from down

the hall. "Dammit, there was an assault in the garage this evening. Where the hell was Security?"

He was on the phone, and still angry, that was for sure. "On a break?" he roared. "You have the supervisor call me back first thing in the morning. Dr. Cameron. Pediatric oncology. Department head."

He turned as Elyssa entered the waiting room, his expression murderous. "Wait here. I want to talk to John." He strode past her.

"Yes, sir," Elyssa muttered. Maybe she shouldn't wait for Dr. Grouch. She could just go home. Her arm throbbed, her head was beginning to pound along with it, and she was exhausted. What did Brett have to be grumpy about? *She* was the one who'd been attacked, not him.

She'd made it to the office door when he stalked up behind her, pushing the wheelchair. "Sit," he ordered.

Elyssa raised a brow. She wasn't a puppy to be ordered around. "My feet are fine. I'll walk."

"Don't argue," he said through clenched teeth, then with visible effort added quietly, "Please."

"Since you asked so nicely." Her legs *were* a bit wobbly. She sat, and he wheeled her into the hall. "I'll drive you home," he said.

"My car's in the garage."

"I'll bring you back to get it in the morning."

"You're awfully bossy," she muttered, then remembered something. "Didn't you say you had a meeting?"

"I canceled it."

In the elevator he punched two. "Where are we going?" Elyssa asked.

"My office. The police are meeting us there."

"Good." Now she'd have something concrete to tell them. They wouldn't be able to brush her off so easily this time.

Two police officers waited outside Brett's office. They introduced themselves as Detectives Sumner and O'Donnell. Sumner was a broad-shouldered, ruddy complected fellow in his late thirties. His partner was older, with graying temples and sad eyes that looked as if they'd seen too much of the seamy side of life.

Brett unlocked the office and invited them in. Elyssa told them what had happened. She knew what to stress—the connection to Randy. After all, sound bytes had once been her specialty.

"Were there any witnesses?" O'Donnell asked.

"Not to the assault. The lights were out in the tunnel, and I don't think anyone passed by."

"Too bad."

Detective Sumner wrote down Elyssa's statement. "We'll take a look in the basement," he said. "Maybe we'll get lucky and find the knife."

Elyssa and Brett accompanied them and waited while the two officers searched. "Sorry," O'Donnell said. "Nothing turned up. We'll file the report, but—" He shrugged and took a step away.

"Wait," Elyssa said. "I'd like you to pass this on to Sergeant Abel Huffstetter at downtown headquarters. I spoke to him recently about reopening the investigation into Mr. Barber's death. This should convince him to pursue it."

"Sure thing," Sumner said. "We'll let you know if we get anywhere on this."

"And you'll be sure to talk to Sergeant Huffstetter?"

"Huh? Oh, yes, ma'am." The two officers left.

Brett wheeled Elyssa back into the hospital. They got her prescription filled, then headed to his car. He drove out of the garage and around the corner. "You're going the wrong way," she said.

"You're staying with me."

Elyssa ignored the pain in her arm and reached over to touch his hand. "For how long? Sooner or later I have to go home." He stared stonily ahead, and she added, "I have a good security system."

She had a gun, too, but a lot of good it did her, tucked

in her dresser drawer awaiting her permit. Anyway, it would have been useless when she was grabbed from behind. What did you do in that kind of situation, ask your attacker to wait while you got your weapon out of your purse?

She lifted her hand to Brett's cheek. "I can't hide from this guy indefinitely. Take me home."

He shook his head. "Stay with me, just for tonight."

Damn, she was too tired to argue. "Okay."

"And tomorrow give me a key. I'll stay at your house."

Elyssa leaned back against the headrest and gave him a sleepy smile. "I guess this is one way to get a guy to move in."

He glanced at her, and something flashed in his eyes. Something beyond anger. "This isn't funny," he said. "It's gone beyond your experience in investigative reporting. Today was a close call. Keep this up and you're going to get badly hurt."

"You're probably right," Elyssa muttered. "Maybe this time Sergeant Huffstetter will listen and get moving on the case." She shut her eyes.

When the car stopped in front of Brett's house, she opened her eyes but didn't move.

"The pain medication's kicking in," he said. "You're dead on your feet."

"My feet are—"

"Fine, I know. Come on, champ." He put his arm around her and helped her up the walk. Inside he asked, "Hungry?"

"A little."

"How about some soup?"

She trailed him into the kitchen and sat at the table. "I didn't know you cooked."

"I open cans." He poked around in a cabinet and held one up. "Chicken noodle. Best medicine." Soon he had it bubbling on the stove.

Sleepily Elyssa watched him. The medicine was working

like gangbusters. When Brett came toward her carrying the soup bowls, she could've sworn for a moment there were two of him. She blinked, and her vision cleared.

He set the bowls down. "Be right back with spoons."

Elyssa listened to the clatter of silverware. "Your kitchen's nice," she muttered. "I like yellow. It's kind of… welcoming. You don't have any plants, though." Her words were slurred. "You should get some plants."

"Don't have time to take care of them," he said, and stopped. He didn't move. He simply stood and stared at her, the spoons dangling from his hand. As if…as if he'd never seen her before.

"What's wrong?" Elyssa asked. She might be groggy but she wasn't so muddled that she didn't notice the stunned expression on his face. "Brett? Are you all right?" When he said nothing, she asked, "Am *I* all right?"

He nodded vaguely. "Yeah, fine. We're both…fine."

"Tha's good. You look funny. Aren't I s'posed to be the one who's woozy?"

Even as foggy as she was, she didn't believe he was fine. Though he sat down across from her and kept up a semblance of conversation, she could tell his mind was wandering. What was he thinking? He wasn't worried about a patient or he'd have called the hospital. And it wasn't anger he was feeling anymore but something else, something she couldn't fathom. Maybe when she was wide awake, she'd figure it out.

After they finished their soup, he helped her upstairs. When Elyssa came out of the bathroom, she found him lying on the bed with one shoe still on, and staring into space. "Your turn," she said.

"Oh, yeah," he muttered, and got up. He stared at his foot as if surprised to see one shoe missing, then kicked off the other and headed for the bathroom.

Elyssa staggered to the bed and sat. Medication had always affected her strangely and this time was no exception.

Maybe she should've told Dr. Halliday she didn't want it. Too late now.

When Brett came out of the bathroom, he frowned at her. "Why are you still up?"

"Checking out the surroundings," she said. To prove it, she glanced around the room. Rosewood dresser, king-size bed sans headboard, a lone night table. "You told me you hadn't done anything upstairs. You were right," she said, stifling a giggle. "Blah. Very blah.

"But I like your bed." She lay down and lifted the corner of the sheet to her nose. "Smells like you." She patted the empty space next to her. "Why don' you join me, Dr.....Cameron? I've...been wanting to sleep in your bed."

The mattress gave as Brett lay down beside her. Certainly close enough to touch her, but he didn't.

"Aren't you going to make love to me?" she mumbled.

"I don't want to hurt you."

She grinned. "You won't. I can't feel a thing."

"I know, so what would be the point?" His voice was laced with laughter. "Turn on your side and I'll hold you."

"Okay," she muttered and fell asleep.

Several hours later, she woke. She sat up, rubbed her eyes and peered at the clock radio on the night stand. Just past midnight.

Instantly Brett stirred. "Are you hurting?" he asked, sitting up beside her.

"A little, but at least my head is clear."

He brushed his hand over her hair. "Want a pill?"

"Oh, please, no. I'd rather have a little pain."

"Want a drink of water?"

Elyssa shook her head. None of those things would do. Her voice unsteady, her tone pleading, she said "I want you." After all that had happened today, that was the medicine she needed. Intimacy—Brett in her arms, their bodies joined.

He drew her against him and kissed her softly. But something was different.

He was there for her physically, but she sensed that emotionally he had pulled away. His hands touched her in all the right places, but his heart didn't seem to be in it. His body moved with hers, but the rhythm seemed somehow off.

Afterward she wondered if she'd imagined the change in him. Maybe she was groggier than she thought. Just now though she was too exhausted to think it through.

She dozed but woke again. This time the bed was empty.

Brett stood by the window, staring out. His body was tense, his fist clenched against the glass. She thought of going to him, putting her arms around him and asking what was wrong, but she sensed he wouldn't tell her.

At the hospital, when she'd come out of Trace's room, he'd been his usual self—teasing, admiring. His eyes had glowed when he looked at her.

Something had extinguished that spark.

What? And why now? Had her injury reminded him how needy a woman could be? In his mind, was she becoming a reincarnation of Denise, a burden too cumbersome to bear?

Could she do something to change that? Or was it too late?

Chapter 12

Brett stared, unseeing, into the night. His thoughts were jumbled, his emotions in turmoil. His life's course was set, and he'd never been tempted to change it.

Yesterday, he told himself firmly, was simply an aberration. Of course he'd been distraught when he'd seen Elyssa pale and hurt. Certainly he'd been upset when she'd admitted the assault was connected to her investigation. Dammit, he wanted to keep her safe. If he had the right, he'd lock her up inside the house and not let her out until she came to her senses and quit this dangerous crusade of hers. Or until whoever had gone after her was safely behind bars. That made sense.

What didn't make sense was this absurd longing for her. And where had that insidious thought come from, that crazy idea that he might be falling in—

Absolutely not!

This was an affair. A *casual* affair. Okay, it was more than casual, but it wasn't love. Couldn't be, he thought uneasily. *Shouldn't* be.

As soon as she was safe, he'd back away from her, scale things down. He wouldn't see her every day. Their encounters would be...casual. That decided, he went back to bed.

But he felt strangely unsatisfied.

He slept and dreamed of his childhood, when life was simple and decisions quick and easy. He wore his high school baseball uniform, stood at the plate and waited for the pitch. He swung and connected, and noisy cheers resounded from the stands.

But it wasn't cheers he heard. It was Elyssa, and she was moaning. He sat up and saw that her eyes were shut. She was having a nightmare.

He stroked her shoulder. "It's all right, sweetheart. You're dreaming."

Her eyes flew open. "Brett," she murmured and let out a breath. "I was dreaming about the tunnel. Silly."

"Not silly. Come here." He pulled her close so that she curled spoon-fashion against him. "Go back to sleep."

Within minutes her breathing deepened. He brushed a finger over her breast. He'd back off from her, but not yet. She needed him now—his protection, his support. He'd stay at her house at night. But just until she was safe alone.

And then he'd be alone, too. He tightened his arms around her, and with the scent of her skin in his nostrils, fell asleep.

Over Elyssa's objections the next day, Brett had called Cassie, told her what happened in the tunnel, and asked if she'd keep Elyssa company until he got there tonight. Elyssa had snapped that she didn't need a baby-sitter, but she did welcome the idea of having Cassie over. Maybe she'd help her figure out what to do about Brett.

When Elyssa drove up to her house, Cassie's car was already parked in front. Elyssa found her bustling around in the kitchen, preparing breakfast. "What are you making?" Elyssa asked suspiciously. "Please don't tell me you're back on health food. I couldn't bear fruit with wheat germ this morning.''

"Pancakes," Cassie said. "With real butter and syrup. And bacon. Welcome to the Invalid-for-a-Day Club. You get to indulge in comfort food for twenty-four hours."

"Thank heaven. Pancakes are my favorite."

"The cook will have everything ready in five minutes." Cassie slapped Elyssa's hand away as Elyssa started to open the package of bacon strips. "I said 'the cook.' That would be me. Sit down and tell me about yesterday."

While her cousin started the bacon, Elyssa perched on a bar stool and gave her a brief summary of the assault in the tunnel.

"No wonder you look upset," Cassie said.

"Actually, I'm upset about Brett. The minute he came downstairs to the emergency room, he started acting different. First angry, then...well, distant."

Cassie looked up and scowled. "I'd say he has a right to be angry. Putting yourself in danger is not a smart thing to do. For heaven's sake, Elyssa, who do you think you are? Xena, Warrior Princess?"

Elyssa laughed. Trust Cassie to give her a dose of what doctors said was the best medicine. "I'm Nancy Drew."

"You're not her, either," Cassie said sharply, "though why I waste time lecturing you, I don't know. You're as hardheaded as a...rhinoceros."

"Mule," Elyssa corrected. "Thank you."

"Now, what else?"

"Brett's pulling away." She bit her lip. "I can feel it."

Cassie flipped the bacon. "I don't buy that. He's too crazy about you."

Elyssa shook her head. "This isn't a serious relationship for him. He's made that clear."

"Bull," Cassie said. "I watch people, watch their body language, and I've seen the way he looks at you. You may not know it, *he* may not know it, but he loves you." Eyes narrowed, she added, "Know what I think? You don't believe a man as wonderful as Brett could really care for you.''

''That's...that's ridiculous,'' Elyssa sputtered.

''Is it? Think about it.''

''But—''

''Nope, the subject is closed. You run it over in your mind for a couple of days. Then we'll talk, because by then you'll see that I'm right.'' She slid the bacon strips onto a plate.

''You always think you're right.''

Cassie brought the rest of their meal to the table. ''Because I am. Now sit down and eat. I have something to tell you.'' When Elyssa had served herself, Cassie said, ''I've decided to move to New York.''

Elyssa's hand stopped with the fork halfway to her mouth. ''When did this come up?'' she asked carefully.

''Oh, I've been thinking about it for months,'' Cassie said airily. She poured syrup on her pancakes and dug in.

''You always talked about that happening 'someday.'''

''Well, someday's now.'' She put her fork down and leaned her elbows on the table. ''The Indianapolis Players are wonderful, a real class act, but I could sit around for years before I get onstage. In New York there are so many opportunities.'' Her eyes glowed. ''I've already spoken to an agent. Ned Sorrells. I heard he takes on a few newcomers, so I sent him a videotape. He called yesterday and said he's willing to talk to me.''

''That's wonderful.'' Not wanting Cassie to see the dismal look in her eyes, she stared down at her plate. She was truly glad that Cassie had a chance to realize her dreams, but... ''I'm gonna miss you,'' she said, forcing a smile.

They ate silently for a few minutes, Elyssa choking down the food she usually savored. ''Where will you live?'' she asked.

''I'll find something.'' Cassie was always confident. ''I'm going to work my buns off,'' she added. ''No distractions.''

"Define *distractions*."

"Anything in pants. I'm not going to get involved with anyone. I may not even date."

"You said that a couple of weeks ago. The next day I called and Nathan answered the phone."

"No, really," Cassie said. "This is my chance. It's what I've dreamed of all my life. I don't intend to go off on a tangent and blow it."

Elyssa hesitated. She didn't want Cassie to think she was pouring cold water on her plans. Nevertheless, she had to say what was on her mind. "One thing, Cass. Give yourself a deadline. Don't stay there indefinitely. Give it a year. Then...well, if things don't work out, come home." She gnawed at her lip, hoping Cassie wouldn't take her words the wrong way.

Cassie thought for a moment, then grinned. To Elyssa's relief, she lifted her coffee cup in a toast. "*Two* years."

"Okay, but not a day more."

"Makes sense." Cassie held out a hand. "Deal."

Elyssa shook Cassie's hand, then made herself let go though she wanted to hang on. She smiled and added lightly, "And then come back and go into business with me."

"Be Coco the Clown the rest of my life? It won't happen."

Elyssa studied her cousin—the sparkling eyes, the bewitching smile, the air of total self-assurance. Add to that a heaping dose of talent. Cassie was right. She wouldn't be back. Cassie would take Broadway by storm.

And there'd be a void in Elyssa's life that no one else could fill.

Two days later Elyssa received a call from Jenny. "I've found something," she said.

Elyssa was glad Brett wasn't here. For this she needed privacy. She opened her desk drawer and took out the tablet she'd been keeping notes in. "Tell me."

"Ever since you found Randy's notes, I've been searchin' through his things. Well, last night I hit pay dirt. I found his appointment book."

Elyssa's heart jumped. "Fantastic. Nobody seems to know what he was doing the...last couple of weeks."

"This may shed some light," Jenny said, her voice as excited as Elyssa's. "The last two weeks of February he had several meetings with a Dorothy Ryder. He had another meeting scheduled for...for March 5...but of course he never...he never made it."

Elyssa wished they were talking in person. Jenny needed to feel a friend's arms around her right now. "Seeing that is tough," she said softly.

"Yeah, I put my hands on that book and I kept thinkin', Randy's hands touched this very spot." She sniffled. "Oh gosh, Elyssa, I'd give anything to have him back."

"So would I."

"Do you know who Dorothy Ryder is?" Jenny asked. Her voice trembled.

"No, Randy never mentioned her."

"There's a phone number, too," Jenny said.

Elyssa wrote it down. "I'm going to the groundbreaking of the new cancer hospital this afternoon, but I'll call her as soon as I get back. Did you find anything else?"

"Yes, remember the note you found about some committee? Well, right after this woman's name he wrote, 'Committee FCCC.' Do you have any idea what that means?"

"No," Elyssa said, and wrote that down, too.

"I found one more thing inside the book," Jenny said, her voice shaking again. "The key to a safe-deposit box."

"Oh, my God. Did you know—"

"No, he never said a word about a box. Heck, we didn't have anything valuable enough to put in a bank box."

What would Randy have stored in a box, especially one that he'd never discussed with his wife?

Suddenly Jenny gave a little cry. "Oh, my God, Elyssa—"

"What? What happened?"

"A...a note just fell out of the appointment book. It...oh God, it says... 'If anything happens to me, open the box and read the notebook." She choked on a sob. "I was right. He *knew* something, something he shouldn't have. And it got him killed."

"We'll find out."

"Yes," Jenny said. "I've already talked to our attorney in Indianapolis and he's arranged it so I can open the box. I thought I'd come in next week, but now...well, I want to get there sooner. I'll come tomorrow morning. Will you go to the bank with me?"

"Of course." They arranged to meet there, and Elyssa hung up.

Tomorrow they'd know. Her hands shook. With anticipation. With dread.

She glanced at the clock. She'd better get moving. The groundbreaking ceremony for the new hospital started in an hour and a half. She would put Jenny's discovery out of her mind, at least for the next few hours.

She opened her closet. Now that he stayed with her at night, a couple of Brett's suits and shirts hung beside her clothes. Looking at them gave her a warm feeling, but she reminded herself not to become complacent about their relationship. It wasn't going to last. Another thought she preferred to erase from her mind this afternoon.

She scanned her wardrobe. This was an important day for Brett. She wanted to look beautiful—well, as nice as possible—for him. Her new blue silk, she decided. Blue was the in color this year. Stores featured it in every shade from powder blue, to the deep navy of the ocean. Her dress was somewhere in between, the color of a misty twilight sky. She took it out, running her hand over the material. She loved the elegance of silk, the feel of it against her skin.

She pictured herself in the dress, pictured Brett running *his* hand over her breast, along her hip. He had such skillful hands. His touch could soothe or electrify. How she wished—

The phone rang.

She checked her caller ID box. The call came from the hospital but not from Brett's office. Hesitantly she reached for the receiver. "Hello?"

"Hi, sweetheart."

It *was* Brett. She let out a breath. "Hi."

"I'm running behind. Can you meet me at the ceremony?"

"Sure."

"Don't park in the garage. Use the valet parking service."

"Okay." He didn't need to convince her. She hadn't once ventured into the garage in the past week. "I'll see you later," she said and hurried to get into the shower.

She made it to the site in time, then stopped to gaze at the bare ground where the hospital would eventually stand. She imagined the building, the lobby, the waiting rooms filled with books and toys...and Brett, in his element, striding through the halls. Chief of staff, she thought. Brett had achieved his goal so young, but he deserved it. He'd be a superb director. Of course he'd be busier than ever, but he seemed to thrive on what others perceived as pressure. She wondered if she'd still be part of his life when he assumed his duties here.

Where was he? She wandered through the crowd of well-dressed—and well-heeled—guests, searching for him.

Several people hailed her—people who still recognized her from her TV years. They assured her she was missed. Several urged her to return to television. She was gratified to know that she'd been appreciated and that she was remembered.

But she realized with surprise that she no longer had any desire to be in front of the camera. In fact, she hadn't

thought about her former career in weeks. There'd been a
time when she could hardly bear to turn on the TV and
watch bright-eyed newscasters spouting out the day's
events. It was a revelation to think that day was over and
to realize she found her work with children, especially
those in the hospital, much more satisfying.

Smiling, she moved through the throng. She still hadn't
spotted Brett. He must be running even later than he expected.

No, there he was.

He stood in the shade of a maple tree, talking to a blond
man who stood with his back to Elyssa. He looked familiar.
As she moved toward them, he half turned so that she saw
his profile. Derek.

Startled, she stopped. Strange, Brett had never mentioned
knowing Derek or anyone else from the TV station. Yet
the two men were deep in conversation.

Her lover and her former lover. What were they talking
about?

Oh, God, she thought as her cheeks flushed, she didn't
want them to spot her. Brett would ask her to join them,
and she'd be wretchedly uncomfortable. Keeping her eyes
on them, Elyssa backed away, stood beside a group of people and tried to look as if she belonged with them. Finally
the two men shook hands and Derek walked away. Only
when he had disappeared into the crowd, did she move
forward.

She waved at Brett, and he hurried toward her and took
her arm. "I was getting worried," he said. "I was afraid
you'd miss the ceremony."

No, she thought, seeing in his eyes what he left unsaid:
I was afraid something had happened to you.

"I was caught in traffic," she told him.

"You valet parked?" When she nodded, she felt the tension drain out of his hand.

He led her toward the chairs that had been set up for the
ceremony. Several rows had been roped off for celebrities

and important guests. "Our seats are here," he said, indicating the front row. "Did you get a program?"

She held it up, then, as they took their places, put it in her lap. "I saw you with Derek Graves," she said. "I didn't know you two knew each other."

"We don't. We just met." He turned to shake hands with a colleague.

She wanted to ask him what he and Derek had talked about, why they'd talked so long and so seriously. "Were you—" Someone tapped the microphone, and feedback, as grating as fingernails scratching a chalkboard, drowned out her voice.

The ceremony began with remarks by Indianapolis mayor, Paul Thoreau, then state senator Gilda Harrison. Her mind beginning to wander, Elyssa glanced down at her program and scanned the list of speakers. Farther down the page she read the names of the hospital board of directors.

Then she noticed a note thanking the work of the Committee to Fund Children's Cancer Center. There she found Brett's name along with several others. She smiled and glanced over at him. He was absorbed in Senator Harrison's words.

She was about to fold the program and drop it in her purse when the committee's logo caught her eye. An oval flanked by a caduceus on either side. In the center of the logo were the Committee's initials: CFCCC.

Elyssa frowned. She'd heard that sequence of letters only hours before. Jenny Barber had read it to her. Straight from Randy's appointment book.

Chapter 13

As Elyssa stared at the program, the letters swam before
her eyes. Surely she'd read them wrong. She blinked,
forced her eyes to focus, and read them again. CFCCC. No
mistake.

The committee, she thought. That's what Randy had
written in the David Brinkley book Jenny had given her.
But surely not *this* committee. There had to be another one,
she told herself as her thoughts careened wildly. The committee for…for something else.

No one at this prestigious hospital could be involved in
something sinister enough to cause a man's death. Of
course not. Randy's investigation had to be about a different committee.

But suddenly she remembered that Randy had done a
story about the hospital several months before his death. It
had been about two men with similar names whose medical
records had been mixed up. He'd talked to her about his
assignment before he'd filmed the spot, and they'd dis-

cussed the best way to approach the story. He'd made several trips to St. Michael's for background material.

He could have met someone here who served on the fund-raising committee or knew something about it. Oh, Lord, maybe there *was* a connection.

Or was she losing her mind? Finding associations that didn't exist? Becoming truly paranoid?

Despite the warm September afternoon, she shivered. Her teeth began to chatter.

"Elyssa." Brett's voice penetrated the fog of confusion and suspicion. "Honey, are you all right?"

"I'm fine," she assured him. But she wasn't.

Dazed, she sat through the rest of the ceremony: several more speeches, Dr. Clark Madigan grasping the ceremonial spade and turning over a clod of earth, the introduction of the new hospital's senior staff. Brett first, of course. Eyes gleaming, he stood, faced the crowd and waved, to hearty applause.

Elyssa had expected to enjoy this afternoon. With Brett in the spotlight, she should have. Instead, she felt sick.

She had enough experience on camera to know how to hide her feelings. She was confident that no one, not even Brett, saw the churning emotions, the bubbling nausea, as she did all the expected things—congratulated Brett, greeted his colleagues, chatted about how wonderful the new facility would be. But when Brett urged her toward the buffet table, she couldn't choke down a single bite. And the champagne she forced herself to sip gave birth to a throbbing headache.

Dr. Madigan cornered her. He was a handsome, broad-shouldered man, just starting to gray at the temples and bulge at the belly. His exquisitely tailored navy suit probably cost enough to feed six starving children for a month. His silk tie was conservative, as was his jewelry. No diamond-studded watch, just a plain gold Rolex. He probably thought he wasn't one to flaunt his wealth, but his clothing and demeanor all but shouted it in your face. Oh, well, she thought, if he worked as hard as Brett, he earned his money.

"Ms. Jarmon, so nice to see you." He took her hand. She wondered vaguely if he noticed how cold her hand was. "I understand you've been entertaining our youngsters."

"Yes," she said, and hoped her speech wasn't slurred.

He smiled at her. His teeth were dazzling white. She wondered if dentists offered professional discounts for whitening doctors' teeth. "How long does your contract run?" he asked.

"Three more months." She had assumed it would be renewed. This wasn't the time to ask.

Madigan glanced to his left, caught someone's eye and took a step back. "Good of you to come. I hope to see you at the ribbon cutting next year."

"I believe Brett and I will be joining you and some others at *A Chorus Line* tomorrow night," Elyssa said.

He stopped. His brows furrowed for a moment, then he smiled. "Yes, of course." Then he walked away.

Elyssa put down her champagne glass. The midafternoon sun beat down, half blinding her. She needed an aspirin, a bed and a dark room. She searched for Brett. As soon as she found him, she made an excuse to leave.

He led her aside. "What's wrong? You're not yourself."

Had she thought he wouldn't notice? No such luck. She pressed a hand against her throbbing temple. "Headache."

He insisted on walking her to the valet parking area. "Are you sure you can drive?" he asked.

"Of course," she muttered through the pain. "The headache's not that bad." Her car pulled up.

Brett opened the door for her. "Lock up," he said, "and call me as soon as you get home."

At her house she went straight to the kitchen, downed two aspirin and went upstairs. She glanced longingly at her bed but didn't lie down. She had things to do.

As soon as she'd called Brett and assured him she was fine, she got out the note with Dorothy Ryder's telephone number. She dialed, waited. "Come on, Dorothy. Tell me I'm certifiable."

A woman's voice answered. "Administrative Offices, St. Michael's Hospital."

Elyssa sat down hard. *Oh, no. No!* "Dorothy Ryder, please."

"I'm sorry," the woman replied. "We have no one by that name in administration."

"I was given this number."

"I haven't been here very long," the woman offered. "Let me check to see if she's been transferred to another department. Give me your name and number, and I'll call you back."

She didn't want to do that. "I'll hold." Portable phone at her ear, she paced the floor. From the window to the wall and back, over and over again. Maybe she'd written the phone number down wrong, she thought hopefully. Pretty unlikely, though. There were too many arrows pointing to St. Michael's.

How long did it take to check on someone? Why hadn't the woman come back yet? Elyssa's heart lodged in her throat as nervous anticipation gripped her. She wanted to know but she dreaded what she'd find out.

She imagined all sorts of scenarios: Randy was ill, he'd had to meet with Dorothy about insurance. But why the note about CFCCC by her name? Was she the secretary to that committee? But then, why would Randy need to see her? Question after question spun through her mind as she crossed the room again and again.

"Hello."

Elyssa jumped and nearly dropped the phone.

"I checked on Dorothy Ryder," the woman said. "She did work here, but she died some time ago."

Breathlessly Elyssa asked, "When? What happened to her?"

"I don't know."

Sensing that the woman was about to hang up, Elyssa

cried, "Wait. I really need to know." Improvising quickly,
she added, "I'm...I'm a family member, a...distant cousin.
Could you check...please?"

"Hold on."

After a few minutes she returned. "Mrs. Ryder died last
year in early March. She was killed in a traffic accident."

"Oh, no!" She didn't have to fake her shock. "My...my
mother and Dorothy were cousins, but they lost touch the
last couple of years. When Mom found out I was coming
to Indianapolis, she wanted me to look Dorothy up. I have
some family memorabilia, pictures of her and Mom
and...and other things. I just feel terrible, and Mom will
be devastated."

She needed more information. "I'd...like to go by and
see her husband. Um, Andrew, isn't it?"

"Hold on." She returned in a moment. "Joe."

"That's right, thanks. I'll give him a call."

Letting the receiver slip through numb fingers, Elyssa
sank down on her bed. *Oh, my God. Another traffic accident.*

Randy's safe-deposit box had better provide some answers to the questions tumbling around in her mind.

Or Brett would have the answers. After all, he was on
the Committee to Fund Children's Cancer Center. But how
much would he tell her?

She spent an hour on the couch with the blinds closed
and an ice pack on her temple, until the throbbing in her
head dulled to an occasional twinge. Then she planned what
questions to ask Brett and how to ask them. She would be
an investigative reporter again, she told herself.

He'd said he would be back late, and it was nearly eleven
before Elyssa heard his key in the door. Her heartbeat sped
up. She wouldn't badger him with questions the moment
he walked in the door. No, she'd make this a normal evening—or what had become normal for them, since he'd
been staying with her. A late night snack, some quiet con-

versation. Then she'd slip in her questions unobtrusively. Casually.

He opened the door and stepped inside. "You waited up for me," he said, smiling. Whatever had bothered him the evening after her accident had dissipated. Or else he hid it well.

He let his medical bag slide to the floor and crossed the room. Dropping down beside her on the couch, he pulled her close for a kiss. "Headache better?"

"All gone." Elyssa put the questions that plagued her out of her mind as she luxuriated in the feel of his arms around her, the whisper of his breath on her temple. With a sigh she rubbed her cheek against his, then drew back. "Want a snack? I have smoked-turkey sandwiches and potato salad. And apple pie."

"That sounds great. I haven't eaten since the reception."

When she'd put the sandwiches together and they were seated across from one another, he asked, "Did you enjoy the groundbreaking ceremony?"

He'd given her the perfect opening. "Yes and no."

His brows lifted. "Tell me about the no."

"I saw something on the program that disturbed me. Do you remember I told you that Randy had written 'the committee' in the book I found?"

"Randy again," Brett muttered.

Elyssa ignored his disapproving look and continued. "Jenny called me today. She found his appointment book. He'd written, 'Committee FCCC,' the same committee that was listed on the program today. Brett, what *is* CFCCC?"

"The Committee to Fund Children's Cancer Center. It's exactly what the name says—a fund-raising committee."

"Are you sure?"

"Absolutely. I'm a member. Have been since it began."

"Tell me about it," she said.

"We solicit contributions from foundations, corporations—anyone with big bucks to help fund the new hospital."

That sounded innocent enough. Then why had Randy scribbled 'Committee' in the book Jenny had given her and then drawn a skull and crossbones beneath it?

"There's more," Elyssa said. "Randy had an appointment with a woman named Dorothy Ryder for the day after he died. Apparently he'd met with her several times. Did you know her?"

"Should I?"

"She worked at St. Michael's."

Brett shrugged. "Honey, hundreds of people work at St. Michael's. I don't know half of them."

"She was in administration."

He picked up his fork and dug into the potato salad. "Name still doesn't ring a bell."

"She was killed last year in March. In a traffic accident."

No response. Brett continued to eat.

Annoyed, Elyssa said, "Did you hear me?"

He finished a bite, put the sandwich down, and said, "You said she was killed in an accident."

"*At the same time as Randy.* Doesn't that strike you as odd?"

"Dozens of people die in traffic accidents every day."

Elyssa watched him calmly finish his sandwich, push the plate away and reach for the pie. Surely he could see that there was a connection of some kind.

He glanced up and saw her expression. "Honey, it's a coincidence, that's all."

"I don't believe that." If she laid it out carefully, he'd see the relationship. "Randy listed an appointment with Dorothy Ryder. Next to it he wrote CFCCC. There must be a link."

Brett shrugged. "Maybe he was interviewing her about the committee."

"But you're on the committee and you said you didn't know her."

"I meant that he could have been getting background on

some of the committee members. You said she was in administration. She'd have had access to that information. Whatever happened to Randy, I'm certain it had nothing to do with the hospital.''

Elyssa stood her ground. "I'm sure it did."

"You're grasping at straws."

The easy dismissal hurt. "I'm not," she insisted. "I *know* there's a connection."

"Elyssa," Brett said in an infuriatingly patient tone, "you're not being logical."

Why did he always discount what she said about her investigation? Hurt spewed into anger. So much for the "casual" conversation she'd planned. To heck with being a cool, detached reporter. Fuming, she glared at him. "What a macho male response, Dr. Cameron. No, I suppose, like a *woman,* I'm being irrational."

"Whoa," Brett interrupted, "don't turn my remarks into a war between the sexes."

"All right, it's not a battle of the sexes, it's an attack on me personally." Wound up now, she stormed, "I'm being *intuitive.* That's what it takes to be a good reporter. You have to see relationships where others think they don't exist. When *you're* working with a patient, don't you ever have to go with your gut instead of your head?"

"Of course. All doctors do at times."

"Well then." She was disgusted with herself for losing her temper, and in truth, she was more confused than ever. Too edgy to sit still, she pushed back her chair and went to stand at the window.

Clouds hid the moon. The night was murky—a dark void like her mind. Here and there she picked out pinpoints of stars but couldn't make out a single constellation. Isolated stars shone dimly, like the solitary, disjointed facts of Randy's case—one here, another there, with nothing to connect the dots. Only Randy had known how they fit together.

Brett came up behind her and put his hands on her shoulders. He kneaded the tight muscles, his strong fingers loosening the knots. Though she was angry with him, she couldn't control her body's response. She melted under his expert ministrations. She sighed and leaned back against him.

"Feel better?" he murmured.

"Mmm-hmm."

"Know what would make *me* feel better?" he asked. "If you'd give up on this whole Randy thing. Let the police handle it."

Elyssa straightened. "They're not interested, even after what happened in the tunnel. Remember I asked Sumner, the guy who came over afterward, to pass the information along to Sergeant Huffstetter? I called the other day and he was pretty evasive. I think he tossed it."

"Did you call Huffstetter?"

"Twice," she said. "But he hasn't returned my call."

"So hire a private investigator or have Jenny hire one. I'm sure you're on the wrong track, but even so, your looking into his death has triggered something." He turned her to face him. "Look at your arm. Didn't that threat the other day get through to you? Dammit, Elyssa, I worry about you every minute. Don't you understand I want you safe? Leave this alone before you really get hurt."

She stepped away from him. "I'm close to an answer, I know it. Jenny found a key to a safe-deposit box. We're going to open it tomorrow."

"God, Elyssa. No."

He reached for her but she returned to the table and began clearing it, rattling dishes and silver in her exasperation. "I won't give up on this until I know the truth." She started for the kitchen. "I can't."

She heard him cross the room and go upstairs. Angry again and frustrated, she carried the dishes to the kitchen and put them in the dishwasher. *Why* was Brett so anxious to stop her just when she sensed she was about to learn what had happened?

Upstairs they undressed silently, avoiding each others' eyes. They got into bed, but they didn't make love.

Elyssa lay stiffly on her side of the bed, staring up at the ceiling. Sleep wouldn't come. Her muscles were tense, her nerves strained. She could tell by Brett's breathing that he was awake, too. But he said nothing. Neither did she. They were at an impasse. Half the night passed before she fell into a fitful slumber.

The sound of rain pelting against the window woke her and she opened her eyes to find herself curled against Brett. Holding her breath, she turned her back to him and edged away.

He reached out and held her still. "Don't," he whispered.

She didn't answer, but she stayed where she was. His body was so warm, his arm around her so solid.

He drew her closer, his hand molding her breast, then the curve of her hip. "I want to kiss you. Turn around."

She couldn't refuse even though she thought perhaps she should. She still needed him, maybe more than she needed answers to the puzzle of Randy's death. Surely as much as she needed air and light. She turned toward him.

Like a flower parched for the taste of rain, she opened her lips to meet his kiss.

It was spellbinding. His mouth moved across hers, slowly, sweetly. The taste of him drove everything else from her mind. Her pulse began to thud, strong and slow. Her bones liquefied, and the hand she'd placed on his shoulder slackened. He murmured low in her ear, then kissed the sensitive spot below her lobe. From there he traveled down to dip his tongue in the hollow of her neck.

She was lost. The sound of the rain faded. Her awareness of the room, the bed, of everything around her dimmed. Brett filled her mind, awakened all her senses.

Nothing existed but this moment. The worry, the fear—nothing mattered but this man, the comfort of his arms, the tender intimacy of his kisses.

They'd made love in so many different ways—with laughter, with passion, with tenderness. But this time all of those emotions—and more—were combined.

Brett slipped her gown off, then put his mouth to her breast. His kiss seared her, rocked her to the core, and she moaned his name. He muttered something hot and sweet and took her nipple deeper into his mouth. He suckled, moving his tongue in an irresistible rhythm, and the heat inside her built and built until it erupted. Until she flew apart, with his name on her lips, in a climax so powerful it staggered her.

Stunned, every muscle lax, she lay in his arms. She'd never responded so strongly, just to having her breast kissed. When she could manage to speak, she murmured, "We didn't even..."

She felt his lips curve against her temple, felt his erection against her thigh. "Yeah, but we could make up for it."

Amazingly, her strength was coming back. She stroked a hand down his back, then leaned over to run moist kisses from his shoulders to his belly, and lower. "Lie back," she whispered. "It's my turn now."

Chapter 14

Brett stood in the bathroom, shaving. He glowered at the face in the mirror, not liking what he saw.

Even their incredible lovemaking couldn't make up for what had happened downstairs last night. He'd hurt her, and dammit, he would probably hurt her again.

Why couldn't she see the folly of what she was doing? Right now she was on the wrong track, but when she realized that, she would head off on another. And another.

Someone didn't want her to keep digging. For whatever reason, she'd stirred up a blaze of trouble that was only going to keep growing until...

He had to stop her. Damn, if he could, he'd chain her to the bed, lock her in the house.

He had no right to stop her.

He had no hold over her, *couldn't* have. He couldn't demand or even say, ''I can't go on without you.'' Because when this crazy investigation of hers was over and she was safe, he'd back away from her. He'd have to before either of them got in deeper. He stared into the mirror, and his bleak face stared back.

It was getting late. He rinsed off his razor and put it in the spot in the medicine cabinet that he'd claimed as his own. Second shelf, on the left. He frowned. Staying here was becoming entirely too comfortable.

Wavering on the brink of something he didn't dare name, he shut the cabinet and finished getting ready for work.

Seated across from Elyssa at the breakfast table, Brett asked, "Where are you off to?"

She glanced out the window. The day had dawned gray and drizzly. "I have some errands to run," she said evasively. She'd made up her mind to go to St. Michael's and find out everything she could about Dorothy Ryder. And she knew just who to ask. Her friend Amanda. But Brett didn't need to know about her plans. What was the point in provoking a repeat of last night's argument? Fortunately, the volunteer coordinator's office was located well away from Brett's department.

"Aren't you and Randy's wife going to the bank today?"

He'd caught her there. Unfortunately, he had an excellent memory. "Yes, this afternoon."

"I want you to promise me something. If you find anything in that safe-deposit box, *anything* that could put you in the slightest amount of danger, I want you to call me."

"And what will you do?"

"If there's information the cops can use to find out what really happened, I'm going to drive you down to police headquarters so we can give it to them."

Elyssa sighed. "Do you think that will do any good? I told you, Sergeant Huffstetter isn't interested."

"Then we'll find someone who is."

She could manage this on her own. "You're too busy. I can drive myself."

"Indulge me," he said. "I want to be sure someone gets to work on this."

So did she. "All right."

He let out a breath. "And if you don't find anything significant, I want you to *give up.*"

"I can't promise you that," she said.

"You are the most incredibly stubborn woman I've ever met," he said, tossing his napkin on the table.

"And you are the most mule-headed man."

"If you mean determined, yes." He glanced at his watch. "I have to make rounds in half an hour." He leaned over to kiss her cheek. "We'll talk more about this later."

Elyssa sat across from Amanda Pryor, sipping coffee. She'd fended off the inevitable question about her bandaged arm, telling Amanda she'd fallen off her bike.

Elyssa had thought of several ways to introduce the subject of Dorothy Ryder, but Amanda saved her the trouble by asking if she'd enjoyed the groundbreaking ceremony.

Perfect. Amanda had opened a circuitous route, but Elyssa figured she'd reach her destination soon enough. "It was wonderful, and watching the building go up will be exciting."

"And knowing your guy has a major role there," Amanda added with a knowing smile.

Detour. She really needed to put a stop to this line of chatter. "He's not 'my guy,'" Elyssa said firmly.

Amanda shook her finger playfully. "Ah-ah, don't try to pull the wool over my eyes. Remember, I'm 'she who sees all.' No one at the ceremony could've missed the possessive way he put his hand on your shoulder, the way he looked straight into your eyes after he acknowledged the applause. Oh, no, my dear, he's definitely yours."

Elyssa's cheeks warmed. No use continuing down this path. She had a more important goal in mind. "I'm impressed with the work the fund-raising committee for the new facility has done," she said. "Brett told me a little about it, and even though I'm not in the news business any longer, I recognize a good story. I thought I'd talk to some of the committee members, even some of the staff, and find out more. Then I can pass the info on to some friends in the media.''

"Good idea," Amanda said. "I'm sure the committee will appreciate the exposure. It could generate more money."

"I know the committee, of course, and I also got the names of some staff. Maybe you could give me some more." Elyssa took a notebook from her bag.

"Lee Anne Scarborough," Amanda said. "She's Clark Madigan's secretary. You should talk to her."

After a few more suggestions, Elyssa said, "I heard of someone else. Dorothy Ryder. Do you know her?"

"I did, but she's dead."

"Oh, dear," Elyssa murmured. "Something sudden?"

"Traffic accident. Such a sad story."

"Really?" She waited, knowing Amanda couldn't resist telling what she knew.

"Her car went out of control and slammed into a concrete wall."

Elyssa had a flash of the night when she'd almost met the same fate, and shivered. The words threatened to stick in her throat, but she managed to ask, "What time of day?"

"Late at night," Amanda said. "She spent the evening at her daughter's and was on the way home. Karen, the daughter, had given birth to Dorothy's first grandchild three months before, and Dorothy was in heaven. She'd show everyone pictures of the baby and brag about how cute the baby was—you know, the whole grandmother routine. And then, in a minute, she was gone."

"She died at the scene then?" Elyssa asked.

"Instantly," Amanda said and sniffled. "It was tragic."

"I wonder how she lost control," Elyssa said. "Was she upset about something that would distract her attention?"

"Oh, no," Amanda said. "Like I told you, she was as happy as could be."

"That is really too bad," Elyssa murmured. "I wonder why I was given her name."

"She and Lee Anne Scarborough were good friends. I imagine she filled in occasionally when one of Lee Anne's kids was sick."

Elyssa nodded. She continued talking for a few minutes, then got up to leave. *First mission accomplished.*

Her next visit was to Clark Madigan's secretary.

As befitted the chief of staff, Dr. Madigan's office was large and opulent, with expensive furnishings and original art on the walls. Lee Anne Scarborough, an attractive woman, probably in her early forties, sat at an imposing desk. She greeted Elyssa with a distant smile that said she was too busy to spare more than a moment for walk-in callers.

Elyssa smiled. She'd breached more formidable barriers than Lee Anne during her days in television. Quickly she introduced herself.

"Oh, of course," Lee Anne said, with more interest. "I should have recognized you. You're doing some work here now, aren't you?"

"Yes, and I was at the groundbreaking ceremony yesterday. I'm so excited about the new facility, and I happen to have a friend who's on the board of a foundation with an interest in children's health issues. I'd love to give him some information about the new hospital, and I thought you'd be just the person who could tell me what financial needs they'd have. I assume, being Dr. Madigan's secretary, you've been involved with CFCCC."

Lee Anne preened a bit. "I know everything there is to know. Here," she said, reaching into her desk, "let me give you a couple of brochures."

"Thanks, and could I ask you some questions? The foundation will want to know about the committee's mission, how they accomplish their goals, and so on."

"I'd be happy to tell you anything you need to know," Lee Anne said.

What she wanted to know was how often the board met and whether Lee Anne had records of the meetings. She slipped those questions in unobtrusively, and when she'd pumped the woman as much as she could, rose and thanked her. "I'll pass this along, and I'm sure you'll hear from my friend soon." She'd better make up a name. "Arnold Wells."

As she started for the door, it opened and Clark Madigan walked in. He was clearly surprised—and not particularly pleased, she thought—to see her, but he covered his displeasure. "Elyssa, how nice to see you again. How can we help you?"

She waved the brochure Lee Anne had given her. "I'm hoping to help *you*." She mentioned the friend and the foundation she'd invented.

Madigan, who was, of course, far more savvy than his secretary, frowned. "I'm not familiar with the Severin Trust."

"Oh, it's small, but they're very interested in children," Elyssa said.

Though she doubted he believed her, Madigan smiled. "We can always use more funding," he said. "Thank you."

"Glad to help." She hurried out and glanced down the hall. She was sorry she had run into Madigan, but she'd be even less pleased to meet Brett. He'd have too many questions that she didn't want to answer.

Relieved that Brett was nowhere around, she headed to the valet parking desk in the lobby and called for her car.

She'd gotten what she wanted from Lee Anne—confirmation that Lee Anne was likely to have inside information about CFCCC. If Dorothy substituted for Lee Anne occasionally, she could have had access as well. *Nancy Drew strikes again.*

Now she would contact Dorothy Ryder's husband. As

soon as she drove away from the hospital, she took out her cell phone, called directory assistance for Joe Ryder's number and dialed. When a pleasant-voiced man answered, she said. "Mr. Ryder, my name is Elyssa Jarmon. Your wife—"

"If you're selling some memorial book, I don't want it." The voice was not so pleasant now. "It's been a year and a half and you people are still—"

He was about to hang up on her. "No, Mr. Ryder," she interrupted. "Your wife was working with a friend of mine from Channel 9."

"Then you've got the wrong Ryder. My wife didn't work at a TV station."

"No, sir, but she was helping him with a story about the hospital."

"I don't know anything about that."

She heard the sound of finality and knew she had to say something—anything to keep him on the line. "I think she was murdered."

Joe gasped. "Who the hell are you?"

"I used to be a reporter. Now I'm convinced the same people who killed your wife have targeted me."

"You think she was killed," Joe said slowly. "Why?"

"Because she had information that could have brought down some very powerful people."

"You really believe that?" Joe asked.

"Yes, and I'd like to come by and talk to you."

There was a long silence. *Please,* Elyssa prayed. *Please say yes.*

Finally he said, "Tomorrow," and gave her the address.

She hung up and braked for a red light. She was on the verge of an answer, she knew it.

Pleased with herself, she opened her window and took a breath of fresh morning air. The rain last night had cooled down the city, and she could feel a hint of fall. Elyssa pictured herself and Brett, curled up before a fire. Would they still be together when winter came?

Suddenly she needed to hear his voice. Impulsively she punched in his office number and asked to speak with him. He was between appointments and came on the line immediately.

"Hi, it's Elyssa," she said.

"What's wrong?"

Damn, her voice was shaking. She cleared her throat. "Nothing."

"Did you find out something about Randy?"

"I haven't been to the bank yet. I was calling to...see what time to be ready this evening."

"Six. I thought I told you."

Whoops. He probably had told her. He sounded hurried. She shouldn't have disturbed him, no matter how much she needed the reassurance of his voice. "Must've forgotten. I'll let you go. I know you're busy." Reluctantly she hung up, wondering how much longer she'd be able to call him like this. How much longer until he decided to move on?

One part of her grieved for the inevitable break. Another said not to worry about tomorrow, just make the most of every moment. Hadn't she learned from Randy's death how easily the future could be snatched away?

Chapter 15

In the lobby of the bank, Elyssa brought Jenny up to date on what she'd learned since yesterday. "Now maybe we'll know the whole story," she said. A few minutes later when they sat down in a cubicle with Randy's safe-deposit box on the table between them, she hoped she was right.

Jenny put her hand on the cover of the box, then drew it away and let out a shaky breath. "I'm scared," she whispered.

"But we have to *know,*" Elyssa said firmly. "Open it."

Jenny shoved the box toward Elyssa. "You do it."

She lifted the cover, and they peered inside. A black spiral notebook lay before them. Elyssa took it out and opened it.

Heads together as they leaned over the table, they began to read:

March 2. I'm writing this in case something happens to me. The dates everything happened are confirmed in my appointment book, but I wanted to write about the events and what I know in detail. Jenny dearest, I hope you never have to read this. I hope I can take care of what needs to be done myself, but if you do read this, take it to the police as soon as you finish.

"You see? He was in trouble. Oh, Randy, why didn't you tell me?" Jenny choked.

Elyssa put an arm around Jenny. Then she turned the page.

February 17. Here's where everything started. I got a call from Dorothy Ryder, administrative offices, St. Michael's Hospital. Met her last year when doing a story on a mix-up in records. She said she had a tip for me, a potentially major story.

"I can almost hear his voice," Jenny said, her eyes filling.

"Me, too," Elyssa said. She read the entry again. "Damn, when I saw those initials on the program yesterday, I was sure something fishy was going on at St. Michael's. I wonder if Derek found out, too, and tried to scare me off. He might have been afraid I'd take the story elsewhere after the way Channel 9 treated me."

"But having someone go after you with a *knife?*" Jenny gasped. "Would he go that far?"

"I don't know. Let's see the rest." Elyssa flipped to the next page.

February 18. Met Dorothy at Burger King. Last month she helped out in the chief of staff's office and saw some notes that led her to believe CFCCC, the Committee to Fund Children's Cancer Center, is involved in fraud.

Elyssa felt a cold chill. "Chief of staff. That's Dr. Madigan." *Brett's friend.*

"Look at this." Jenny read aloud:

Here's the history of this committee. They were formed to raise funds for the new hospital but also managed to get authority for site selection.

They convinced the hospital to switch from the location they had planned to build on, to a new one. Dorothy thinks some members of the committee owned the site.

"Would that be illegal?" Jenny asked. "A conflict of interest or something?"

"I don't know." Elyssa turned the page.

February 20. Met with Dorothy again. Here's what she's figured out. These men—she hasn't figured out who yet—bought the land cheap, formed a corporation called Hastings and sold the land to the hospital for an inflated amount. They made $5,000,000 profit on the deal.

"Hastings Corporation," Elyssa mused. "Why does that ring a bell? Wait, the notes in the book. The number 1066—that was the year of the Battle of Hastings."

"Good grief," Jenny said. "I'd never have remembered that, but Randy would have. He loved history."

"I sure didn't," Elyssa said. "But our high school teacher drummed that date into our minds." She grimaced. "Randy must have written the note in the Brinkley book to himself. It would've been a pretty obscure clue for someone else to decipher."

"But why would this Hastings Corporation have anything to do with Randy's death?" Jenny said. "It's just a real estate deal, isn't it?"

"Seems to be at first glance. But think about it. These guys buy the land for peanuts, they bury their names in some kind of corporation. Maybe they even have one or two people who aren't involved with the hospital as a front. *They* own the land, *they* choose that land for a new hospital, *they* set the price and then make a killing.

"If a TV reporter got hold of that information and made it public, think of what would happen. Even if they weren't charged with anything, they might have to give the money back. And their reputations would be ruined. Maybe they'd have to leave the hospital and start all over somewhere else. And what hospital would want them on staff after a scandal like this? Nope, if Randy went on the air with that story, they wouldn't be happy."

Jenny put her hand to her mouth. "Unhappy enough to…to kill him?"

"Maybe Randy will tell us." Elyssa turned the page.

February 23. Dorothy called. She thought someone was following her, said to be careful.
February 25. I thought she was overreacting, but she was right. Someone started following me, too. I saw a black Chevrolet behind me several times today. I don't think it's coincidental.

Jenny began to cry. "Why didn't he tell me? I'd have made him go to the police." She picked up the notebook and shook it as if she were shaking Randy. "Why didn't he have enough sense to go to the police on his own?"

Thinking of her own not-so-pleasant experience with the authorities, Elyssa shook her head. "I'm sure he planned to, but he had no real proof," she said, and wondered if the police would have believed him if he had contacted them.

"Yeah, I guess this is just what they'd call hearsay," Jenny said, then glanced down at the notebook. "Oh, Lord, look at this." She pointed to the page.

February 27. Dorothy called from a pay phone, told me to watch my butt. Someone went through her desk at work last night. Lucky she's been keeping her notes at home. I knew I was right about someone tailing me. Made an appointment with a lawyer to draw up a will. Also going to apply for a gun permit.

Jenny sniffed again, and Elyssa squeezed her shoulder. They continued reading, absorbed by the unfolding drama.

February 28. Met Dorothy in the park. She's going to "work late," one night this week, slip into Madigan's office and copy notes. She hasn't even told her husband what she knows. Doesn't want him involved— same way I feel about Jenny. Dorothy says these men are extremely powerful, with connections throughout the city. Even have pawns at the TV station. Derek Graves for one. The worst of it is I talked to him when I started this.

He's been telling me to back off this investigation, that it might be too hot to handle. Says a story like this could get the station sued. Now I know why. He's in it up to his neck.

"Derek. Why am I not surprised?" Elyssa muttered. "I knew he was a rat."

"And he knew everything Randy was doing," Jenny said, her eyes wide with horror. "But would he—?"

"Maybe, for enough dough. Someone must've paid him off." She remembered the new BMW in his parking space at the station.

"But would he have hurt you?" Jenny asked. "You two were still involved."

"Maybe he thought Randy had told me something," Elyssa said. "But he couldn't have known I'd be in the car that night." She pondered that for a moment, then said,

"No, I happened to be in the wrong place at the wrong time. If someone thought Randy had confided in me, they'd have come after me long ago. No one bothered me until I talked to you and started investigating."

"Until you told Derek what you were doing," Jenny said.

"True, but I don't think Derek's in charge. He was probably just the errand boy. Someone else made that decision about Randy, someone with a lot more to lose."

"Now they're after you," Jenny said, shuddering.

"They won't get me," Elyssa said with more confidence than she felt. "Tomorrow I'm going to see Dorothy's husband. I'll bet you Dorothy left behind the proof Randy never got. Then I'm going to the police, and this time they'll listen."

"*We're* going," Jenny corrected.

"Not a chance. You're not involved."

"How can you say that?" Jenny asked, her cheeks flushed. "Of course I am."

"Not the way I am," Elyssa said. "Derek knows you're suspicious. I'm sure he *doesn't* know you're in town."

Jenny's usually sweet expression hardened with determination. Elyssa searched desperately for a way to curtail her friend's resolve. "Your children have already lost one parent. Do you want to take a chance on their losing both?"

Jenny dropped her eyes and shook her head. "But you—"

"I'll be fine," Elyssa insisted. "Let's hope Randy wrote down some names." She turned to the next page.

"There they are," Jenny said, pointing.

March 1. Dorothy isn't sure how many members of CFCCC are with Hastings. She's sure of these: Dr. Clark Madigan, hospital chief of staff, Dr. Avery Stevenson, neurology. Thinks Gavin McRae, hospital administrator, is another. Doesn't know how many more or who they are.

Elyssa read the note again. "Madigan," she murmured. Brett's mentor, the man he revered almost as a father. How could such a man be involved in…murder?

The entry continued on the next page.

We should have the proof in a couple of days. Then we're going to the D.A. and the cops. I hope we both make it till then.

But neither of them had, Elyssa thought.

And what about her? Would *she* make it until she delivered the information to the authorities?

Had Randy learned any more? Did Dorothy ever figure out who the other Hastings members were? She turned another page. Nothing. They'd read the last entry.

"Elyssa," Jenny said urgently, "we've got some of the names. Why wait until you see Mr. Ryder tomorrow to turn this over to the police? Go today."

"I can't." Not until she spoke with Brett. He was on the fund-raising committee. If she went public with this information, his reputation could be ruined along with the others. No, she had to talk to him first.

Elyssa shut the notebook and placed it carefully in her briefcase. "Let's go."

She kept the briefcase under her arm, grasping it tightly as they walked out of the bank. "I'll talk to you tomorrow," she said and headed for her car. She checked the back seat and, once inside, locked the doors and drove cautiously out of the parking garage. She avoided the freeway and kept a wary eye on the rearview mirror. Driving had never been so scary. Every cross street, every intersection seemed fraught with danger.

An SUV loomed on her left, and Elyssa glanced at the driver. A harried-looking woman with a carful of preschoolers. She posed no threat. But the black sedan with a lone man at the wheel pulling into the street from a parking lot seemed ominous. Elyssa swerved into the right-hand lane and into a crowded supermarket parking lot. The black car drove past.

She put a hand over her racing heart. Should she forget about waiting and go straight to the police?

The dashboard clock showed four-thirty. Brett was due home in an hour, and they'd planned on dinner alone at Maison de Ville before they met the Madigans and several other couples at the theater. Ironic, Elyssa thought, to be socializing with the man who might well be responsible for two deaths and, by random chance, for her own near death.

She had to talk to Brett, had to see if he knew anything else. Suddenly another thought, almost too frightening to imagine, leaped into her mind. If these men were as ruthless as they seemed, could Brett be in danger, too? Because he was associated with *her*. She had to warn him.

Resolutely she drove out of the parking lot.

At home she checked every door and window, made sure the security system was on, then called Brett. She would tell him she'd learned something incriminating, but she'd give him the details later. She couldn't blurt out what she knew about Madigan over the phone. Brett needed to hear that in person.

"He's in surgery," his secretary said. "I was just going to call you, to tell you he probably can't go out to dinner."

"Thanks." She was relieved that their dinner plans had changed. She couldn't tell Brett her news in public. She'd fix a light meal for them at home. She went down to the kitchen and got out an omelet pan.

What about the rest of the evening? What should she do? Stay home and talk to Brett? Go to the theater as planned so Madigan wouldn't suspect she was on to him? Yes, she'd go.

She put on her makeup, then, since she had some time, she slipped on a robe, curled up on her bed and reread Randy's notes. When she finished, she glanced uneasily about the room. Someone had ransacked Dorothy's desk. If they suspected she had evidence, they'd have no compunctions about searching here. Leaving the notes in her briefcase, the logical place to keep them, was far too risky.

Where, then? Under the mattress, in the linen closet, behind a book? Every place seemed too obvious. She finally settled for a plastic container filled with penne pasta. She shoved the notebook inside, piled the noodles around it until she was certain it was hidden, then put it back on the pantry shelf.

That done, she went back upstairs to dress. She yanked a sleeveless black silk dress off the hanger, rifled through the closet until she located the matching jacket, then slipped on a pair of high-heeled sandals, fastened on crystal earrings and a matching bracelet. She was halfway down the stairs when she realized the shoes were navy. With a sigh she trudged back up and exchanged them for black. Her mind was so full of what she'd learned today, she could have put her dress on inside out and not noticed when she looked in the mirror. She checked herself again. Okay, she was passable.

With nothing else to do, she turned on the six o'clock news and tried to concentrate on the latest bulletins from Washington. But she couldn't. She turned off the TV and paced the room. If she kept this up much longer, she'd wear a path across the hardwood floor.

How would Brett react to today's developments? No matter. She had to broach the subject tonight. The longer she waited to go to the authorities, the greater the chance that, incredible as it seemed, these people would strike again.

Suddenly something she'd forgotten sprang into her mind. Her encounter this morning with Clark Madigan. Had he checked to see if the Severin Trust was real? If he had, surely he'd realize she was fishing for information about the committee. The evening at the theater took on a sinister cast.

She could still back out.

No, she decided. Nothing would happen to her in a public place. The theater was the safest place to be. She'd spend the evening observing Clark Madigan and his colleagues. Maybe she'd learn something more, something useful.

Elyssa checked her watch. Six-twenty. When would Brett get home? If he showed up more than ten minutes from now, they wouldn't even have time for a snack before they left.

She went to the window to watch for his car, stood there for a few moments, then trudged back to the couch. Darn, she needed time to explain to him what she'd learned, time to convince him that he might be in as much danger as she.

Six twenty-eight. Time was running out.

Chapter 16

At seven Brett charged in, cleaner's bag in hand, and raced upstairs. Elyssa clenched her hands in frustration. She'd have to talk to him in the car. With no time for finesse, she'd need to be fast and blunt.

He came down, freshly shaved and perfectly turned out in a navy suit and crisp white shirt. Nervous as she was, she wasn't so distraught that she couldn't appreciate a man who looked as if he'd stepped out of *GQ*.

Straightening his tie, he stopped to survey her. The way his gaze traveled over her from head to toe made her blood heat. It was so easy for him to distract her, even without trying. With a smile of masculine approval, he murmured, "You're beautiful." The smile widened into a devilish grin. "Let's stay home."

He was teasing; she knew he wouldn't back out of the evening. Regardless, this wasn't the time for sexual repartee. Elyssa shook her head firmly. "We're late."

"I could have that dress off you in thirty seconds flat."

"Forget it, Doctor. Let's go."

As they walked out to the car, she told herself to curb the teasing banter. Every second counted. It was seven-twenty. She had twenty minutes in the car, five more if traffic was heavy.

No time for a graceful lead-in. "Brett, have you ever heard of Hastings Corporation?"

"Sure," he said, maneuvering around a Lexus. "They were the original owners of the land where the new hospital's going up."

"Do you know the names of the Hastings partners?"

Someone behind them honked, and Brett stepped on the gas. "No, but I'm guessing you do."

"Some of them." She let out a nervous breath. He wasn't going to like this, but she had to tell him. She plunged ahead. "Gavin McRae, Avery Stevenson...and Clark Madigan." She saw him flinch, but before he had a chance to comment, Elyssa continued. "Do you know how much they made on the sale?" He shook his head. "Millions. *Five* million to be exact."

"Any owner hopes to make a profit," he said slowly.

"The hospital had another site in mind. They could have gotten it for far less, but Hastings manipulated the trustees into purchasing *their* land. Property they'd bought below market value. That's breach of trust."

"Maybe, but that's not my expertise. It's an attorney's call." Stopping at a red light, he turned to her. "Is this what you found in Randy's notebook—that members of the fund-raising committee were also the owners of the property?"

"Yes, and a lot more."

"Have you spoken to the police?"

"No, I wanted to talk to you first."

He turned to her. "What do you expect me to tell you?"

"I don't know," Elyssa said. "What I do know is that Randy found out about this through Dorothy Ryder. She was the leak. And when the Hastings group realized he knew, they had him killed. Had Dorothy killed, too."

"You can't believe that men like Clark and Avery would kill someone."

"Maybe not personally, but they could have hired—"

"Come on, honey. That's ridiculous."

"I don't think so," Elyssa said stubbornly. "Could they have defrauded the hospital?"

"Unlikely," Brett answered, turning a corner. "But even if they did—and I seriously doubt it—the rest of what you're saying is way off base. Face it, your friend fabricated something—"

"He didn't."

"All right. Dorothy did."

Didn't he get it? "They were both killed because of what they 'fabricated.'"

"Honey, I can't argue with you about the cause of Randy's death. Truth is, we may never know."

There he went, discounting her again. Her hands clenched. "And the threats to me?"

"I can't dispute those, either, but to imagine that they came from Clark Madigan is ludicrous."

She was so frustrated she felt like crying. "Brett, you're in denial."

"And you're obsessed with Randy's death. That's natural." He held up a hand to quiet her. "But think. Clark is a *doctor*. Physicians don't take lives. They save them. The man is respected, admired, not only for his professional expertise but for his compassion, his involvement in charity, his—"

"You're wearing blinders," Elyssa protested. "You can't see past what he's done for you." She glanced out the window. They were less than ten minutes from the theater. She had only a short time left to convince him that what she knew was true, and she wasn't doing a good job of it so far.

"You don't know Clark Madigan," Brett countered. "I do."

Elyssa grimaced. "Randy was a respected reporter and I knew *him*. He didn't waste time on off-the-wall stories."

Brett didn't comment on Randy but said, "Once you've talked to Clark this evening, gotten to know him a little, you'll realize what a fine man he is."

"He'll be wearing his public persona, which could be as fake as a three-dollar bill."

Brett continued in a soothing voice, which irritated her all the more. "Give him a chance, sweetheart."

"What if *you're* in danger?" she asked. "What if you become a target of these people?"

"Now you're really out in left field. 'These people' are my friends."

She spoke slowly, carefully. "Maybe your pal Madigan wasn't the mastermind, but Randy was killed because he knew something about Hastings Corporation. Now I'm getting threats because I'm looking into it. Someone thinks I'm getting too close to the same information he had. Maybe they think he told me something before he died. The point is, I'm in danger because of Randy. Doesn't it make sense that because you're close to *me,* you'd be in danger, too?"

"No."

She felt like shaking him. "Think of the money involved," Elyssa argued. "Money can make people do monstrous things."

Brett made a turn and the theater loomed up before them. "Madigan doesn't need the money," he scoffed.

"Everyone needs money." *Even you,* she thought, suddenly remembering his remark about overextending himself to get the house he wanted.

Another thought surfaced. Until now Brett had insisted she go to the police. But since she'd suggested his friends were implicated in Randy's death, he was suspiciously quiet about contacting the authorities. He could have insisted on forgetting the theater, turning around and driving to police headquarters. Instead he was trying to persuade her she was wrong.

Frustration, confusion and doubt swirled through her. Half-remembered phrases swam into her mind. The afternoon he'd taken her to his house and commented that he'd spent more than he could afford, but, "Some unexpected funds came through."

Their discussion at the breakfast table this morning. "If you find anything in that safe-deposit box, I want your word that you'll call me."

On the surface, neither of those remarks sounded suspicious, but they could mask other motives. Sinister motives.

Unspoken thoughts suddenly crystallized.

The timing of that midnight call. The same evening she told Brett about her suspicions, about her plan to find out what had happened to Randy.

Brett and Derek, heads together, at the groundbreaking, talking far too intensely for new acquaintances.

The constant refrain from Brett: "Back off. This investigation of yours is too dangerous."

Dangerous to whom?

And then the thought, bright as a neon sign suddenly lit up—how many times had she asked herself why a man like Brett, who could have anyone, would want her?

Could Brett's interest in her be a fraud? A scheme to divert her from delving into Randy's death? He'd tried to deter her or maybe even to distract her with his lovemaking.

At that moment Brett reached for her hand. She stared at the fingers covering hers. She could hardly feel his touch; all her nerve endings had gone numb. Now she realized the car was no longer moving but was parked in the garage next to the theater. "Elyssa," he said, but her mind was so fogged she barely heard him.

Gently he turned her to face him, then took her hand again. "Honey, I know you want closure on this, but you have to accept what happened, forget it, and go on."

He couldn't have said anything worse, and in that coaxing tone as if he were speaking to a child. The haze in her mind cleared, anger erupted, and she pushed his hand away. "Don't patronize me, Brett. I'm not a kid playing pretend games. I'm a reporter."

"You can't be an objective one when you're involved in the story."

Fury almost robbed her of speech. Folding her arms across her chest like a barrier, she forced out her words. "But I can be persistent."

"If you're so convinced of what you told me, why didn't you go to the police today?" he asked.

"Because of you, dammit. I was afraid for you." When he responded with a questioning look, she added desperately, "I don't want you to be hurt, professionally or personally."

"Why should I be hurt?"

"I don't know. Please, Brett, tell me anything you know about this corporation."

"I've told you all I know." He stared at her, a puzzled frown on his face. "Why are you so angry with me?"

"You've been trying too hard to get me to stop this investigation."

"For your own safety."

"Or someone else's?" she asked.

"What do you mean? Whose?"

Like lava gushing from a volcano, the questions spewed out. "Are you protecting someone? Yourself?"

Silence. Her words lay between them like stones tossed into a pond, causing ripple after ripple. Mutely she stared at Brett, saw the shock on his face.

"You know me better than that," he said softly.

She thought she did. Now she wondered disconsolately if she only knew a good actor. "Can you ever really know someone else?" she muttered.

He didn't answer.

They sat without moving or speaking, both staring straight ahead. Somewhere outside a horn honked. Footsteps sounded, hurrying past, and a woman's shrill voice intruded. "Hurry. I told you we were going to be late." Then silence.

Now what? She had to go on with her plans. Hadn't she promised herself she'd observe Clark Madigan this evening? That, by God, was what she would do. She'd just bragged about what a great reporter she was. A reporter was like an actress. Personal problems were hidden and the face in the camera lens was untouched by private emotions.

"It's nearly eight," she said stoically. "Let's go."

The door locks clicked open and Brett got out of the car. For an instant he stood, jaw clenched, his hand on the door as if he meant to slam it. Then she saw him pull himself together. He shut the door quietly—too quietly—and came around to the passenger side, where she still sat frozen.

"Come on." His face was blank, his voice controlled.

"Brett—" she began.

"Later," he said, and reached into his jacket pocket for the tickets. A muscle jerked in his cheek.

Not touching, eyes averted, they walked side by side into the theater. The lobby was deserted except for a few late-comers hurrying to the auditorium doors. Elyssa was glad she and Brett were late. She couldn't greet his friends or carry on a conversation. Not yet. She doubted he could, either.

The usher led them down the aisle, and, with murmured apologies, they slipped past another couple and took their seats as the house lights dimmed.

The overture began. Elyssa had seen *A Chorus Line* for the first time a number of years ago and loved it. But not tonight. She kept her eyes on the empty stage as music filled the auditorium. Anyone watching would think she was enthralled. But in her lap she dug the fingernails of one hand into the palm of the other.

Horrified at what she'd said to Brett, Elyssa wondered how she would get through the rest of the evening. She wanted to go home and—

Hide? Cry? Most of all, she wanted to erase the past ten minutes.

She wished Brett had shouted at her as they walked through the garage. Anything would have been better than his cold reserve.

Thoughts flitted through her mind, faces swam in and out of her imagination. Randy, Derek, Brett. Always Brett. When she'd read Randy's notes, her first concern had been to protect Brett. Why had she never suspected that *he* might be involved in the events surrounding Randy's death? That was easy. Because she was in love with him. And wasn't love blind?

What kind of fool had she been all this time, trusting him so much? Gullible enough to give him a key to her house. And worse, the key to her heart.

The curtain rose, the line of actors took their places.

The play began.

Over the actors' voices, Cassie's words replayed in Elyssa's ears. *You don't think a man as wonderful as Brett could love you.* It was true. Even as she tumbled head over heels for him, even as he showed her he cared for her, she hadn't been able to believe it. He'd said he couldn't commit, but in every way he'd showed her commitment. He'd given her his attention, his protection, his devotion. Was it all pretense, as make-believe as the actors spouting their lines on the stage before her? Had she fallen in love with a...criminal?

Or was her own self-doubt the culprit? Two years ago she would never have suspected that Derek—or any other man she might have been involved with—would play her false. But she'd been on top of the world then, her confidence in herself soaring. After the accident everything changed.

More than her face was damaged that night. The accident stole her belief in herself. She'd thought she'd regained her sense of self-worth, had said as much to Cassie, but maybe she'd been wrong. Were her misgivings about herself the reason she distrusted Brett?

He shifted in his seat, his sleeve brushed her arm, and she turned to glance at him. He stared straight ahead.

Why hadn't she asked him to take her home where they could talk this out? What did she think she could accomplish here when her emotions were in tatters?

If Joe Ryder gave her information that showed Brett was involved in Hastings along with his colleagues, what then? Would she have the guts to go to the authorities and turn him in, or would she destroy the evidence, pretend she'd never seen it? If she did, how could she justify her actions to Jenny? To herself?

Her accusation had stunned him. At least it appeared to. Did that prove he was innocent? Or deceptive?

He dropped his program, bent to retrieve it, and as he straightened, glanced at her. His eyes were bleak.

He wasn't angry. He was hurt, and she'd done it. With one word—*yourself. Are you protecting someone? Yourself?*

Working in the media, she'd known the power of words. How could she have allowed that word to slip out? Even as she let it fly, she wanted to take it back, but she was too late. She saw the word's force, watched it pierce Brett's heart with arrow-like precision.

More than anything now, she wanted to reach for his hand, to feel it close, warm and reassuring, around hers. But she didn't. Confused and miserable, she moved as far away from him as possible.

She couldn't watch the play anymore. She could only look at Brett. She wanted to memorize everything about him. Now, because she might never have another chance. Tears misted in her eyes, clogged her throat.

Beside her Brett felt her gaze but didn't turn to her. She'd come at him straight out of left field, back there in the car, slammed him right in the gut. In the heart.

Funny, from the moment he'd become involved with her,

he'd worried that someday he might hurt her. It hadn't crossed his mind that *she* might do the hurting. And how deftly she had, attacking his honesty, his integrity—the very qualities he prized most in himself.

Only a few weeks ago she'd said she trusted him. How did she define *trust?*

Dammit, he'd ignored his own warnings and nearly fallen in love with her. Hadn't he promised himself long ago to devote his life to medicine and forget relationships? One disaster should be enough in any man's life.

Surreptitiously he glanced at Elyssa. She'd given him an out with her crazy accusations. He didn't have to listen to them anymore. He could leave her at her door and go on with his life. Forget her siren's voice, her warm laughter, her caring and her intelligence. And the way she cradled him deep inside her. Yeah, he should be relieved, not aching as if she'd cut out a piece of his heart.

Applause rippled through the theater, and the lights came on. Intermission. Automatically he stood.

Simon Martinez, seated on his left, put out a hand. "Didn't think you'd make it. Did you have an emergency?"

"No, a procedure that took longer than usual." He introduced Elyssa to Simon and his wife, Helena. Just as if this were a normal evening. Just as if his life weren't falling apart.

The four of them started up the aisle. "Isn't the music wonderful?" Helena bubbled.

"Great," Elyssa said.

Brett merely nodded. He'd missed the entire first act. He was surprised at Elyssa's enthusiastic agreement. He'd have sworn she was as distracted as he.

Their group gathered in the lobby. When the Madigans came up, Brett saw Elyssa tense, but he was certain no one else noticed.

"Well, Elyssa, we meet again," Madigan said, taking her hand in both of his.

Brett watched Elyssa smile and make small talk, as if she were delighted to be with these people. When he knew she thought some—if not all—of them were guilty of fraud, and worse. What an actress. She said her cousin Cassie was talented? Cassie wasn't even in Elyssa's league.

Madigan smiled genially and said, ''Elyssa stopped by my office today to pick up some information. She's hoping to interest the Severin Trust in our fund-raising activities.''

Brett glanced sharply at her. What was she up to?

Suddenly he wondered if she'd suspected his colleagues all along. Was that why she'd agreed to go out with him in the first place? So she could observe them all close up, gather evidence for her case against them? And him, too?

He wished he'd known Randy Barber. Was Elyssa's friend a nutcase? Or had he really uncovered dirty dealings and paid for his discovery with his life?

Could Randy—and Elyssa—be right?

He looked at his mentor's smiling face and thought of all Clark had accomplished, all he stood for. A criminal? Impossible.

Elyssa and Helena Martinez excused themselves to go to the ladies' room. Brett wandered away from the group and found a quiet corner, turned his back to the crowd and stared morosely out the window.

The skies, which had cleared that morning, had clouded again. He remembered last night. He and Elyssa, cocooned in her bed while rain lashed the windows and the wind moaned. He remembered the smell of Elyssa's hair, the touch of her breath against his cheek. And their wild, sweet loving…

''Brett.''

Startled, he turned. Dr. Herbert Raines, chief of surgery, stood behind him.

Brett stared uncomprehending at his colleague's outstretched hand, then shook it. He responded automatically to Raines's comments about the performance tonight. He wished Raines would go away. He wasn't in the mood for small talk.

Neither apparently was Raines. "I'm disturbed to see you with that news reporter again," he said bluntly. "She stirred up a scandal a couple of years ago, blabbing about tests ordered in the E.R."

This seemed to be a repeat of the conversation Brett had had with Madigan when he first began seeing Elyssa. He hadn't appreciated Clark's intrusion into his private life, but at least Clark was a close friend. Raines wasn't. In fact, Brett didn't like the man. And tonight, with his temper already on edge, he didn't think he could handle this conversation civilly. He answered just as bluntly. "Elyssa's not a reporter anymore, and this conversation is off-limits." He swung around.

He'd taken one step when Raines put a restraining hand on his arm and said sharply, "Are you feeding her information about St. Michael's?"

That stopped him. He stared pointedly at the hand on his arm. When Raines removed it, Brett said coolly, "That's a strange question, Herb, since I just told you she's no longer a reporter."

Raines gave him a skeptical look. "She's spending a lot of time at the hospital."

"But not as a reporter. She dresses up like a clown and entertains kids in the cancer unit."

Of course, he thought, she'd also targeted the hospital in her investigation into her friend's death. And knowing Elyssa's tenacity, she'd probably started inquiring about that woman in administration who died last year. God, was that what she'd been doing in Clark's office today? But Raines had no reason to know that, and Brett wasn't going to tell him.

Raines shook his head, then smiled paternally. "Take my advice, Brett. Break it off with her."

No matter that barely an hour ago he'd halfway decided to do that very thing, Raines's remark was not only inappropriate, it was profoundly disturbing. Brett's eyes narrowed. "Break it off with her," he repeated. "Why?"

"Madigan doesn't like her. None of us do."

"Clark hardly knows her. Why does he dislike her?"

Raines shrugged. "Maybe he carries a grudge about the black mark she put on his hospital with that story a few years ago. Maybe she just rubs him wrong."

"And the rest of you?"

"Same thing. We have long memories." Again he put a hand on Brett's shoulder. "Forget this one and find yourself another woman. They're all alike—"

"Back off."

The steel in Brett's voice halted Raines. He turned away but not before saying coldly, "Do yourself a favor, Cameron, and remember that Madigan hates to be crossed. I didn't see your name on the Budget Committee…"

"So my career's on the line?"

Raines smiled, almost pityingly. "You're still on as director of the new hospital. Prestige appointment, done deal. But you know, what's done can be undone."

"Is that a threat?"

"Of course not. Just friendly advice."

The two men's eyes met. Raines said nothing more. He walked away.

Brett watched him stroll over to Madigan. The two men spoke for a moment, then Raines ambled over to a group standing near the snack bar and joined in their conversation. Madigan remained where he was, took his cell phone out of his pocket and made a call. Then he, too, joined the others.

Brett glared at his colleagues. He felt as if he were a freshman in some kind of high school social club and had been chastised by the seniors for dating the wrong girl. Who exactly did these men think they were, dictating his private life?

Was the world going mad? Suddenly nothing made sense. His colleagues disliked Elyssa for no apparent reason. Damn, he'd gotten the impression that Madigan was over his aversion to her. He'd have to sit down with his mentor and have a frank discussion about that.

And he and Elyssa needed to talk, too, later tonight, about her bizarre accusations about Madigan and the rest. Okay, maybe he could accept the idea that they'd manipulated the hospital for their own financial gain, but murder? That was too outrageous to even think about.

Where was Elyssa, anyway? As the house lights blinked, he scanned the lobby, then spotted her and Helena coming out of the rest room. He hurried to catch up with them. Still not speaking to each other, they returned to their seats.

The second act was half over when he felt a familiar vibration in his pocket. His cell phone.

Why was his service contacting him tonight? He wasn't on call.

He tapped Elyssa on the shoulder, mouthed, "Phone," and slipped out to the lobby. "Cameron," he snapped.

"This is St. Michael's, sir." He didn't recognize the operator's voice. She must be new.

"Singh's on call tonight."

"I'm sorry, doctor," the operator said nervously, "but Dr. Singh's wife went into premature labor. He told me to page you."

"What's the problem?" Something that could be dealt with over the phone, he hoped. He and Elyssa needed to talk. As soon as possible, not when he was half-dead after a late-night trip to the hospital.

"Mark Haley, sir. He went into cardiac arrest a few minutes ago. They're trying to stabilize him...."

"I'm on my way."

The talk with Elyssa would have to wait. He tore his program in two and scribbled a note to Rob Tyler, an OB-Gyn who was new to Indianapolis: "Emergency call. Can you drop Elyssa at her home?" On the other half of the program he wrote a quick explanation to Elyssa. He found an usher, gave him the notes, then dashed out of the theater.

Chapter 17

"**M**essage for you, ma'am."

Elyssa took the folded paper from the usher and squinted at it in the darkness: "Emergency. Rob Tyler will take you home."

Why had Brett gone to the hospital? He'd mentioned that he wasn't on call when they'd made plans for the evening.

He didn't say he'd see her later. She wondered if he planned to come over.

She'd met Rob Tyler briefly one day at the hospital. He was a gynecologist, new to Indianapolis. With his specialty, he wouldn't be involved in the new children's cancer center, and he hadn't been here long enough to be a Hastings partner. She supposed he was harmless. And, considering the alternatives—waiting alone at the theater for a cab or asking Clark Madigan for a ride—Rob was her best choice.

She peered down the row at Madigan. How much had Lee Anne, his secretary, told him about their discussion at his office this morning? If only she'd read Randy's notes *before* she went to the hospital, she'd never have chanced talking to Lee Anne.

She no longer pretended to watch the play. She clasped her hands tightly in her lap and tried not to shiver. The darkened theater felt ominous, the people around her menacing. She'd never felt so alone. So defenseless.

His mind occupied with Mark Haley, Brett took the stairs two at a time to the second floor of the hospital. He expected to see a flurry of activity around Mark's room, but the hallway was dark and still. Dammit, had they lost the boy?

Approaching the nurses' station, he slowed and stared in surprise. Annie MacElroy, the night charge nurse, and another RN were sitting behind the desk, quietly chatting. A radio turned low played songs from the fifties.

Annie, gray-haired and grandmotherly, who often stated that she'd entered the nursing profession with Florence Nightingale, looked up and grinned. "Why, Dr. Cameron, how come you're paying us a visit so late? And all dressed up, too?"

He didn't smile back. "Where's Mark Haley?"

Annie seemed surprised at the question. "Asleep in his room, I imagine. He had some pain earlier, but—"

"What the hell are you talking about?" Brett growled, and saw Annie flinch at his unusual vehemence. "My service called fifteen minutes ago and said he arrested."

"A-arrested?" Both nurses jumped up. Brett strode down the hall and they followed. He shoved Mark's door open. The room was dark, the young man sleeping peacefully.

"Doctor, I told you—" Annie began, but Brett was already on his way back to the nurses' station.

"What in hell is going on here?" He grabbed the phone and called his answering service. "This is Dr. Cameron. Who paged me fifteen minutes ago about my patient, Mark Haley?"

"I'll check on it," the operator said. In a few moments she returned. "No one, sir," she said.

"What did you say?"

"Um, nobody called you." She sounded apprehensive.

"That's impossible."

"I've checked the records for the last hour."

"Dammit." He hung up and glared at Annie, who hovered in the background. "Did someone on the floor call?"

"Janie's checking, but I don't think so. Mark is fine. Why would someone call you?"

"Exactly what I want to know. Well?" he said as the other nurse approached them.

She shook her head. "The call didn't come from here."

In the dark theater he hadn't noticed the incoming number on his cell phone, but now he checked the last received call. It hadn't come from the hospital. Then, where? He used the hospital phone and called the number back.

The phone rang and rang. He was about to hang up when a man's gravelly voice answered. "Yeah."

"Who is this?"

"Who ya want?" the man said.

"I got a call from this number. I'm trying to figure out who made it."

"Good luck. This's a pay phone, man. Corner of Eighth and Garner."

Brett hung up. Then he called Singh, the doctor who *should* have been on call tonight.

Singh picked up on the first ring. Brett heard the sound of a television in the background. He explained what had happened and that he'd been told Singh's wife was in labor.

"Labor? I don't understand who would have told you that. She's not due for six weeks. She's spending the weekend in Chicago with her sister."

"A mix-up, I guess," Brett said. He disconnected and walked toward the elevators. Whoever called had to know the names of Brett's patients, had to know Singh's wife was pregnant...

Someone wanted him out of the way, wanted Elyssa alone. Someone...who knew too much. Clark Madigan?

Lord, everything Elyssa had told him must be true. He bypassed the elevator and ran for the stairs, checking his watch.

Thank God the play wouldn't be over yet. He'd get her out of the theater, drive her home, and apologize like crazy on the way. For doubting her, for doggedly defending a man he'd worshiped for years and who didn't deserve his adulation. At home he'd give her fifteen minutes to throw things into a suitcase, then he'd get her out of there to somewhere safe.

Where? She'd be no safer at his house or at Cassie's. Or anywhere in Indianapolis. He'd call his sister Gina, send Elyssa to stay with her for a few days. Meanwhile, *he'd* turn over all the information she had on Hastings to the police.

"Dr. Cameron, Dr. Cameron!" A breathless voice stopped him in mid-stride.

With one hand on the exit door, he turned and saw Annie running down the hall. Behind her came Ramon Guiterrez's mother, her face ashen, her cheeks tear-streaked.

"It's...Ramon," Annie said, puffing. "He turned blue and...we...we can't get a pulse."

"Oh, Doctor, thank God you're here. My boy..."

"Come on." With the two women behind him, he raced down the hall toward Ramon's room.

The play would be over soon. Rob would drop Elyssa off, and she'd be home alone. At least he could do something about that. As he ran, he flagged down one of the nurses' aides. "Page Dr. Robert Tyler and ask him to take Ms. Jarmon to his home. Tell him it's urgent."

The curtain closed, then opened again as the cast received a standing ovation.

"Elyssa." She jumped at the sound of her name, then turned. Rob Tyler, seated in the row behind her, beckoned.

She joined him and met his wife Debbie, seven months pregnant with their second child.

When their group congregated in the lobby, Dr. Madigan headed straight for her. "Where's Brett?" he asked.

"At the hospital."

"An emergency? Too bad. Patricia and I will drive you home." He sounded so friendly, so sincere, that she suddenly wondered if Randy might have been wrong in his accusations. Maybe Dorothy Ryder was a woman with an ax to grind, who had it in for Madigan and lied to Randy about the doctor.

But then, why were Randy and Dorothy both dead?

The doctor put a hand on her shoulder. His touch made her want to flinch, but she didn't let herself react. "Thank you. Rob and Debbie have already offered."

Madigan squeezed her shoulder lightly. "Take care, my dear."

Was there a sinister undertone to his remark? She watched as he sauntered away, chatting with a couple whose names she couldn't remember.

She was about to follow the Tylers when Madigan glanced over his shoulder. His eyes bored into hers. Gone was the genial facade. His stare was cold, merciless.

She felt as if she were caught in the crosshairs of a high-powered rifle. She stood, unable to move, until she heard Rob's voice behind her. "Coming, Elyssa?"

With an effort, she broke the contact with Madigan and turned. But as she crossed the lobby beside the Tylers, she could feel his eyes still on her, feel the uncompromising force of his gaze. She had to steel herself not to run.

In the connecting garage, they walked up a flight of stairs to reach the Tylers' car. Elyssa watched as Rob put a hand under Debbie's elbow and helped her up the steps. At the top he asked, "You all right, honey?"

"Yes, Dr. Tyler. Pregnancy's a natural condition." She shot him a mischievous smile. "But you'd know that, wouldn't you?"

"Smart mouth," he muttered and kissed her cheek. "It's different when the baby growing in there is yours. Even if it's the second time."

So, Elyssa thought, it *was* possible to be a physician and have a happy family life. Why couldn't Brett see that? Then she reminded herself that what Brett understood or didn't, might no longer matter. Their relationship was very likely damaged beyond repair.

The Tylers were a pleasant couple, and any other night she'd have enjoyed spending time with them. Debbie chatted animatedly about the new home they'd bought, her newfound interest in gardening and the next Broadway musical coming to town. "I used to do little theater back in Oklahoma," she drawled. "I could belt out those Broadway songs with them best of them, couldn't I, honey?"

Rob grinned. "Sure could." His cell phone shrilled and he answered. When he hung up, he grinned at Elyssa. "Brett doesn't take anything for granted. I guess he was afraid I didn't get his note. That was a message to be sure and take you home."

"Elyssa, would you like to stop for coffee?" Debbie asked. "Knowing the medical profession, I bet Brett won't be finished for hours."

Debbie had said the last thing Elyssa wanted to hear, that Brett would be late...if he was coming at all. She dreaded sitting alone in the house, but she didn't have the wherewithal to spend another hour socializing. "Thanks, but I have to be up early. Another time, though."

When they pulled up in front of her house, Rob offered to walk her to the door. Ordinarily she'd have turned him down, but tonight she welcomed his courtesy. He waited while she turned off her alarm system and unlocked the door, then, with an amiable good-night, he left her.

As she locked up, the phone began to ring. *Brett.* She hurried into the kitchen. It wasn't Brett. The number on her Caller ID printout was unfamiliar. She hesitated, her hand hovering over the receiver. The ringing stopped.

She'd just stepped back into the living room when the phone rang again. This time she answered.

"Dr. Cameron, please."

She didn't recognize the woman's voice, and she had no intention of admitting she was home by herself. "He's in the shower," she said. "Is this an emergency?"

"No."

She reached for a pad and pencil. "May I give him a message?"

"Uh, no, thanks. I'll call back later."

Elyssa hung up and hurried back to the front door to reactivate her security system.

Brett pulled up in front of the Tylers' house and jumped out of the car. He was halfway to the door before he realized the house was dark. He pressed the bell. No answer. Frantic, he pounded on the door.

It opened, and a sleepy Rob Tyler blinked at him. "What—?"

"Where's Elyssa?"

"Calm down, pal. I got your message. We took her home."

"Home?" Brett shouted. "I told you to bring her here."

"That's not the message I got."

Brett swore. No time to explain. Leaving Rob gaping in the doorway, he swung around and raced to his car.

The house seemed too empty to Elyssa. She thought of calling Cassie and asking her to come over, but didn't. She shouldn't be so dependent on her cousin. Soon Cassie would be on her way to New York. "Get used to it," she ordered herself, dropped her purse on the coffee table, kicked off her high-heeled sandals and wandered back to the kitchen.

She poured herself a glass of wine and stood at the counter sipping. The final melody from *A Chorus Line* drifted through her mind. Apparently she'd paid more attention than she thought. She hummed softly, thinking about what she'd done for love.

She'd wanted to protect Brett from Clark Madigan, but instead she'd spoiled everything. Was she a fool? Should she have trusted him? Or had she fallen in love with the wrong man—again? She set the wineglass down carefully; she felt like throwing it against the wall.

Maybe she'd call Cassie after all. She had her hand on the phone when a sound from upstairs stopped her.

Brett must have finished quickly at the hospital, come home and parked in the garage. Even with suspicion still gnawing at her, she felt a flash of relief at the thought that he was there. Now they could talk things through.

Going to the kitchen door, she called, "Brett, I'm home."

He didn't answer, but she heard his footsteps in the upstairs hall.

No, not his. Too heavy. Or was she imagining?

She held her breath. Listened.

Another step. Not Brett's.

Someone was there, and he was coming down. Fast. She saw the shadow of a man, huge and menacing, against the stairway wall.

The back door, she told herself. *Get out.* Eyes still on the stairwell, she tiptoed backward toward the door.

A black boot appeared on the step.

She froze as fear ripped through her. But worse than the fear, more horrible by far, was the recognition.

A black boot! Just like the one she saw long ago…in Eagle Creek Park.

The man on the stairway came into view. She could see him clearly now, even the malevolent grin on his face. *Out of the shadows, the light will dawn,* the psychic had said.

The entry hall light went out. *Lights out, love.* That's what he'd said to her, just before…before he kicked her down the hill.

In a flash everything that happened the night in the park came back: the crash, Randy's last words, his death and the face of the man who tried to kill her, too. The man who now advanced across her living room with a gun in his hand. She covered her mouth to keep from screaming.

She wouldn't give him a clear target. Hands shaking, she shut the kitchen door and pressed the light switch, leaving the room in darkness. She knew her way around the room; he didn't.

Did she have time to get to the back door, set off the alarm? No, he would open the kitchen door, switch on the light and shoot. She dashed around to the back of the center island.

She reached for the carving knife beside the cutting board. It wasn't there.

She grabbed the skillet she'd gotten out earlier and ducked down. Thank God she'd splurged on the island when she remodeled the kitchen.

She heard his footsteps coming closer, then a bump and a curse. He must have tripped over her shoes. But that didn't delay him for long. Closer now. He must be nearly to the kitchen.

He opened the door and chuckled. "It's lights out for good this time, love. The guys at Hastings want you wasted."

She'd heard that voice before. On the phone in the middle of the night. And in the hospital garage.

"Let's cooperate," he called, then flipped on the light. "You give me what you have on Hastings and I'll make it quick and easy for you."

She didn't answer.

In the silence her heart pounded like a drum. Could he hear it?

A sound came from the living room. The click of a door key, the turn of a knob.

No! Elyssa scrambled over and peered around the side of the island.

The man whipped around, distracted as the front door swung open, and Brett, clearly visible in the light from the porch, dashed inside.

"Brett," Elyssa screamed. "Get out. He has a gun."

Chapter 18

In the entry hall Brett froze, the sight before him nearly stopping his heart. Ignoring the man's weapon, he raced across the room.

Everything seemed to happen at once.

He heard a shot, felt the air stir as a bullet whizzed by him. At the same time Elyssa bolted around the kitchen island, brandishing a skillet.

"Get back," Brett shouted as the man fired and missed him again, but she kept coming. One more step and she raised her arm and slammed the frying pan on the gunman's head. With a crash, he toppled to the floor.

Looking dazed, Elyssa stared down at the man, now stretched facedown in her kitchen doorway.

Brett didn't spare the gunman a glance. Seething with terror and rage and another, darker emotion he didn't want to face now, he kicked the man's gun away, then rushed to Elyssa. "Are you all right? Are you crazy, running at him like a maniac?" he shouted. "Dammit, he had a gun."

"What was I supposed to do, you jerk, stand there and let him shoot you?"

He couldn't answer; his throat was clogged with shock and rage. He ran his hands over her frantically, checking for injuries. He didn't know what kind he expected to find—he knew she hadn't been shot, but he just needed desperately to touch her, to reassure himself that she was all in one piece.

He pulled her into his arms and clutched her close. He wanted to shake her, yell at her, but he did none of those things. He doused the inferno boiling inside and gave her what she needed, what he needed, too. "It's all right, baby," he whispered. Then he buried his face in her hair and drew in her scent.

She could have been killed. A minute more and the intruder might have snatched her away forever. In the instant when he'd seen her with a gun pointed at her heart, he'd known *his* heart.

His voice cracked with emotion as he drew back and asked, "What happened? How did he get in?"

She said nothing, only gazed at the man on the floor. Finally she whispered, "Is he...is he dead?"

Hating to let her go, he knelt beside her attacker. His own hand shook badly as he quickly checked the man's pulse, then lifted his lids and examined his pupils. "Unconscious. Looks like you gave him a concussion."

He rose and took Elyssa's icy hands. His own weren't much warmer. "What happened?" he asked again. "Can you tell me?"

Elyssa still didn't answer. She glanced at the man, then at Brett and said in a flat, detached voice, "We need to call the police."

"I'll do it," he said, watching Elyssa carefully. She seemed so fragile, he feared she would shatter. He wanted to hold her, never let her go. But she was right; they had things to do first. Gently he guided her to a chair, then called 911 and told the dispatcher they needed someone to deal with an attempted homicide.

While he spoke to the dispatcher, Elyssa got up, wandered over to the man and stared down at him as if transfixed.

When Brett finished his call, he muttered, "I should tie him up." The man was big, with rock-solid muscles, and Brett didn't want to have to wrestle him to the ground if he woke up.

"I have a rope in the utility closet," Elyssa said.

"Come and show me." He was afraid to leave her alone.

They brought back the rope, and Elyssa watched as Brett secured the man's wrists and ankles.

He rose from the floor and took her hand. "Come and sit down," he urged, but she didn't move.

As a siren sounded in the distance, she looked into Brett's eyes. "I know that man," she said. "He killed Randy."

Stunned, Brett wondered if she could be imagining or if perhaps she was hysterical from shock. "Elyssa," he began, but she shook off the hands he put on her shoulders.

"I saw him in the park that night," she said, her voice rising. "I remember."

"When? How?"

"Remember when Mariah said, 'Out of the shadows, the light will dawn.' She was right. I saw him coming downstairs, from the shadows into the light...and I knew." She grasped Brett's hands, held tight. "He...he kicked me down the hill."

"My God." Brett stared at her as the wail of the police siren grew louder.

"His voice," she continued. "I heard it that night on the phone, in the garage. He—"

A loud knock interrupted her. "Police," shouted a man's voice.

Brett opened the door and two officers, a man and a

woman strode in. "Detectives Sara Perkins and Mike Miller," the woman said. "What happened here, sir?"

"That man." The word seemed too pallid for the dregs of humanity stretched out on the floor. "He broke in and—"

"I'll tell you." Elyssa's face was chalk-white, but her voice was steady.

Brett sat beside her on the couch and took her hand. He should have been here through all of this. Instead Elyssa, all alone, had faced down a killer. He felt sick inside.

Detective Perkins took down their names. When Elyssa gave hers, Miller brightened. "I thought you looked familiar," he said. "Didn't I used to see you on television?" Elyssa nodded. "I never forget a face," he remarked as he wandered over to look at the man on the floor. "This guy's out cold. What'd you hit him with, Doctor?"

"*She* hit him."

Detective Miller glanced at Elyssa. "With—?"

"The, um, frying pan."

A chuckle escaped, and Miller said, "Lady, you wield a mean skillet."

"The pan was on the counter," she said softly. "I don't know why I picked it up…maybe to use as a shield or…or to throw at him. I didn't even realize I was still holding it, but when I saw him turn toward the doorway and point the gun, I knew he was going to shoot Dr. Cameron and well, I just…went for him."

She'd run straight at a man holding a gun. Without a qualm, to protect *him,* Brett thought. He shuddered, imagining what could have happened, what he could have lost.

"Why don't you start from the beginning?" suggested Detective Perkins.

"Dr. Cameron and I were at the theater. He had an emergency and left for the hospital…."

Brett flinched. "There wasn't an emergency. Someone set me up to get me away." He heard Elyssa gasp, and put his hand over hers, holding it comfortingly while he explained what he'd found at the hospital.

"Then a real emergency kept me there," he finished. Bile pooled in his throat as he pictured what he would have found if he'd arrived here a minute later.

Detective Perkins turned to Elyssa. "Did you let the guy in?"

"No, I don't know how he got into the house."

"Check the security system, Mike," Perkins said.

"On," he called.

"Has it been on all evening?"

Elyssa frowned. "Let's see. I turned it off when I came in. The...the phone was ringing, so I left the system off and went to answer. A woman asked for Dr. Cameron."

"When did you turn the system back on?"

"As soon as I hung up."

"Two minutes, max," Miller said. "Still enough time for him to get in. I'll take a look."

"What happened next?" Perkins asked.

"I heard him upstairs," Elyssa said and shuddered. "I was scared to death."

After a few minutes Miller returned. "Window's broken in an upstairs bedroom. He must've been waiting on the back porch roof. I didn't see anything out of place up there, but why don't you come up with me, Ms. Jarmon, and check."

As they returned, the doorbell rang and Elyssa saw Perkins let two men in. "Crime scene unit," the detective explained. The men went about their business, bagging the intruder's gun, removing the bullets from the entry wall.

Elyssa said to Perkins, "Nothing upstairs was disturbed."

"Okay," she said, "either your guy was compulsively neat, or robbery wasn't the motive."

"No." Both Elyssa and Brett spoke at the same time.

The police officers glanced at each other. "What, then?" Miller asked.

"Murder," Elyssa said firmly. "I believe all this is related to the death of a friend of mine, Randall Barber. The case was closed because it appeared to be a traffic accident. But I have new information that proves it wasn't. I found some incriminating information about a group called Hastings Corporation, and I guess the word got out." She explained, then pointed to the intruder. "He was there the night my friend was killed. And tonight he mentioned Hastings Corporation. He said, 'Hastings wants you wasted.'

"A few days ago Randy Barber's wife found a key to a safe-deposit box," she continued. "When she and I opened it, we found a notebook that explains everything. I'll get it."

She stepped gingerly past the unconscious man and went into the kitchen. They all watched as she took a canister out of the pantry and dug a notebook out of it, scattering pasta on the floor, then returned and handed it to Detective Miller.

He scanned the book and whistled. "Pretty serious allegations."

And, Brett thought, *he* hadn't believed her. He winced. He'd been in denial until the truth had slapped him in the face. And even then, he hadn't been here when Elyssa needed him.

"I may have even more evidence," Elyssa continued. "The woman Randy was working with—I'm supposed to see her husband tomorrow morning."

"We'll pick up whatever he has," Miller said. "Call him in the morning and let him know. Call Mrs. Barber, too. We'll want her in for questioning."

"And we'll need you to come down to headquarters tomorrow and make a formal statement," Detective Perkins said. "Cancel anything you have going for the day. You, too, Doctor. These Hastings guys'll think tonight's plan worked. If they don't suspect anything, we'll have an easier time rounding them up."

"Sure thing."

"But you have to go in—" Elyssa began.

Brett cut her off. "No buts," he said harshly. "You're not facing this alone." Not this time. "What time do you want us there?" he said to Miller.

"Nine, and when you call the hospital, use your cell phone. You can make the other calls from headquarters." He walked to the gunman's side. "Help me roll him over, would you, Doctor?"

"Sure." They rolled the man, none too gently, onto his back.

Miller let out a whistle. "Victor Gray. I've run into him before. He's a for-hire thug. You brought down a professional, Ms. Jarmon." He grinned at Elyssa. "With a frying pan."

Gray moaned and opened his eyes.

"Victor," Miller said, "you woke up just in time to hear your rights."

He knelt beside the glowering man and recited the Miranda warning, then untied the rope and replaced it with a pair of handcuffs. With Brett's help, he pulled Gray to his feet. "Okay, buster, you're on your way to lockup."

He and Brett steered Gray across the room, and Elyssa followed with Detective Perkins. The police officer opened the door, then turned back. "Keep your blinds closed. And to be on the safe side, I'll have a squad car on the street to keep an eye on the house the rest of the night. We'll see you two tomorrow."

Brett stood as Elyssa shut the door behind them. Emotions—too many, too strong—pummeled him from every side. With everything that had happened this evening, he felt battered. How much worse must Elyssa feel?

She turned, leaned against the door and shut her eyes. Brett went to her, took her in his arms. For a long moment she was utterly still, then she began to tremble. Her breath caught on a sob. "Oh damn, I hate to do this. Just give me a minute."

She tried to pull away, but he held her fast. "It's okay,

honey. Let it out," he said, and led her back to the couch. His own throat was clogged, his breath unsteady, but he murmured to her as she cried. He wasn't sure what he said, only that his words were comforting to her. And to him.

Hearing her cry tore at his heart, but he knew she needed to give in to her emotions. So he held her as she wept, deep, wrenching sobs that finally subsided to hiccuping sighs. Brett reached into his pocket for a handkerchief and silently handed it to her. She wiped her eyes and blew her nose.

"Better?" he asked, and she nodded. "Want some tea? Brandy?"

"No," she said quickly. "Don't go." She looked up at him sheepishly. "Hold me a little longer."

"As long as you want." *Forever,* he thought, then quickly brushed the thought away. "You saved my life," he said softly.

"Yeah, I guess."

"With a frying pan." He laughed and kissed her forehead. "My hero."

"You saved me, too," she murmured, her voice quivering. "He'd have shot me if you hadn't opened the door."

"Don't talk about it." He stopped her words by covering her mouth with his and kissing her desperately.

"I didn't think you'd come back," she said softly when he drew away. "You didn't believe me—"

"I was *wrong.*" He repeated his chilling conversation with Herbert Raines.

Elyssa straightened, her eyes now bright with purpose. "These people won't get away with what they're doing. Tomorrow the cops are finally going to stop them for good. Madigan, too." She touched his cheek. "I'm sorry."

"Don't be. He'll have to pay for what he did."

"You care for him."

"Cared," he corrected. "I made a mistake." One among many.

"I made one, too," she said softly. "I accused you of trying to protect Madigan...and yourself. I hurt you."

"You did." The words she'd spoken, the feelings they'd evoked seemed so long ago, he barely remembered them. "Now I understand."

"I don't think you do. I have a confession to make," Elyssa said, her expression somber. "I didn't trust you because I didn't trust myself. I thought you'd been seeing me to distract me from learning the truth."

"Funny," he said. "This evening I wondered if you'd gone out with me to pump me for information."

"Oh, Brett, no."

He framed her face with his hands, looked deep into her eyes. "I asked you out because from the first time I saw you, long ago on TV, before any of this happened, I wanted to be with you." He bent to kiss her softly, tenderly. "You were my fantasy. You still are."

She put her arms around him. "Make love with me. Right here. Right now."

He undressed her slowly. "You're so lovely," he murmured. At her sound of disagreement, he said, "Yes, you are. And not just your body—though I like it very much—but you're beautiful inside, too. Your thoughts, your words..." His voice broke as he thought again of how close he'd come to losing her. How empty his life would be without her.

When she lay naked on the couch and he, too, had discarded his clothes, he told her without words—with his lips, his hands and his body—all that she meant to him. He kissed the hollow of her neck, cupped her breast and lifted it to his eager mouth, caressed her belly, her thighs.

What if he'd never had another chance to love her like this? If the worst had happened and he'd lost her, he would always have known it was his fault.

Tonight he would give her everything. Whatever she needed, whatever she asked for, and more.

Gently, he parted her thighs and kissed her. With his lips

against the very core of her, he gave her more than he'd ever given, more than he'd dreamed he could.

Her muscles tightened, her body arched. And then he heard her cry out his name, and with his mouth still pressed against her, he held her while she climaxed.

She clutched him. "I want you...inside."

He knelt over her and plunged deep. She closed around him, hot and sweet. She was better than any fantasy, more glorious than any dream, he thought as his blood pulsed and his heartbeat quickened. And his cry echoed hers as he found his own release.

Once wasn't enough. He needed her again. And again.

Sometime during the night they stumbled upstairs and into bed. Even in sleep they didn't let go of each other.

When Elyssa woke the next morning, Brett was already up. The aroma of coffee drifted upstairs.

She lay still for a moment, gauging her emotions. Relief, that was number one. Relief that finally everyone—the police, Brett—was taking her seriously. The proof hadn't been pleasant, but if the people who killed Randy were put away, it would be worth the pain.

Hope, that was the other feeling. She and Brett had been through so much together, maybe he was ready to think of a future. The way he'd loved her last night made her think so. Feeling lighter than she had in days, she got out of bed.

When she came downstairs, she heard his voice. He sat on the couch, talking quietly on his cell phone and making notes on a pad of paper.

"How's Darcy doing this morning?" he asked. "Still vomiting? Watch her through the day. We'll think about lowering the next dose or trying a different mix. We'll decide when I'm back." He paused to listen. "I don't know. As soon as I can." He disconnected and looked up. His face was grim.

"What's wrong?" Elyssa said.

"New kid with an inoperable brain tumor, another one

whose family wants to pull him out of a clinical trial, and one who's having an adverse reaction to her chemo." He rotated his shoulders and sighed.

"You need to be there," Elyssa said.

"Wrong. I need to be with you."

The words were right, but something in his tone disturbed her. "Need, want. Two different things."

"Dammit, Elyssa. Don't second-guess me. I need *and* want to be here, okay."

Frowning, she sat on the chair across from him. "But something's bothering you."

He got up and began to prowl the room. "Yeah, you're right. I came down this morning and the first thing I saw was the bullet holes in your wall."

He pointed, and Elyssa stared at the fractured plaster around the two small cavities. She put a hand to her heart. Last night with so much happening, she hadn't thought much about the shots Victor Gray had fired. Now, seeing the aftermath in her very own house in the bright morning light shocked her. She and Brett could have been on the receiving end of those bullets.

But they weren't. They were safe. And the wall could be repaired. "It can be fixed," she said. "I'll call—"

"That's not the point," Brett said.

"What is?"

"I wasn't here when I needed to be. I went to the hospital."

"Of course you did. How could you have known what was going to happen here?"

"I should have listened to you. I should have guessed." He stopped pacing to stare out the window, his shoulders slumped. "But I didn't put it together until I got to the hospital and realized the emergency call was a set-up. And I almost didn't get back in time." He drew back his clenched fist, and for a moment Elyssa feared he'd plunge his hand through the windowpane.

"Because there was a real emergency."

She saw now that it wasn't anger he was feeling, it was

guilt. She went to him, put her arms around him and laid her cheek against his back. "You needed to stay at the hospital."

He spun around and took her by the shoulders. His fingers bit into her flesh, but she didn't flinch. "I know, but that doesn't make me feel any better. I should have taken you there with me."

"You didn't know that. Besides, you got here in time. That's what matters. Do you hear me?"

He nodded, and then his cell phone rang. She listened to him answer questions, give orders...and she wondered. Had he accepted what she'd said? She told herself to believe he had. If not, they'd talk about it later. There was no time now. They were due at police headquarters in less than an hour.

At headquarters she phoned Joe Ryder.

"Your call yesterday was a shock," he said. "I never let myself think that Dottie's death was anything but a traffic accident, but you got me wondering."

She heard the sadness in his voice. "I know that was tough for you," she murmured.

"Yeah, it was like going through her death all over again." He sighed. "I...I went through her desk—hadn't been able to do that before—and I found a disk you'll want to see. It tells everything Dottie knew."

"You can give it to the police. They'll be coming by to talk to you this morning. And I want to thank you, Mr. Ryder."

"I should thank you," he said. "Now that I know what happened, I want those bastards—excuse me, but I don't know anything else to call them—to get what they deserve."

"So do I."

Next Elyssa called Jenny and told her what had happened last night. "And I remembered the accident," she said.

She heard Jenny gasp, then her friend said, "Will you tell me?"

"I'd rather do it in person. But I do have a message for you. From...from Randy."

"Oh." Jenny's voice quavered. "G-go on."

"He said..." Elyssa's voice shook, too. "He said, 'Tell Jenny I love her.'"

Jenny said nothing, but Elyssa could hear her sobbing. She bit her lip. Maybe she'd done the wrong thing. She should have waited until they were together to tell Jenny her husband's last words.

Then she heard her friend's choked voice. "Thank you," Jenny said softly. Then more sobs.

"Are you going to be okay?" Elyssa asked.

"Yes, I just need to be alone and cry awhile. I'll talk to you later."

Elyssa hung up as Mike Miller came toward them. His eyes were red-rimmed and bleary, his dark brown hair disheveled. "I guess you've been working all night," Elyssa said.

"Comes with the territory." He smiled. "Like yours, Dr. Cameron."

"Yeah," Brett said but he didn't return Miller's smile.

Miller led them through a maze of desks occupied by harried-looking cops. At the door to a small interview room, he stopped. "I'll want statements from each of you separately. Doctor, why don't you have a cup of coffee while I talk to Ms. Jarmon?" He nodded to a coffeemaker on a small corner table. "Be warned. It's bilge."

Brett shook his head.

Elyssa smiled. "I'll pass, too. But you go ahead."

He poured himself a cup. "Before we start, I'll bring you both up to date on what's happened since last night. We ran your visitor's prints and I was right. He's Victor Gray, 'a professional hit man'—*his* words, by the way. Once he heard we had enough evidence to nail him on Randall Barber's murder, he decided to cooperate."

"What about the woman who called and asked for Brett?" Elyssa asked. "She had to be part of the plan."

"Yeah, according to Gray, she helps him out from time

to time. But don't worry about her,'' Miller said. ''We picked her up about an hour ago.''

He motioned Elyssa into the interview room. There, he took her through the events of last night, then backtracked to her accident and what had happened since.

''You know,'' she said, ''just the fact that you're listening to me makes me feel vindicated.''

Miller raised a brow, and she said, ''I came here after I got run off the road and tried to get the investigation to Randy's death reopened. I tried again after I was attacked at the hospital. No one paid attention.''

Miller sighed. ''What can I say? We're overloaded, and often the police don't react until something serious happens.''

''I think being threatened with a knife qualifies as 'something serious.' But I don't want to get into a discussion of that with you.''

''Neither do I. By the way, where can I reach Mrs. Barber?''

She gave him the name of Jenny's hotel and left so Brett could take his turn.

Before they began, Brett said, ''You told us Gray is cooperating. Define *cooperate*.''

''He confirmed a good deal of what Ms. Jarmon's friend said, and he gave us names. Do you know them?'' He referred to a list, reading out one name after another.

Hearing them sickened Brett. These were men he knew and worked with, men he respected: Herbert Raines, neurologist Avery Stevenson, hospital administrator Gavin McRae, Eric Lowe, a banker Brett had never met…and Clark Madigan. ''How would a man like Dr. Madigan, a pillar of the community, find a hit man?'' Brett asked.

''You'd be surprised,'' Miller said. ''Those 'pillars' are often rotten on the inside. And if you have the money, you can buy anything, even a killer.''

Brett shook his head. Such things were outside the realm of his imagination.

Here was the ''cancer'' Mariah had spoken of so vehemently. Like the real disease, this malignancy had gone unnoticed until almost too late. Truly too late for Randy and Dorothy. But at least they'd caught it before it spread any further.

Elyssa looked up as the interview room door opened and Miller beckoned her back inside. She scrutinized Brett's expression as she took a seat. He was still angry at himself, she thought. Well, that was normal, wasn't it? People were upset by events they couldn't control. Hadn't she felt the same way when she couldn't help Jenny?

Brett would get over the self-blame. She'd help him. After last night—staring down a killer and prevailing against him—she felt powerful enough to accomplish anything.

"What happens next?" Brett asked.

"We get the D.A. involved."

"I'm glad to hear that," Elyssa said. "I appreciate all you've done."

"You've made it easy for us. Ever done any crime reporting?"

"Never been interested."

"You could make a career of it if you ever go back on television," Miller said.

"Thanks, but I think one 'adventure' is enough for me." She smiled. It was good to feel relaxed again. "So we can go back to our real lives now, right?"

"Um, not yet," Miller said grimly, and Elyssa felt a flutter of anxiety. What now?

"The two of you stay inside the rest of the day," the detective said. "You should be safe there. We'll station a plainclothesman outside your house just in case."

Brett looked up sharply. "In case, what? You have Gray locked up."

"We're concerned that Madigan may have hired a backup. And if Victor Gray knows, he's not telling."

Chapter 19

"Not another killer," Elyssa muttered. The relief she'd experienced since she'd seen Gray led off in handcuffs last night evaporated, replaced by that same prick of fear she knew so well. She'd had only twelve hours of peace. Now the fear was back, like a harsh throbbing in her stomach.

She wondered if Brett was afraid, too. She looked at him. No, not frightened. He was furious.

He sprang to his feet. "Hell. How long will this go on?"

"No longer than necessary," Miller said in a tone that brooked no argument. "With luck we'll round up these fellows before the day's out: We're not looking at white-collar crime anymore. Conspiracy to murder's a dirty business. So go home. Don't use your phone. If you have to make a call now, use ours."

"What about visitors?" Elyssa asked. "I have to get hold of my cousin, have her come over and pick up some equipment."

"No problem."

Elyssa called Cassie and quickly filled her in on what

had happened, then Miller walked them back out through the squad room. She spotted her old friend Abel Huffstetter across the room and wondered if he knew what had happened last night. And if he did, was he embarrassed at the way he'd treated her? Granted Abel hadn't had the information Miller and his partner had now, but he'd been a jerk when she tried to talk to him.

At the door they shook hands with Miller. "I'll call when I know something," he promised.

On the way home they said little. Brett felt as if he were on a Tilt-A-Whirl ride at a carnival, as his thoughts spun wildly in too many directions. From Elyssa to Madigan to last night's emergency. He'd made the only decision he could make at the time, but he'd almost lost Elyssa. Where did he go from here?

By the time they reached her house, their police protection was in place, a spiky-haired blond man in a dusty Ford Taurus. Brett slowed, and the cop nodded to them.

At the door Brett went in first. "Come with me," he said, tugging Elyssa's arm. "I want to check all the rooms." Even though the cops were nearby, he wasn't taking anything for granted.

When he was satisfied that the house was empty and secure, they returned to the living room. Elyssa flopped down on the couch, hugging her knees and staring at the closed blinds. Finally she got up, went into the kitchen and returned with a glass of water.

As she came into the living room, there was a thud near the door. She jumped as if she'd been shot. The water glass fell from her hand and shattered.

Brett hurried to her and put his arm around her. She was trembling. "Honey, it's all right. That was the mail coming through the slot."

"Oh, God." She put her hand over her mouth. "I've heard that sound a thousand times. I shouldn't be so jumpy. I..." Her voice trailed off as she looked in dismay at the tiny shards of glass scattered on the floor. "Damn, I have to stop this."

"Hey, don't beat yourself up. You have every right to be edgy." He led her away from the broken glass. "I'll clean this up. You sit down."

When he returned with a broom, she was going through the mail. She tore open an envelope and began to laugh. "Look at this. My gun permit came. I am now licensed to carry a weapon." She made a paper airplane with the sheet and sailed it onto the coffee table. "That's irony for you."

"Yeah."

"I already bought the gun. It's upstairs in my nightstand." She sat down on the couch, picked up the permit and smoothed the paper. "I wonder, if I'd had it on hand, would I have shot Victor Gray?"

He came and sat beside her. "Would you have?"

"I...think so, although the frying pan was less bloody, wasn't it?"

He pulled her close. "For the rest of my life that scene will be etched in my memory—you flying out of the kitchen like an avenging angel, waving that frying pan."

She smiled and snuggled close to him. But within minutes he felt her tense again. Damn, he had to do something to get her mind off their situation or she'd make herself sick. "How about a game of cards?" he said.

"Okay." She went to the corner cabinet and rummaged in the drawer until she found a deck. "Gin rummy."

"Strip poker," he countered. She made a face, and he said, "Okay, we'll settle for gin." If he kept her occupied and upbeat, maybe the tension he saw in her shoulders would lessen.

He sat down at the game table so that he faced the ruined wall. He didn't want Elyssa staring at the reminder of last night and worrying that something as bad or worse might happen. "Penny a point," he said as she shuffled.

"Cheapskate," she huffed. "Dollar."

"Optimist. I don't want to clean you out. Dime."

"Agreed."

She dealt, and they concentrated on the game. Or pretended to. Though they bantered and teased each other, he knew neither of them had the heart.

They stopped for lunch, nibbling halfheartedly at roast beef sandwiches. Brett sat where he could keep an eye on the door. Ears straining, he listened for sounds from the street, from the back of the house. After lunch they returned to their card game. As the minutes crawled by, Brett's muscles screamed with tension.

His frustration must have showed because Elyssa laid down her cards. "Your fist is clenched."

"Is it?"

Elyssa leaned back and grimaced. "Spit it out, Brett. I know you're angry about staying home from the hospital. Why don't you just say so?"

He stared at her in surprise. "Honey, I'm angry about a lot of things, but missing a day at the hospital isn't on the list."

"What is?"

"You have to ask?" he said in disgust. "Last night you were nearly killed, I find out the man I've idolized for years may be responsible, now you may have a second hit man after you. Why the hell would I be angry about the damn hospital?"

"I thought—"

"You thought wrong." Ruthlessly he forced his temper under control. "Elyssa, I—"

The doorbell rang twice. "That's Cassie's ring," Elyssa said and got up.

"We're not taking chances. I'll get it."

When he opened the door, Cassie breezed in, an armful of bangle bracelets jingling. She blew him a kiss, then took Elyssa by the shoulders. She studied her cousin thoroughly, critically, then grabbed her and pulled her close for a long, hard hug. "You idiot," she said, her voice breaking, "I told you that you'd get in trouble playing *Murder She Wrote*. Coming face-to-face with a killer. Good God."

Brett watched the way the cousins interacted as Elyssa reassured Cassie that she was all right, then gave her instructions about today's birthday party. The closeness between them shone like a beacon. They were closer than many sisters; they seemed to read each others' thoughts, one sometimes finishing the other's sentence.

Cassie bundled the equipment she needed in her arms, then dropped everything on the floor to hug Elyssa one more time. Over Elyssa's shoulder, her eyes met Brett's. "Keep her safe," she said fiercely, then without waiting for an answer, she grabbed the equipment and hurried out.

Cassie seemed to siphon all the energy from the room when she left. Elyssa sighed. "Lord, I'm going to miss her when she leaves for New York," she murmured.

"Heading for Broadway, huh?" Brett said. "When's that going to happen?"

"Soon. Not having her here will seem so strange." Quickly she straightened her shoulders. "But I'll get used to it. Bet my long-distance bills go through the roof."

She *would* handle Cassie's absence, Brett thought. Elyssa was strong and resilient enough to handle anything.

He winced as he thought of Cassie's last words to him: *Keep her safe.* So far, he'd done a damn poor job.

The ghost of Denise snickered in his ear, *Poor job? Haven't you always?*

Yeah, he thought. He'd never done a good job when it counted. Good doctor, lousy husband.

But he wasn't planning on being a husband again. Okay, make that lousy lover, poor excuse for a friend. Elyssa deserved better.

"—need to keep busy," Elyssa was saying, her gaze straying to the grandfather clock in the corner. "I think I'll bake brownies. Wanna help?"

"I don't bake."

"With the manual dexterity it takes to be a doctor? Come

on, Cameron, you'd be a natural.'' When he raised a brow, she added, ''Okay, we have two choices—we bake or watch *The Young and the Restless*.

''Okay, we'll bake. And afterward we'll do something manly. We'll…arm wrestle.''

''In your dreams, Doc.'' She led the way into the kitchen.

While she got out the mixer and the ingredients for brownies, he checked the back door, then, moving the blind just slightly, peered out the front window. The afternoon had turned gloomy. A fine rain, almost a mist, fell softly, obscuring the view. Brett could barely see the Taurus across the street.

He hoped the officer inside the car had good eyesight and would spot any suspicious characters. Of course, the car itself would shout ''cop'' to anyone skilled in recognizing and avoiding the law. But maybe that was the point. It would warn off anyone who was after them.

''Why haven't the police called?'' Elyssa muttered.

''Probably too early. Come on, let's bake.''

Since Elyssa insisted that brownies weren't real unless they were made from scratch, baking kept them busy. And Brett found it distracted them, as well. Despite his need to stay mentally alert, despite his consciousness of the agonizingly slow passage of time, he was well aware that Elyssa was inadvertently turning him on. When she stood on tiptoe to reach into an upper cabinet, her blouse tightened, displaying the curve of her breast. She hummed softly while she worked, and the sound evoked memories of midnight loving. Even the movement of her hands as she measured and stirred was sexy.

It occurred to him that he'd never spent an afternoon like this with a woman. Certainly not with Denise. He'd always been too busy, and Denise hadn't been particularly domestic. The nearest she'd come to baking had been to pick up a cake at the bakery.

Being with Elyssa in the kitchen, with the sound of rain

pattering softly against the window and the smell of chocolate melting on the stove, was homey. Was...intimate. As if he and Elyssa belonged together.

He knew this afternoon was just one moment out of time. But he could savor it, store it away to relive in lonely moments.

They worked in easy harmony, he chopping nuts, Elyssa breaking and mixing eggs, then adding them to the creamed butter and sugar. "My mom used to bake brownies on winter Saturdays," she said with a half smile. "Cassie and I would help, or make a mess, depending on your viewpoint."

She reached for the vanilla, opened the bottle and held it to her nose. "Mmm." She offered it to him. "Want a sniff?"

Eyes locked with hers, he circled her wrist with his fingers and lifted the bottle. "Smells good," he said hoarsely, "like the soap you use." He took the bottle from her and set it on the counter.

She swayed, leaning closer. With only a gentle tug, he had her against him. She smelled of vanilla...of woman.

"This is no way to bake," she laughed. But she seemed in no hurry to move away. Instead, she nibbled at his jaw.

"I want a taste."

She glanced at the mixing bowl. "Not yet."

"Of you." If he didn't kiss her now, he'd surely die of hunger. He lowered his mouth to hers and sampled, then reluctantly let her go.

She returned to her baking—mixing, then pouring the batter into the pan. Brett leaned against the table, watching her. She seemed at home, at ease. And desirable. He'd never realized how sexy a woman could look with flour on her nose.

When the pan was in the oven, she turned to him. "Wanna lick the bowl?"

Who could turn down an offer like that? They dived in. Though licking the bowl brought out the little boy in him, he was quickly distracted, and the adult, aroused male took over. He grabbed her hand, eyed her chocolate-tipped fingers and pulled them into his mouth one by one, licking, sucking. Then while the rich aroma of baking wafted from the oven, he turned his attention to her mouth.

"You have chocolate here," he said, licking one corner of her mouth, then sliding his tongue across her lips. "And here." She sighed his name, and the whisper of her breath in his mouth aroused him even more. "Put your arms around me," he murmured.

"They're covered with flour."

"Do it, anyway." She rose up on tiptoe and twined her arms around his neck. Her lips parted, invited his tongue. He held her closer, teased her tongue with his, until she moaned and fisted her hands in his hair to pull him nearer, urge him deeper.

The doorbell rang. They both jumped.

"Who could it be?" Elyssa whispered, the color draining from her face. She slid open a drawer and grabbed a carving knife.

"Put that down. Stay back," Brett ordered, afraid she might rush the wrong person—maybe a kid selling candy to raise money for his school.

Someone rapped sharply on the door. No, not a kid. Someone with a heavy hand. Through the frosted glass, he saw the shadow of a man. Who?

Keeping out of sight, Brett moved cautiously along the wall, edging toward the door.

The man knocked again and called, "Ms. Jarmon, it's Alvin Staples, your surveillance."

Elyssa started forward, but Brett shook his head. The man's word wasn't enough. He pulled a handkerchief from his pocket and wiped the condensation from the window. Yes, it was the cop. Brett opened the door but kept the chain on. "Yes?"

"Just wanted to let you know we're changing shifts. Next car'll be a Honda Civic."

"Thanks," Brett said. "Have you seen anyone lurking around?"

"Stopped one guy. He said he was the neighbors' gardener. Had lawn equipment in his truck." At Brett's dubious look, he added, "That was before the rain. He left when it started coming down."

"Okay," Brett said, but he wasn't completely satisfied. Anyone could get his hands on a lawn mower. Still, he had to trust the plainclothesman's competence.

He shut the door and pulled Elyssa back into his arms. "Your heart's thudding."

"The cop scared me. I thought—" She burrowed into him, clutching him tightly. "Kiss me."

He did and she whispered, "Harder."

One word was all he needed. He devoured her mouth, lifted her to her toes, fitting her body flush against his, wanting her closer still. Moaning, she strained against him, and her need fired his.

Danger was a powerful aphrodisiac, he thought dimly as his heart pounded and his blood thrummed. He was painfully aroused, harder than he ever remembered.

With a groan he swung her up in his arms and carried her upstairs.

No time for niceties, he shoved her skirt up, then jerked her panties down while she fumbled with his zipper. Not fast enough, he thought, not nearly.

Clothes tangled around them, they came together. Their mating was harsh, primitive, but it was what they needed. Panting, cursing, driving each other harder and higher. She was scorching hot inside, the muscles that sheathed him flexing, rubbing, squeezing. Then she cried out with her release. And with a gasp—of triumph or despair—he let himself go.

Later, they snacked on burned brownies.

Chapter 20

The call from Mike Miller finally came at eight o'clock.

"It's him," Elyssa mouthed, and Brett hurried into the kitchen to pick up the extension.

"All clear," Miller said.

She was almost afraid to believe him. With the portable phone at her ear, she went to peek out the front window and saw the Honda driving away. Legs shaking, she dropped into a chair. "What's happened?" she asked.

"We were damn lucky," Miller said. "We got a warrant, and we confiscated CFCCC's and Hastings' files. Clark Madigan's personal files, too."

"Fast work," Brett commented.

"Yeah, the disk Joe Ryder gave us was damning. It got Judge Parker's attention. He issued the warrant in a flash, and we were able to walk into Dr. Madigan's office and surprise the hell out of him."

Elyssa's head swam. So much to take in all at once. What she and Jenny—and no one else—believed for so long was true. Vindication at last.

For her, this was a victory. For Jenny, too, though it would be bittersweet. But Jenny would finally have closure.

And for Brett? This had to be painful.

Still listening to Miller, Elyssa went into the kitchen. Brett stood with his back to her. She went to him and put her hand on his shoulder. He turned, and she saw everything in his eyes—relief, pain, uncertainty. She touched his cheek, and he put an arm around her and pulled her close to his side. "Are you okay?" she mouthed, and he nodded. But she knew that he wasn't and wouldn't be for some time.

"What about the other Hastings partners?" he asked.

"We rounded 'em all up and brought 'em in for questioning. Took damn near half our units." Miller chuckled. "Of course, the Hastings guys all have high-powered lawyers. This place looked like a bar association convention for a while.

"But you can rest easy now, Ms. Jarmon. It's over. I don't think any of those jerks will be bothering you again."

"Thank you," Elyssa said softly.

"I'd like to talk to you and Mrs. Barber again tomorrow," Miller continued. "Eleven o'clock?"

"Sure."

"The D.A.'s office will probably want to see both of you, too," he added. "They'll be in touch."

Elyssa and Brett hung up and stood looking at one another. The nightmare was over for her. For Brett, there was still so much to deal with—chaos at the hospital, grief at the loss of an idol, the future of his own career. She saw that in his eyes, in his stance. But he said nothing.

So she put out a hand and clasped his. "You can go back to the hospital now," she said softly.

"Tomorrow's soon enough." He lifted her hand to his lips. "Tonight I want to be with you."

Before they went to bed, Brett opened the door and stepped outside into a rain-washed world. A sliver of moon shone in the dark, cloudless sky. Autumn was only a few days away, and he felt its bite in the air.

Everything felt clean, fresh. It was a time for beginnings. And endings.

In bed they made love slowly. The frenzy of early afternoon had abated, leaving tranquility and tenderness in its wake.

This time, as if she sensed his inner turmoil, Elyssa took the lead. She undressed him, kissed him, murmured to him—soft words of love, of comfort. Then she slipped out of her clothes, knelt over him and took him deep into herself. She set the pace, moving so slowly they seemed to float and then spin into space and gently down. Afterward, she held him, and for a while he was completely at peace.

Now she lay beside him, her head on his shoulder, her hand resting against his heart. Sated with love, exhausted from the events of the past two days, she slept deeply.

But Brett's calm didn't last. Eyes open, he lay in bed, warring within himself, visited by the demons of the dark. Thoughts he'd avoided now churned in his mind.

Guilt tore at him. The other night he'd gone to the hospital. He could have taken her with him, but he hadn't. Elyssa had gone home. And faced a killer.

His choice. His fault. Again.

Choices. His life had been filled with them. Opposing goals—professional aspirations and personal ones—had tugged at him.

Medicine, his earliest dream. Planted by the pain of his cousin Aaron's death, its roots were strong. He'd never deviated from the path he'd set for himself as a young boy. From child to man, his aspirations remained unchanged.

He thought of his years in medical school. The late nights, the constant studying, the drive to be the best. His hard work had paid off. He'd graduated at the top of his class, won honors, and been chosen for a residency at one of the country's top hospitals.

He remembered the thrill when someone called him Doctor for the first time. Remembered the fear, common to new residents, that he was a fraud, that he'd never be able to live up to his dream. And the growing confidence as he found he *could* do what he'd set out to. And do it well.

He thought of the obligations he'd undertaken with pride, with joy. And the responsibilities still to come. Responsibilities to hundreds, maybe thousands of sick children. For the first time in his professional life, the weight of them lay heavy on his shoulders.

He'd sacrificed so much for his profession. His time, his unborn child, his wife. He'd almost, God help him, sacrificed Elyssa, too.

How did he balance the scales? Medicine on one side and on the other, one woman. The woman who owned his mind, his heart, his soul.

Before they'd gone to the theater—a lifetime ago, it seemed—he'd come here from the hospital, and Elyssa had been waiting when he opened the door. Seeing her there, he'd felt as if he'd truly come home. And for a few minutes he'd thought there was a chance for them. He'd imagined the future: coming home to her every night, raising a family, sharing a life.

How could you build a marriage when every day your obligations to your patients and your wife were constantly at odds? When you were continually faced with impossible choices?

At the hospital the other evening he'd made the only choice he could...and still he felt he'd failed.

He'd sped here from the hospital, praying all the way he wouldn't be too late. Then, standing in Elyssa's doorway again, filled with horror and guilt, he knew. A future for them was a futile dream.

Now, in the moonlight, he turned to her, drank in her features, pressed his lips against the soft skin of her cheek. He wanted forever with her. But it couldn't be.

At least he'd kept his promise to himself. He'd stayed

with her until she was safe. No more questions plagued her. No more threats. She could get on with her life.

She deserved far more than he could give her. She deserved a man who'd be there for her in every way, not one who had to fight himself to give her what she needed.

The pain of loss making his heart feel heavy, he shut his eyes and finally fell into a dreamless sleep.

Elyssa frowned across the table at Brett. Something was wrong.

Although he appeared relaxed, she was too attuned to him not to recognize signs of tension: the way he gripped his coffee cup, his fixed expression as he stared down at the table. Was he angry because she'd kept him away from his work for so long? Yet he seemed in no hurry to leave.

"Don't you have rounds this morning?" she asked.

He looked up, blinked. "Hmm? No, I canceled."

She'd never known him to do that. Puzzled, she said, "But everything's all right now. You don't have to stay with me."

His expression was grim. "Elyssa, the other night—"

"Please don't talk about that," she said. "It's over, and you don't owe me a morning because of what happened."

"Owe you?" he said bitterly. His hands tightened on the coffee cup until the knuckles turned white. "I left you alone, then you made yourself a target on my account—"

"So you do think you owe me," Elyssa murmured. Damn, she didn't *want* him to feel that way. Who wanted a man to spend time with you to settle a debt? "Pay up then, Doctor," she said, keeping her voice even. "Go back to work."

He shoved the coffee cup aside and got up to pace the room. She'd seen him do that before when he was stressed. He stood at the window for a moment, then turned to face her. "You don't understand what I'm trying to say."

Something in his tone sent cold chills through her. Her

stomach clenched. "Maybe I don't," she said slowly. "Why don't you explain."

"I wasn't here for you the other night."

"You had no way of knowing what would happen. Face it, Brett. You're not Mariah."

Eyes bleak, he continued as if he hadn't heard her. "I was— God, I was almost too late."

"You were just in time. You distracted him, caused that one moment of indecision that gave me time to go after him." She tried to smile, to speak lightly. "I think we're a pretty good team."

He shook his head as he walked to the table. "I'm wrong for you. I can't give you what you deserve."

The chill spread through her body, turning her to ice. She was surprised she could speak. "What do you think I deserve?"

"A man who can give you all of himself. A man who doesn't have to make choices—"

"Don't confuse me with Denise, Brett." Her words were dagger sharp. He didn't flinch but she knew they pierced him. "I haven't asked you to make a choice," she said.

"You need more than I can give you," he went on doggedly.

She hated that. Detested his taking control over *her* thoughts, *her* feelings. "Stop it," Elyssa cried, her voice rising. "Don't tell me what I need. If I want more from you, I'll let you know. You don't have the right to decide for me."

"Dammit." His hands slammed the edge of the table. Coffee cups clattered, and a spoon fell to the floor. "I can't be the kind of doctor I need to be *and* the kind of lover I need to be."

Every word seemed wrenched from somewhere deep inside him.

Her anger drained, and pain, raw and wrenching, took its place. "Oh, I misunderstood," she said quietly. "You were talking about what *you* need. At least that's honest. I'd rather you'd be straight with me than pretend to be noble.''

He looked as if she'd slapped him. ''Noble? I'm anything but that,'' he said bitterly. ''Dammit, I'm a failure at relationships.''

''I don't think so.''

''I do,'' he insisted. ''I tried once. I couldn't make it work.''

''And you'll never give yourself another chance. You made that clear early on.'' Her eyes never leaving his, she asked, ''Has it ever occurred to you, Dr. Cameron, that you could be wrong?''

He shook his head. ''I know myself.'' Then he murmured, ''I'm sorry,'' and turned away.

Elyssa used every ounce of strength to hold herself together as he walked out of her house. Out of her life.

She listened to the sound of Brett's car starting, then driving away and waited for tears to come, but they were frozen inside.

She shouldn't be surprised that he'd gone, she told herself. Brett had never offered her commitment, never suggested their affair would last. He'd told her medicine was his life.

''Damn you, Brett Cameron,'' she muttered.

She couldn't blame the breakup on her face. Or on anything she'd done. No, the only thing she could fault herself for was being fool enough to imagine she could change Brett. She'd wanted to believe that what he felt for her was strong enough to last. Mistake.

The house was silent, empty. Her mind was empty, too. She couldn't think what she was supposed to do next. She sat motionless as minutes ticked by.

Finally she stirred. ''You've dealt with loss before,'' she reminded herself. ''You can handle this.''

Okay, she'd make a list, then stand up, put one foot in front of the other and get through the day.

The list was easy: find someone to repair the bullet hole in the entry hall wall; check to see that she had everything ready for tomorrow's birthday party; call Jenny about the appointment with Detective Miller. She had enough to keep her busy for a while.

She only wished she didn't feel so cold.

She started by calling Jenny. "How are you?" Elyssa asked.

"I'm fine. Goin' to the police station yesterday wasn't as bad as I imagined. Actually, it was a relief to finally talk to someone who believed me. By the time I left, I felt as if Randy was a hero."

Elyssa wondered if Jenny would get on with her life, find a new relationship now. How long did it take to get over a loss as devastating as hers?

How long did it take to get over a man you loved who simply walked out of your life?

How did you manage? One minute at a time, she guessed. And she did get through the day.

And the next. That included a visit to the district attorney's office, where she spent several hours answering questions. She was happy to cooperate in building a case against Madigan and his cohorts, but at the same time she longed to put the whole experience behind her. Every incident she recounted brought memories of Brett.

On the day she was scheduled to entertain the children in the cancer unit, she considered calling and canceling. What if she ran into him? She picked up the phone, dialed the hospital...and slammed the receiver down.

No! She would not allow him that kind of control over her life. She'd made a place for herself at St. Michael's, and she wouldn't relinquish it on his account. If she ran into him, she'd give him a cool nod and walk on by.

But she didn't see him. Perhaps he was avoiding her. *Good,* she thought. *Let him.*

She stopped at Trace's room. He was being discharged. Tomorrow he would go home.

The walls were bare now, the posters taken down. An open suitcase sat on the dresser with a pile of comic books beside it. Trace sat up in bed, playing with a Game Boy.

"Hi," Elyssa said. She took her hand from behind her back. "Brought you a going-away present."

His eyes lit up. He unwrapped the box in typical boy fashion, shredding the paper and tossing it on the floor. "Wow, *Toy Story 2*. Thanks." He scrambled over and opened the nightstand drawer. "I have something for you, too." He held out a small box.

She opened it and found a clown figure. "It's lovely. Thanks."

"There's something else."

She looked in the box again and found a photo of Trace. His head was bald, his skin sallow, but he was grinning.

"It's so you'll remember me," he said.

Her eyes filled. "No way could I forget you," she said, and hugged him hard.

They talked for a few minutes, and he promised to come and see her when he came back for a checkup, then she left. She glanced back from the hallway and saw him engrossed in his game. Though he didn't look up, she blew him a kiss.

She stopped at rooms of several children too sick to come to her show. Then she gathered her equipment and trudged back to her car.

By the time she got home, she was exhausted from the effort of smiling and pretending that everything was fine. At least she had her clown makeup to help hide the circles under her eyes.

Even alone at home she couldn't escape Brett. News about the scandal at St. Michael's dominated the airwaves and the front page of the *Indianapolis Clarion*. The officers of Hastings Corporation, or Madigan's Mafia as the media had dubbed them, had been relieved of their staff positions at the hospital, pending investigations by the district attorney and the state medical association. All this was thanks to the information provided by banker Eric Lowe in exchange for legal immunity. His four cohorts' files had been confiscated and their personal banking records seized.

Derek's role in the scandal also came out. In return for a sizable payment, he'd funneled information about Randy's investigation—and hers—to the Hastings group. Perhaps he hadn't suspected that these men were desperate enough to do away with Randy, but after the fact he'd certainly known. Yet he'd admitted nothing to Elyssa. Instead, he'd ratted on her, too. Being his former lover hadn't protected her. "Bastard," Elyssa muttered. For a fee, he'd been willing to hand her off to a hit man.

As head of the new hospital and a member of the fundraising committee, Brett was interviewed constantly. It seemed to Elyssa that she could hardly turn on the TV or pick up a paper without seeing his face.

And there was no way she could keep herself from watching and reading. Or remembering and wanting.

When he showed up on the ten o'clock news, she searched his face for clues to his emotional state. She saw lines of fatigue around his mouth, and his expression was grim, but that could be because he was upset about the chaos at the hospital.

She flipped off the TV and trudged upstairs to bed. She'd been managing the days fairly well. The nights were another matter.

The bed seemed so large without Brett lying next to her. And she still couldn't get warm. She lay down, pulled the blanket up to her chin and huddled under it, shivering.

She wondered if Brett was equally cold.

Chapter 21

"Why don't you come to New York with me for a few days?" Cassie asked, leaning back on her living room couch. "Getting away will be good for you. You've been pining over Brett for a week now."

Elyssa put down her coffee cup. "I'm not going to pine anymore."

"Good, then come with me. Give yourself a treat."

"I'm too busy."

"Come on, Elyssa. With all you've been through, you deserve a vacation."

Elyssa shook her head. "I have two projects in the works. I've been talking with the director of social services at St. Michael's. I'm going to start a training program in clowning for volunteers."

Cassie's mouth dropped open. "Good grief, Elyssa, this town has a dozen other hospitals. Why St. Michael's? You'll run into Brett every time you're there." She gave a disgusted snort. "What do you do, sleep on a bed of nails, too?'' When Elyssa only laughed, Cassie asked, ''Have you seen him?''

''Just once. Yesterday, from down the hall.'' And her heart had caught at the sight of him. ''He was talking to a family.'' She remembered the way he'd put his hand gently on the mother's shoulder, how she'd looked up at him with a face full of hope.

''Did you talk to him?''

''No, he was half turned away. I don't think he saw me.''

''Bummer,'' Cassie said. Then she asked, ''What's your second project?''

''Brett.''

''Huh?''

''You heard me. I'm going to talk to him, or rather talk *at* him.''

''Well, hallelujah.'' Cassie raised her cup in a toast. ''When did you decide this?''

''Last night, after I saw him on TV for the thousandth time. I realized that when he walked out, I was so stunned I didn't say everything I should have. At first I was just numb and doing my best to pick up the pieces and go on without him. Then I started to get mad. Every day I've gotten a little angrier, and now I'm plain furious.'' Her fists clenched. ''He's a stupid, stubborn, senseless man. I feel like beating *him* with a frying pan.''

Cassie applauded. ''Bravo. Tell him while you're still mad.''

''I'm going now.'' Elyssa checked her watch. ''It's after five. He should be getting through for the day.'' She stood, shoved her chair in and grabbed her purse and car keys. ''I've waited long enough for him to wake up. I'm going to talk some sense into him.''

As Elyssa headed for the door, Cassie asked, ''Do you know what you're going to say?''

Her hand on the doorknob, Elyssa stopped and grinned. ''Having an actress in the family has its benefits. I've learned a lot from you. I've rehearsed every line.''

Cassie grinned back. "Good, but don't be afraid to ad-lib if you need to."

Damn her, Brett thought. Damn Elyssa for her magic. It went beyond her shows for the kids. She'd bewitched him, too.

For the first time in his life, medicine wasn't enough. He'd spent the week working longer hours than usual—longer than necessary—to no avail. His self-inflicted wound still festered.

Yet he didn't know how to heal it. He still feared that a lifelong commitment was impossible for him, but, dammit, he *wanted* to make one.

Lost in thought, he moved slowly down the hall. He thought of getting away from the hospital and taking a walk, but his stomach reminded him he'd skipped lunch. He stopped at the line of vending machines near the cafeteria, dug in his pocket for change and bought a candy bar. *You'd lecture your patients if they didn't eat three meals a day,* Elyssa's voice chided.

Dammit! He tossed the candy bar in the trash, went into the cafeteria and bought a bowl of soup.

"Brett." He turned and saw Rob Tyler hailing him. "Come join us," Rob called, and Brett took his tray to the table where Rob and Debbie were having a snack.

"In for a checkup?" Brett asked Debbie.

"No, just catching up with the father of my unborn child."

"We tell each other we've got to stop meeting like this," Rob said cheerfully, "but with my hours, sometimes it's the best we can do."

Brett stared thoughtfully at Debbie. "Does that bother you?" he asked. "If I'm being too personal, tell me to shut up...but...it's important."

"I don't mind your asking," Debbie said cheerfully. "Yes, sometimes I wish Rob kept regular hours, like a banker. But I knew what I was getting into—I was a physical therapist at the hospital where he did his residency. So, to answer your question, no it doesn't bother me.''

"What will you do if the baby comes and Rob can't be there?" Brett asked.

"Grin and bear it." She chuckled at the pun. "I have to do the work myself, anyhow. He just gets to cheer me on."

"You two are damn lucky," Brett said.

"Don't kid yourself," Rob said. "Luck has nothing to do with it. Marriage is hard work." He smiled into his wife's eyes. "But it's worth it."

Brett took a spoonful of soup. Once when he'd hit rock bottom during the grueling days of his residency, he'd told Madigan he didn't think medicine was worth the sacrifice. The older man had simply said, "Go home and ask yourself how badly you want to be a doctor."

Brett had searched his soul, come back and answered that being a physician was the most important thing in his life. And Madigan had replied that anything that important was worth the sacrifice.

Now there was something—some*one*—in his life as important as medicine.

This past week all Brett's illusions about Madigan had come crashing down, and he'd been filled with bitterness and disgust. Now, he thought, maybe the man had left him something of value to remember after all.

Elyssa pulled into a parking space in the hospital garage.

Her steps firm, she headed toward the tunnel entrance. Nothing to fear there anymore; it was just a tunnel.

A feeling of power surged through her. Not the power she'd had as a television personality, but a new strength. The past few months she'd gained the courage and the fortitude to get on with her life. And to take it in the direction she wanted to go.

Within a few minutes she arrived at Brett's office. Seven days had passed since she'd seen him. Without hesitation she opened the door.

Jean, his secretary, looked up and smiled. "Ms. Jarmon," she said, her smile growing wider. "Dr. Cameron's with his last appointment. He should be finished in ten minutes."

"I'll wait." She sat down, picked up a copy of *Time* and opened it. She didn't bother trying to read, just stared at the pictures until they blurred before her eyes.

Ten minutes crept by. Fifteen.

The door opened, and a man and woman, followed by two teenagers, came out. Brett would be in his office now, winding down for the day.

Elyssa didn't wait for Jean to call her name. She got up and marched into the inner hallway.

She rounded the corner...and came up short against a warm body. Against *his* body. She gasped as he grabbed her shoulders to steady her.

"What are you doing here?" he asked.

This wasn't what she intended—bumping into him like an idiot because she wasn't watching where she was going. But this was the scene she'd been handed. *Wing it, babe.* She raised her chin. "I have something to say to you."

"And I want to talk to you."

Of all the answers he might have given her, this was the least expected. She thought he'd said it all last week, and she almost reminded him of that, but changed her mind and walked silently to his office.

Halfway across the room she halted and turned. She didn't want to sit and leave him standing. It would give him an edge.

He shut the door, took a step toward her, stopped. They stood face-to-face, an arm's length away from each other. Not quite close enough to touch.

She *wanted* to touch him, to feel the warmth and solidity of his arms around her. Instead, she stood still, holding on to her anger. To her power. "I—"

"I was—"

Their voices collided.

Brett stopped. "Go ahead." His eyes were dark with some unreadable emotion.

"Sit down."

He blinked, sat on the couch. Elyssa remained standing.

Her heart thrummed in her chest. This was the most important moment in her life. "The other morning you walked out on me without giving me a chance to say how I felt."

"I was trying to do the right thing."

Her anger ratcheted up a notch. "That's my point." She put her hands on her hips. "You don't *know* what's right for me. Only I know that." She glowered at him and took a step closer. "Were you playing Bogart's part in *Casablanca?* 'We'll always have Paris. Here's looking at you, kid'? Then you walk away." She took a breath. "Dammit, Brett, you never gave me a chance to say what *I* wanted out of this relationship."

His mouth curved, just a little. "I guess you're going to tell me."

Damn right, she thought, riding the wave of newfound power. "I don't need you with me every minute," she told him. "I'm my own person, and I give you the right to be who you are. I don't want you to change. I love you just the way you are."

Stunned surprise showed on his face. Then he said, "May I have a turn now?"

"Sure." Whatever he said, she would deal with it.

He took a breath. "These past few days have been hell. Pushing you away was the biggest mistake I ever made. God, I was a fool."

Astonishment, then relief washed over her. Her knees suddenly felt weak, and she stumbled back and dropped into a chair. "Yeah, you were. But I forgive you."

He laughed, came to her and put out a hand to pull her to her feet. "Come here."

Elyssa saw again the Brett Cameron she'd met that first day, the man who pursued her with such fierce determination. He flashed that grin she loved and drew her close.

"I've been dying for the taste of you," he murmured, and kissed her. Again and again. Until her heart was pounding and her breath was nearly gone. "I love you, too," he whispered. "More than I can tell you."

"Then show me."

A knock on the door startled them. "Doctor," Jean called.

"Come in."

Elyssa tried to back away, but Brett held her fast.

The door opened, and Jean came into the office. "Oh, excuse me." Her cheeks flushed. "I, uh…"

"It's okay," Brett said. "What did you need?"

"Um, Dr. Baron said to be sure and remind you of the breakfast meeting tomorrow."

"Thanks." He sounded as if being found in his office with a woman in his arms was a natural occurrence.

Jean backed toward the door, then stopped and grinned at Elyssa. "Thank heavens you're back, Ms. Jarmon. He's been a bear for the last week." She scurried out and shut the door.

Elyssa chuckled at Brett's sheepish expression, then he joined in her laughter.

"Come and sit down," he said. He sat beside her on the couch and took her hands, his expression serious now. "I realize now that medicine's only half my life. You're the other half." He raised her hands to his lips and kissed them.

"I need you," he said softly. "I want us to be together. Forever. As husband and wife. Will you marry me?"

She looked at their joined hands. All her dreams, all she wanted was here beside her. She smiled into his eyes. "Yes," she said. "I've always been good at sharing. I know medicine will sometimes take over your life, but I can deal with it as long as I know you love me."

"Always," Brett said, and sealed his promise with a kiss.

Epilogue

"This year's clinical award is presented to Dr. Brett Cameron of the new Children's Cancer Center in Indianapolis for his innovative and well-conceived program for the treatment of children with Ewing's sarcoma."

Applause sounded throughout the hotel ballroom, and Brett rose from his chair at the head table to accept the award. Elyssa's heart swelled with love and pride as she clapped and rose with the others for a standing ovation.

Her eyes rested on him as he stood at the podium. *Mine*, she thought. After a year of marriage, she sometimes still found it hard to believe that he really belonged to her. Though she shared him with his profession, the bond they'd formed was sure and strong. She laid a hand on her stomach and the new life growing there.

"...and I'd like to thank my wife, Elyssa, for her love and support. She's encouraged me all the way. And given me a life to come home to," Brett said. He turned and met her eyes for a brief, charged moment.

Later, after making their way through the crowd, accepting congratulations and good wishes from other conference attendees, they went upstairs. "Tired?" Brett asked as he opened the door to their hotel room.

"Not a bit. I'm too excited and proud to be tired."

He laid down his plaque, unfastened his tie and tossed it on the dresser, then reached for her.

Elyssa held him away. "Wait, I have an award for you, too." She opened a drawer, took out a package and held it out to him.

"What's this?" He unwrapped it and pulled out a small gold cup.

"Read it."

He turned the trophy around and read the inscription. "To the World's Best Husband." He swallowed, and his eyes were moist as they met hers. "Thank you."

He opened his arms and she went into them. "You're welcome," she murmured as he pulled her close for a long, delicious kiss.

A kiss that meant love and trust. And commitment.

* * * * *

Silhouette®

INTIMATE MOMENTS™

is proud to present

Romancing the Crown

With the help of their powerful allies,
the royal family of Montebello is determined
to find their missing heir. But the search for the
beloved prince is not without danger—or passion!

**This exciting twelve-book series begins in January and
continues throughout the year with these fabulous titles:**

Available at your favorite retail outlet.

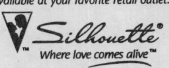

Silhouette®

Where love comes alive™

Visit Silhouette at www.eHarlequin.com

SIMRC

When you're looking for a great miniseries,
look no further than

Silhouette®

INTIMATE MOMENTS™

This month, don't miss

CHARMED
AND DANGEROUS

by Kylie Brant

*Impossibly sexy, fiercely determined, these men give their all
to the fight for justice—but will they succumb to love?*

HARD TO RESIST, IM #1119 (December 2001)
HARD TO TAME, IM #1125 (January 2002)

THE *Delaney* HEIRS

by Carla Cassidy

Look for the next exciting installment...

*The will has been read. Destinies have been decided.
And the Delaney siblings are about to discover what
family really means.*

TO WED AND PROTECT, IM #1126 (January 2002)

Available at your favorite retail outlet

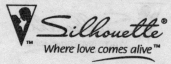

Silhouette®
Where love comes alive™

Silhouette —
where love comes alive—online...

eHARLEQUIN.com

buy books

♥ Find all the new Silhouette releases at everyday great discounts.

♥ Try before you buy! Read an excerpt from the latest Silhouette novels.

♥ Write an online review and share your thoughts with others.

online reads

♥ Read our Internet exclusive daily and weekly online serials, or vote in our interactive novel.

♥ Talk to other readers about your favorite novels in our Reading Groups.

♥ Take our Choose-a-Book quiz to find the series that matches you!

authors

♥ Find out interesting tidbits and details about your favorite authors' lives, interests and writing habits.

♥ Ever dreamed of being an author? Enter our Writing Round Robin. The Winning Chapter will be published online! Or review our writing guidelines for submitting your novel.

All this and more available at
www.eHarlequin.com

Silhouette

INTIMATE MOMENTS™

and NATIONAL BESTSELLING AUTHOR
RUTH LANGAN

present her brand-new miniseries

THE LASSITER LAW

Lives—and hearts—are on the
line when the Lassiters pledge
to uphold the law at any cost.

Available November 2001
BY HONOR BOUND (IM #1111)

Eldest brother Micah Lassiter discovers the dangers of
mixing business and pleasure when he falls for the
beautiful woman he's been hired to protect.

Available January 2002
RETURN OF THE PRODIGAL SON (IM #1123)

Ex-C.I.A. agent Donovan Lassiter learns the true meaning
of love when he comes to the rescue of a young widow
and her two small children.

And coming in spring 2002
Mary-Brendan and Cameron Lassiter's stories

Available at your favorite retail outlet.

Silhouette®
Where love comes alive™